UNBRIDLED POWER

An IAN BLACK *Novel*

****

Richard *and* Barbara Osborn

RICHARD AND BARBARA OSBORN

For our family members and friends who put up with us
while we wrote this book

Thank You for your patience

✱✱✱✱✱✱✱✱✱✱✱✱✱✱✱✱✱✱✱✱✱✱✱✱

Pages 342 to 345 contain pictures and charts on the Bomarc-C missile and the possible intercept options. Page 346 contains a Glossary of Abbreviations.

Britannia-American Books
ISBN: 9780692503379

BritanniaAmericanPublishing@yahoo.com

PREFACE

For more than two centuries, since the United States of America was created, power has been transferred peacefully between presidents, after fairly clean elections. There is no known incident when a president tried to stay on, beyond his term of office. Yes, FDR was elected president for four terms, but it was legal, at that time, under the constitution, and there was no hint of scandal.

Most Americans believe in the democratic form of government, where elections are held and the winners installed in office, without any incident. However, our system of government has never been tested, where a holder of the office has decided not to leave.

All freedom loving Americans should ponder the following question and then decide if they believe that it could ever happen here?

What would happen if a president decided that he would stay in office, regardless of election results or if the election was cancelled?

In this novel, the president decides that he can ignore laws, with impunity, and stay in office as long as he wants. He found out that he can change the rules and bypass Congress.

The dictum "Power Corrupts and Absolute Power Corrupts Absolutely" is once again proven to be correct. Whether one is talking about Roman Emperor Nero, French Emperor Napoleon Bonaparte or the German Fuehrer Adolf Hitler, the dictum has been proven multiple times throughout history.

This page intentionally left blank

1

Mission Bomarc

Early on a Monday morning in November, a few weeks after a devastating Islamic terrorist attack on American soil, Ian Black was sitting in his corner office at Boeing Aircraft, the largest aerospace company in Washington State, drinking his usual cup of coffee. He didn't look his age; most people thought he was in his late forties, but in reality he was sixty-two. His hair was full, brown, with a tinge of gray and neatly trimmed. He sat upright in his chair, like the proud, former United States Air Force colonel he was. He had retired from the Air Force seventeen years ago and had gone to work for The Boeing Company, where he was frequently promoted for excellent work. He was now an Executive Vice President of the company and head of the Defense Systems Division.

As he sipped his coffee, he thought about the documentary, "The Secret Committees", he had watched on CNBC the night before, concerning the financial crises that had happened over the past fifty years. Throughout the program, there was a hint of conspiracy, by mysterious groups trying to manipulate the stock markets and various nations' currencies.

One example given of manipulation was how the price of Brent crude oil has always been controlled by four, large oil companies. Another example was the way George Soros, and other groups, became rich on Black Monday, in September 1992. They bet against the English pound, and Soros alone is estimated to have pocketed considerably more than one billion dollars. The last crisis mentioned in the documentary was the late 1990's Asian financial meltdown, and the rumors about mysterious groups trying to take advantage of the chaos.

This documentary reminded Ian of the conversation he overheard in a Berlin café, back in 1962. At that time, he was in the British Army Intelligence Corps and was waiting for a colleague, from the BND German secret service. Two men were sitting at the next table and were discussing, in low voices, how their cabal was attempting to manipulate the Italian markets. By listening to the waiter and their discussion, Ian determined one was a German, Lutz Schiller, and the other was a Swede, named Borge,

Suddenly, Ian's phone rang, and he quickly came back to reality. Looking at the caller ID, he realized it was the president of the company, so he immediately picked up the handset.

"Good morning, Ian Black speaking."

"Ian, this is Patrick. I'm sending an Air Force Colonel, Alan Burgess, to your office, and he should be there in about thirty minutes. He's an assistant to the President's National Security Advisor and wants to discuss a very important, hush-hush project. Just one thing, Ian, make sure there's enough profit in it for the company."

"Okay, I'll take care of him. Do you know what the project is about?"

"Not exactly, as he was very secretive. He did state, however, that it is a high priority project for the president.

He mentioned that it concerned a missile defense system for the protection of the United States. The colonel expressed the desire to talk directly to the man that could help him. I told him you were that person."

"Thanks, boss." Ian responded, with a smile at the telephone, which he then hung up.

Ian called his administrative assistant, in the outer office on the intercom.

"Alicia, there'll be a Colonel Alan Burgess here soon. When he gets here, please show him in immediately."

"Yes, Mr. Black," Alicia replied.

Ian figured he had about twenty minutes before this colonel would get there, so he started to scan the voluminous list of emails on his computer. He read the ones that looked important and put the others aside, for future reference.

It wasn't long before there was a knock on his office door.

"Come in," Ian said in a fairly loud voice.

Alicia opened the door and ushered in a man who appeared to be in his mid forties, tall with black hair and dressed in a blue U. S. Air Force uniform. Ian stood up, came around his desk and approached the man.

"Colonel Burgess I presume. I'm Ian Black, head of the Defense Systems Division." Ian said, as he held out his hand with a warm smile.

"You're correct, Mr. Black. I am Colonel Alan Burgess and I report to the President's National Security Advisor. While we talk in private, will it be acceptable to you if I call you Ian? You can call me Alan."

"Certainly, Alan, what can I do for you on this cold, wet and windy day?"

"My assistant, at the NSC office in the White House, stated that you served in the British Army and the United States Air Force. How on earth did you manage that?"

RICHARD AND BARBARA OSBORN

"Well, I was born in England to an American mother and English father, and this hereditary fact allowed me to serve in both militaries. The British Army, over a five year period, sent me to Cyprus and then Berlin, as an Intelligence Officer. When my father died in 1963, my mother returned to Tennessee and I followed a few months later. Then, a U.S. general, I had met in Berlin, managed to get me a commission in the Air Force and I was sent to Vietnam as a go-between the CIA and the USAF. Just before the Falklands War, the White House "drafted" me and I became a liaison between President Ronald Reagan and Prime Minister Margaret Thatcher. I ended up as a colonel and retired from the service seventeen years ago, to join this company," Ian responded.

"Well, you certainly have an interested background, Ian. I can't match that. Anyway, since my time is short here in Seattle, I'll get straight to the point for my visit. After the recent major attack by terrorists, the president wants to build eight bases around the coast of the United States, to protect the nation from a similar attack. The president believes it's important to have this defensive weapon, in case Al Qaeda or another terrorist group manages to get within range of our coastline and launch weapons of their own. The concern is that ships or planes, owned by terrorist countries or organizations, could get close enough to the United States mainland, to launch an attack using high explosives or even nuclear material.

We want to know if your company would be interested in manufacturing up to sixty Bomarc missiles, with a new guidance system. Since the last ones built were a Bomarc B model, we would probably call the new one Bomarc C. This new guidance system should include a global positioning system and a terrain contour mapping capability. Your company would be required to design the new guidance system and manufacture from fifty to sixty missiles."

"I'm not that familiar with the Bomarc, even though I did hear of it some time ago and I know our company was the prime contractor. Let me bring in an expert who probably can shed some light on this missile system."

Ian picked up the phone and called his chief engineer responsible for any Boeing Phantom Works project, at this facility. The Boeing Phantom Works was a company organization that worked on mainly classified military products, where development speed was generally important. It was similar to the Lockheed Skunk Works that developed the U-2, F-117 and other high technology aircraft.

"Charlie, this is Ian. Can you come up to my office right away? We need to talk about a missile system called the Bomarc."

"I'll be there immediately, Mr. Black." replied Charles Aylott.

In a few minutes, there was a light tap on Ian's office door and Charlie entered, without waiting for a response. He was an older man, about sixty-nine years old, with grey hair that needed trimming.

"Colonel Burgess, this is our chief boffin and he works on all our Phantom Works projects. If anyone knows anything about the Bomarc, he does. Correct, Charlie?"

Colonel Burgess and Charlie shook hands, with "Glad to meet you."

Ian went on, "Charlie, I'm sorry I called you a boffin. I reverted back to my English heritage for a second. In England, we used to call the chief engineer, a boffin. It's actually a complementary term."

"That's okay, Mr. Black. I understand. Anyway, I'm called all kinds of names behind my back and to my face. What can I do for you?"

"Let me give you the low down on why I'm here. I assume both of you have top secret clearances?" Colonel Burgess asked. After Ian and Charlie nodded, the colonel continued. "Charlie, the president believes it is important to have a defensive weapon in case Iran, or a client terrorist organization, tries to get within range of the United States and launch weapons of their own design, including WMDs. They wouldn't need highly accurate weapons, to wreak havoc on the U.S. As you are probably aware the Bomarc B, with its four hundred mile plus range, was originally designed to destroy Russian bombers, like the Tu-95 Bear and the Tu-16 Badger, over the ocean.

The plan is to build eight bases that will house long range, fast missiles to destroy any of the aforementioned threats, out at sea. In addition, they also need to have a high altitude and a quick launch capability; the Bomarc missile designed and built by Boeing, in the 1960's and 1970's, came to mind. My first, two year, Air Force assignment, was at an East Coast Bomarc base, before the program was shut down."

Charlie replied, "I was in on the development of the B version, after the A version failures became problematic. I believe we still have all the design drawings and documentation in our vaults. Since you're only asking for new guidance modules, the design time should be fairly short, especially if we "steal" designs for GPS and TERCOM from other programs."

"That sounds promising, Charlie." Colonel Burgess responded.

"I have two important questions, before we go any further." Ian said. "Does the Administration have the funding for such an undertaking – missiles, equipment, and shelters? Also, what is the projected timeframe for completion of all eight bases with missiles?"

The colonel replied, "The president has access to all kinds of funds, so that will not be a problem. This has high priority in the president's plans. As far as the time frame, we're talking about three years to have the bases built and operational. In order to make this attractive to your company, we're willing to award a cost-plus-incentive fee, sole source contract. The most important factor in the planning is that we need these bases to be operational within three years."

"Where are the bases going to be located, colonel?" Ian asked.

"Present planning calls for three on the East Coast, three on the West Coast and two on the Gulf Coast. One of the East coast bases will be located near Camp Lejeune, in North Carolina. The exact locations of the other bases are still being worked out. By the way, I forgot to mention that all of your personnel who work on the project, named "Red Moon", must have at least a secret clearance."

"That shouldn't be any problem; most of our management and engineers already have clearances. One other question, concerning this proposed system, is how would the missiles be launched and by whom? This may determine how the guidance systems are developed." Ian queried.

"The eight new CIM-10C bases will be placed under the direct control of the JSS and the SOCC. They could launch and control the missiles directly by entering target data automatically from the SOCC, either by satellite or by cable. That's as much as we've determined right now."

"I think that will be enough for us to work with." Charlie responded.

Reverting to formality, the colonel asked, "Mr. Black, can your company develop and forward to me at the NSC, in one week, a rough estimate for the guidance system development costs and the expected cost for manufacture of each missile? This assumes the quantity will be the sixty units, I mentioned earlier."

"Colonel, I believe we can do that as long as you don't hold us to the exact amount. It would be, as you said, a rough estimate."

"That will be great. I'll expect your answer next Monday. I have to leave now because I have to get back to Washington by this evening. Thank you both for your time."

Colonel Burgess exited Ian's office, after he shook hands with him and Charlie.

After he left, Ian turned to Charlie and said, "We had better get to work. We've only got one week to put together a proposal. Why don't you go down to the documentation area, to determine what drawings and specifications are available on the Bomarc B program."

"Right away, boss." Charlie said as he left Ian's office.

Ian sat down at his desk and thought about the challenges that would be connected with this Red Moon project.

****

After the project had been completed, within the scheduled three years, and the president had the required eight Bomarc missile bases, Ian decided it was time to retire from business life and head back to Tennessee. He left on a "high note", since the program, with the sole source contract, had increased the company's profits substantially.

2

Cayman Fishing Expedition

A few years later, a taxi pulled up to the General Aviation Terminal (GAT) at the Owen Roberts International Airport, located on Grand Cayman Island, and out stepped Ian Black, onto the sidewalk, in front of the building. He paid the cab driver and strode into the terminal looking for the bar area, where he could get a drink.

Ian still didn't look his age; most people now thought he was in his early fifties, but in reality he was sixty-eight. His brown hair had turned silver gray, but it was still full and neatly trimmed. As always, he walked with military precision and gave an aura of being a leader of men.

He walked up to the "Visitors" booth, where there was a pretty young hostess, who smiled at Ian as he approached.

"Where can I find the lounge, Jasmine?" he asked, as he looked at her name tag.

"It's over there, sir," responded the hostess, as she pointed to an area that overlooked the fleet of business jets, located on the parking apron.

"Thank you," Ian said, with a smile, as he went toward the lounge.

He entered the café/bar area and found a seat, from which he could watch the planes land and take off. He glanced at his watch and noted that he had forty-five minutes to wait before Peter Miles would turn up. The flight to Nashville was scheduled to depart at around 4:00 pm local time. They had flown down here in Peter's business jet to do some deep sea fishing. He was Ian's first cousin once removed, and he owned a successful Country Music recording company in Nashville. While he was down here in the Cayman Islands, Peter wanted to take care of some personal financial issues, in George Town.

As Ian sat there drinking his beer, he started to reminisce about his early days in the British Army and the United States Air Force. Because his mother was an American and his father was British, he had dual citizenship and could live in either country. As a lieutenant, his first tour of duty with the British Army Intelligence Corps was in Cyprus, during the late 1950's Emergency. While there, he quickly learned how to fly an Avro Shackleton four engine plane, when both pilots became disabled. When the Cyprus Emergency ended with a peace treaty, he was stationed in Berlin about six months before the East Germans constructed the Wall. He had a short affair, with a German girl who just happened to be the mistress of Erich Honecker, and Ian obtained advance information, about the Wall and when it was going to be built. Even though the intelligence wasn't acted upon, he became a "hero" to his superiors.

Ian came out of his day dreaming and returned to the warm, sunny July day.

The waitress approached his table and asked, "Do you want another beer, sir?"

Ian looked down at his glass and was amazed that it was empty. He must have drunk it all, as he reminisced.

"Yes, please," he replied.

Soon, she reappeared with the beer, saying, as she placed it on the table, "Here you go, sir."

"Thanks," Ian responded.

At that moment, a large business jet landed on runway two six, and once it pulled off the active runway, taxied toward the General Aviation Terminal.

As it approached the GAT, Ian finally got a glimpse of the jet as it made its way to the parking apron by the Terminal. It was larger than most of the business jets he had seen before, and he noticed that it had no markings on it. As it came to a stop, immediately, three stretch vehicles, two limousines and one large SUV, drove up close to the aircraft, and out of the first one stepped a man dressed in a striped business suit and tie. He waited close to the aircraft, as the **Island Air** ground crew of the GAT rolled up a portable passenger ramp.

When the aircraft's door was opened from the inside, the man, who was later identified as an assistant to the former U.S. Senator Harry Thornton, walked up the stairs and entered the plane. In a couple of minutes, he reappeared with six burly looking men and came down onto the tarmac. They were a stern group and you could tell by the look on their faces, and the bulge under their jackets, that they took their job seriously. They were well equipped to do what they had to do, if any danger came between them and their employer. Once they were deployed on the ground and had secured the area, they signaled the plane that is was safe for the passengers to deplane.

Immediately, a man in flowing white robes appeared in the doorway. He was a tall, imposing man, in his late forties, with a black moustache and piercing dark eyes. He paused for a moment, adjusting his eyes to the bright sunlight, and then descended briskly down the portable stair ramp to the waiting middle limo, followed by his retinue of wives and servants. Harry Thornton's assistant and two bodyguards got into the lead vehicle and the rest of the people got into the rear stretch SUV. All three vehicles proceeded out of the airport area and drove toward George Town. The Middle Eastern man was well known in the Cayman Islands, and his group had already been cleared by the Cayman Immigration and Customs officials.

Just before they drove off, Peter Miles entered the Terminal and found Ian sipping his second beer. He thought that was a good idea and ordered one for himself.

"Hi, Ian, have you been waiting long?" Peter asked.

"No, only about thirty minutes. I've been sitting here drinking some beer and watching the aircraft arrive and takeoff. Do you know who owns that large aircraft out there?" Ian inquired. "One man that exited the plane was wearing long, flowing white robes, so I assume he was some big shot from the Middle East. He was followed by several people, including women, and he was met by a well dressed man who seemed to be acquainted with him."

"I don't know, but let me ask this guy coming toward us. I bet he can tell us. His job requires him to keep track of just about every important person who visits the island. It's his business to understand what is going on in this town," Peter responded.

A trim, well dressed man, with a moustache, approached their table, as Ian and Peter rose to greet him.

"Ian, may I introduce you to Superintendent Robert Lee of the George Town police department."

Then turning to the newcomer, Peter said with a laugh, "Bob, this is Ian Black, a friend of mine and he's clean as a whistle, as far as I know."

Ian and Bob shook hands, saying "pleased to meet you" to each other and then sat down.

"Ian, you're not a native born American, are you? I detect a slight accent." asked Bob.

"Actually, Bob, I'm not. My father was English and my mother was an American. I guess I'm half and half."

"Where were you born?"

"I was born in Richmond. How about you Bob? You sound somewhat British to me", Ian replied.

"Yes, as a matter of fact I am. I was born in Hampton, lived in East Twickenham and started out going to Broomfield House School in Kew. After attending King's School Canterbury, I joined the Metropolitan Police Service and managed, after a couple of years, to get on the Scotland Yard's Flying Squad. It was great experience, and then one day I saw an advertisement for a police superintendent here on the Islands. I came out to the Cayman Islands a few years ago and have been here ever since. It's a great job and I enjoy every minute of it."

"I also started out at Broomfield House School and had a friend with the last name of Lee. It's been a long time, but I think his first name was Howard, if my memory serves me well. Is he a relative of yours by any chance?"

"Well, yes, he actually is. He's my father. It's a small world isn't it?"

Peter turned to Ian and Bob. "Ian, I hate to interrupt you two, but we have to get going. We need to get back to Nashville by nightfall.

"Okay, Peter but I have one last question of Bob here.

"Bob, do you know who that large plane out there on the parking apron belongs too. He looked like an Arab, since he was dressed in long, white flowing robes."

"Yes, I think I do Ian. I was advised yesterday that he was probably going to land here this afternoon. The plane belongs to Prince Ahmad Hassain of Saudi Arabia, a very wealthy oil man. He comes here now and again, very discretely. What he does here I don't know, but when he arrives, we seem to get a few other planes with no country of origin on them. In addition, a couple of large yachts arrive in the harbor with Panama registration. All the owners appear to be friends of the former U.S. Senator Harry Thornton and stay at his estate. The only visitor I have become acquainted with is a German industrialist by

17

the name of Karl Schiller. He comes here every four years and stays at Thornton's estate on the edge of town. That's about all I know. They never cause me any trouble, but it's all very mysterious."

When Ian heard the name Karl Schiller, he thought back to the two men he overheard in Berlin, many years ago. One was named Lutz Schiller. He wondered if somehow they were related, even though Schiller was a very common German surname.

"Thanks for the information Bob. It's been great to meet you." With that Ian shook Bob's hand and bade him goodbye.

"I'm ready to go now," Ian told Peter, who was looking pensively at his watch, since they were supposed to leave at 4:00 pm and it was already 4:15 pm.

"Its' been a pleasure meeting you again, Bob. If you'll ever in Nashville, please look me up." Peter quickly added.

"I certainly will."

"Come on, Ian, The pilot is waiting for us in the plane."

Ian paid the bar tab and followed Peter out to his business jet, parked on the BAT parking apron. They climbed in, and then the engines were started up.

The pilot came on the intercom:

"Gentlemen, please fasten your seat belts. We'll be taking off shortly. It should be about a two and a half hour flight, and the weather is excellent all the way, so we don't expect any bumps."

Soon, they were winging their way over the Gulf of Mexico, toward the Florida Panhandle and then on to Nashville, Tennessee; a distance of approximately thirteen hundred miles. Since Cuba required a fee for flying over her territory, the pilot flew the plane around the restricted area surrounding the island.

3

Secret Committee Meeting

Meanwhile, the limo drivers, who knew their ultimate destination, needed no instructions as to how they should get there, since Senator Thornton's assistant was in the lead vehicle. They sped through the Grand Cayman Island capital of George Town and ended up on the bluff above the city. They turned off the paved highway onto a gravel road and drove about one hundred yards, to a high iron gate, which was the entrance to a walled estate. There was a guard house at the gateway with three men posted outside, all armed with machine guns. Senator Thornton's assistant identified himself and his passengers to the guards, who then passed all three vehicles through the gate. The long driveway went on for several hundred yards through lush gardens full of trees, flowers and ornate statuary dotting the landscape. There were ponds and waterfalls along the way. It was a picturesque setting leading up to the stately mansion that was the center piece of the compound.

The first two limos came to a halt at the bottom of the steps, which led up to the front door. Two more armed men were standing on guard at each side of the portal. Senator Thornton's assistant got out of the first limo, went back to the second limo and waited for the driver to open the door. As soon as the door was opened, the prince got out and ascended the stairs to the entrance of the mansion, followed by the senator's assistant. The stretch SUV, with the wives and servants, drove to the quarters they had been assigned.

At that moment, Harry Thornton, himself, came out of the front door and greeted the prince.

"Prince Hassain, it is a pleasure to see you again. It has been quite awhile, since you were here last. I'm glad you could make it to this important meeting of the Committee. We certainly need your advice.

"Thank you for inviting me to your beautiful estate. I'm glad I could fit it into my busy schedule," replied the prince, arrogantly.

The Saudi prince was the last to arrive for the meeting, and the senator led him to where the others were gathered. It was late in the afternoon, and some of the other guests already had their evening cocktails in their hands. The prince never drank back at home, as it was against the religion of his country, but here, however, he could indulge himself with a glass of Jack Daniels, neat, and not watered down, as some people drank their whiskey. There was idle conversation, as he entered the main meeting room.

"Prince Hassain, great to see you again," said Karl Schiller, in a thick German accent.

Karl was a wealthy industrialist from Bonn, Germany. He had been one of the last to join the International Economic and Financial Development committee, known as the Committee to its members. He had actually been recruited by the prince. They both had a strong interest in, and would benefit from, the downfall of democracy in the United States and the resulting financial fallout. The overall mission of the Committee was to promote power in political leaders they could control and, by causing an increase in the socialist programs of the major economies, increase their own wealth dramatically.

Other Committee members in the room included: Jun Matsui, a Japanese banker; Wei Chan, a Chinese government official; Leo DiMaggio, the head of one of the strongest mafias in the US; Andras Nagy, a Hungarian international financier; Giorgios Demas, a Greek shipping magnate; Boris Petrokov, the head of the Russian secret service; Martin Hunt, an American media mogul; Charles Toole, an Australian mining magnate. Each of the Committee members had a mutual interest, which was to see the U.S. government become a dictatorship, run by the Committee.

They all greeted the prince and then continued their conversations. At a half past six, their host came into the room.

"Thank you all for coming, and welcome to my home. Please be seated and we will begin our meeting," said former Senator Harry Thornton.

At one time, Harry Thornton had been a powerful man in the U.S. Senate. His downfall and disgrace came, after it was discovered that he had been laundering money brought in to the U.S., by a Mexican drug cartel. It also didn't help matters, when it was discovered that the distinguished senator from California, and father of four, had a mistress in the Cayman Islands, half his age. He had wrongly believed that his party would support him and gloss over his indiscretions, like they had done so many times in the past for others in his party. They had even looked after and protected a former president, for having a blatant affair with a young intern, while he was in office. But no, they had not turned a blind eye when Thornton was indicted. Many of them disliked the senator, some for his arrogance and others for his total disregard for the well being of his constituents.

"We are here today to put into place the first step in our plan," Harry Thornton continued. "Leo DiMaggio will now brief you on what this step will be. Leo."

"Gentlemen" Leo began, "you all know that we have been searching for the ideal candidate to run for U.S. president. I believe we have found the person for our purpose. He is a young lawyer who, a few years ago, joined the legal department of a firm located in Boston. In school, he was a mediocre student, but was hired because the owner of the company, and his father, were in the war together. He recently ran for Congress from Illinois and won handily, with the assistance of a bright lawyer, Valda Lewis. He is married to his college sweetheart and has three small children. In addition, he is ambitious, arrogant and thinks very highly of himself. I believe he can be controlled for our purpose, by letting him believe he is the savior of the American people. His father was killed in the Vietnam War; a war that his father did not believe in, but was forced to fight in. This young man is very bitter, and he believes that the capitalist government of the U.S. should be replaced, with a socialist one. All we have to do is convince him that the only way, to make the desired changes he wants, is for him to become president. His name is Edward Tuckwell."

A murmur went up in the room.

"*Who the hell is Edward Tuckwell?*" they all thought, except Prince Hassain. He knew Edward Tuckwell very well, since they had been roommates in university. He knew that Leo's assessment of him was exactly correct. The prince had always thought that Edward Tuckwell was arrogant, even to the point in thinking that he and the prince were good friends. As if he, the richest man in his country and a prince, no less, would consider someone like Edward his equal. Most of the Committee's thinking had been to run someone well known for president.

They all thought, "*How do you win an election with someone, no one has ever heard of?*"

"Fellow Committee members," Leo said, regaining their attention. "I know what you're thinking. Yes, he is an unknown, but that is the beauty of it. He is untarnished by today's standards; he is young, attractive and impressionable. Most importantly, he is mesmerizing when he speaks; even when he doesn't believe in what he is saying. At the last convention held by his Party, he gave a rousing speech that was the talk of the attending delegates. People who have seen him at work in court say he's brilliant. It is believed that he could sell the Golden Gate Bridge to Donald Trump and make him believe he really owns it. Besides, there are ways one can manipulate and rig an election; you just have to have the correct people with the right connections. I believe we have the right people here in this room to pull off such an election. Of course it will have to be carefully planned and initiated. We would also have to have a person in place to keep an eye on things after he's elected, someone he trusts. Someone he knows and feels like has his best interest at heart."

After that last remark, Leo stood silently for a few minutes, letting all he had just said sink in and filter through their minds. *"After all, these colleagues weren't where they were by making hasty and poorly thought out decisions,"* he realized. Someone coughed in the room, but no one said anything. They had worked long and hard leading up to this moment, and needed to make sure their selection, for a particular candidate, was the correct decision.

Breaking the silence, Harry Thornton spoke, "Gentlemen, I recommend we sleep on it. In the meantime, you can have the proposed candidate checked out and make an informed decision tomorrow. Right now, I suggest we go to dinner and have a pleasant evening together."

They filed out of the room and followed the senator down the long hallway to the large magnificent dining room. Harry had spared no expense in having the mansion decorated, and this room was his pride and joy. The dining table could easily seat twenty people. At the end of the room, there was a huge ornate fireplace located in the center of the wall, and above it hung a large gold leaf framed mirror. The fireplace was hardly used however, since the weather was usually pleasant and mild on the island. The walls were filled with original paintings of the Masters. The china, crystal and silver were the finest money could buy. Some he had acquired legally and others by not so honest means. He felt it was his right to have these beautiful things. It didn't matter that they were gains gotten over many dead bodies and ruined lives. He was proud to show off his treasures to this illustrious group. Surely they would show him the respect he deserved and craved. After all, they were in a league above the other peons, who thought they ran the world. Fools all of them, the Committee would bring them to their knees.

They sat down and began their six course dinner. By the end of the evening, the guests were full of excellent food and premium wines. They felt a sense of utopia and comradeship. Without a doubt, each of them would sleep well tonight, and then get up refreshed for tomorrow's critical meeting and vote.

4

The Choice

The following day promised to be full of sunshine and gentle breezes, according to the weather forecast, and it would be just right for a game of golf or a cooling swim in the pool. Curiously, no one had been seen on the grounds or on the golf course. Breakfast had been served in each guest quarters, and there seemed to be an odd silence over the estate. However, Leo wasn't worried; in fact, it was a good sign. The members of the Committee were being cautious and doing a thorough investigation of her nominee. They had to be positive that he was the one, or all their posturing, and hard work, would be for naught. When they put their plan into action, they had to be certain of its outcome. If they failed, it could mean the downfall for all of them.

Around six o'clock in the evening, they began to gather once again, in the grand parlor of Harry Thornton's home. They were unusually quiet and subdued, unlike the evening before. With a drink in hand, they waited for the arrival of their host and Leo DiMaggio.

At exactly half past six, the two of them arrived together, and everyone sat down expectantly.

Leo nodded to the Committee members in the room and began to speak.

"Gentleman, I believe we have all had a fair chance to think the situation over and come to a decision on how to vote. Does anyone have any questions?"

Karl Schiller stood up and said, "I have checked out this Edward Tuckwell and I believe he may be an excellent choice for our purpose. Also, I believe it will take a great deal of careful planning to accomplish what we have in mind, and therefore we will need someone who can control the situation from the inside. None of us can overtly be involved or implicated in any way."

"I agree", said Prince Hassain. "We need someone he trusts and will listen to. Do you have someone in mind?"

"Yes, I believe I can answer that," said Harry Thornton. "Valda Lewis, whose name was mentioned yesterday, has performed legal work for Leo and, in addition, she is also a friend of Edward Tuckwell. When he was hired by the legal department of Overseas Transit in Boston, she took him under her wing and was his mentor. When he ran for Congress, she was by his side, as an advisor. I am reasonable sure he will listen to her, so I recommend that we put her in charge of controlling him and overseeing the operation. I have complete confidence in her ability to complete the task to our satisfaction."

There was whispered conversation in the room; there were some who weren't really comfortable with giving that much responsibility to a woman.

Harry Thornton spoke again, "If you all agree, then I think it is time to put these issues to a vote. Do you concur?"

There was a murmur of assent.

"Then" said Harry Thornton, "All of you in favor of Edward Tuckwell as our candidate, raise your hand."

Several hands went up into the air and, when the others looked around and saw who had voted yes, they also raised their hands in favor. It was unanimous. They had all done their homework on Edward Tuckwell, and he seemed to be the best choice they could make. For sure, time was running out for them to make their move, so he would have to do.

"Now" said Harry Thornton, "I say we vote to support this Valda Lewis, as the liaison to Edward Tuckwell. She will be working closely with Leo here, to put our plan into action"

He knew if he inserted Leo into the equation, the members, who were uncomfortable with a woman in such an important position, would have their misgivings laid aside. He was right. They voted one hundred percent to put Valda Lewis in charge. It was decided that she would report to Leo, and he in turn would report to Harry Thornton. The former senator from California would keep the rest of the Committee informed and issue time lines, for what their involvement would be to get Tuckwell elected.

Harry Thornton continued, "Since we have accomplished what we came here for, the meeting is now adjourned. We will meet again in four years on August 25th through 29th, unless there is an urgent matter to be dealt with. If it is appropriate at that time, we will have Valda Lewis come to the meeting, with Leo, to give us a report. Thank you all for coming."

With this important business laid to rest, the mood lightened, more drinks were passed around and the conversation became more congenial. Dinner that evening was an elegant repeat of the night before. When they all returned to their guest quarters, it was with a feeling of excitement and anticipation for the coming months ahead.

5

Persuasion and Agreement

Before Leo had gone to the meeting in the Cayman Islands, he had called Valda Lewis in Boston and mentioned that he might suggest Edward Tuckwell's name for his group's potential candidate.

"Valda, this is Leo. I'm going out of town for a few days to attend a meeting of a group I belong to. Every four years we look for a candidate to support for president. This year I'm going to promote Congressman Tuckwell to the group. What do you think? I've seen him in action and he seems to have a lot of drive. In addition, he's a great orator who I believe can hypnotize the uninformed voters."

"Leo. It's great to talk to you again. It's been awhile. As far as Tuckwell is concerned, I don't think you could have selected a better candidate, especially in this year of fiscal breakdown and overseas entanglements. I support your choice."

"I appreciate your approval of my choice. This brings up another matter concerning our group's support of a candidate. If they do give their votes of assent to Tuckwell, we'll need someone to help run his campaign and keep an eye on him. Would you be willing to take over a year of absence from your job, if your company approves it? If not, would you be amenable to quitting your job, as long as we make up for your lost pay?"

"Yes, Leo, I look forward to helping out if need be. I'll probably quit my job, although I believe they'd hire me back in a second, if I became available."

"Good, that's settled then. I'll call you when I get back from the meeting. I'm sorry I can't tell you anymore about the group I'm involved with. They're very secretive."

"That's okay, Leo. I trust you. I'll look forward to your call in a few days. Bye."

****

Leo DiMaggio flew back on Sunday afternoon from the Cayman Island meeting to Chicago, where he ran the Atlas Group of companies. Almost immediately, he called Valda Lewis, in her Boston apartment, to inform her about the Committee's decisions.

The phone rang in Valda's apartment and she picked it up.

"Valda, speaking."

"This is Leo and I've just returned from my meeting with the group. They're going to support Edward Tuckwell for president and they want you to be his advisor. They also want you to keep an eye on him, to make sure he doesn't stray from the objective. In turn, you'll report to me on how the campaign is going and financial matters. Is that okay?"

"Of course, I'll be glad to help as I said the other day. I'll call Edward right now and have him fly to Boston, so I can put the proposition to him. I would rather do it in person, than on the telephone that can be bugged."

"That's a good idea, Valda. Let me know what he says, after you tell him that there's a group willing to support him for president."

29

"I'll do that. Bye for now, Leo."

Immediately, Valda dialed Edward Tuckwell's number in Chicago and his wife, Leslie, answered.

"Edward Tuckwell's phone, May I help you?"

"Leslie, this is Valda Lewis speaking. Is Edward available?"

"Hi, Valda, I'll get him for you."

In about ten seconds, Edward came to the phone.

"Hi, Valda, what can I do for you?"

"I've got something very important I want to talk to you about. Would you be able to meet me on Tuesday, here in Boston? It's too sensitive to speak about over the phone. Plus, one never knows who's listening."

She sounded mysterious and piqued Edward's interest. He quickly looked at his appointment schedule and was disappointed to see his assistant had booked him for a charity luncheon, in his district on the same day.

"Hmm," he thought, *"Valda would never have asked him on such short notice, if it wasn't something really important. She had never steered him wrong before. She was one of the few people he trusted, besides his wife."*

Edward replied, "Okay, I've looked at my calendar and I can be there on Tuesday. I'll book a flight and get back to you, with the time and flight number. Can you meet me at the airport?"

"Sure. I'll pick you up and we can go for breakfast. I know a great, quiet restaurant, where we can talk in privacy."

"Sounds, good, see you then."

****

On Tuesday morning, Edward Tuckwell caught the 7:00 am flight from Chicago O'Hare to Boston Logan airport. He had been lucky to get a seat. Generally, the early morning commuter flight was full with business people. The plane arrived on time, for a change. He exited the terminal and found Valda waiting at the arrival loading zone. The security police were about to chase her out of there, because she had been waiting too long.

Edward climbed into her car and said, "Good morning, it's great to see you again."

"Good to see you too, it's been awhile," Valda replied. "I've decided it would be best to have breakfast first and then we can talk business in a park, where no one can listen in."

"Okay by me," said Edward. "You must have something really important to discuss."

"Yes, in fact I do."

Valda stopped at a small restaurant that she knew served an excellent breakfast. After they had ordered, they talked about the weather and politics in Washington.

The waitress brought their food and they ate fairly quickly, so they could leave and get down to business.

After leaving the restaurant, Valda drove to Copley Square Park at Boylston and Dartmouth. She was lucky to find a spot in a nearby parking garage, and then she walked with Edward to the park. They found a seat that was not close to any other bench. She glanced around to make sure no one was within listening range.

"Edward, I'll come straight to the point. How would you like to run for president? Recently, there was a meeting of important, international people who want to support a candidate, and they have selected you. This group believes that you are the right person to take this country forward, in a new direction. The troubles, facing this country right now, call for someone with a new vision. What do you think?"

Edward could not believe what he was hearing. *"Run for president?"* he thought. This was a dream he had for as long as he could remember.

He would promise the people the "moon", if he had to. He knew that if he could entice enough uninformed people to vote, by offering them free goodies from the government, he could win. Julius Caesar and Adolf Hitler had demonstrated that this would work.

"Yes," he said, "I would run, if I have enough backing. Are they willing to donate enough funding to finance the campaign?"

"Yes, they are," Valda said, with emphasis. "We'll have to find ways to hide the donations, as some funds are from foreigners, which is against US election laws."

"This all sounds great. I'll need a couple of days to think about it and then I'll let you know. Is that okay?"

"Yes, but no more than two days. If you don't accept the offer, the organization has someone else in mind."

She drove him to the airport and dropped him off at the departure area.

"Edward, don't forget to call me in two days. If you are going to run for president, we need to get organized as soon as possible."

Edward nodded and said," I promise I'll call you by Thursday morning. Would you be on my team if I run for president, like you were when I ran for Congress?"

"Absolutely, I wouldn't miss it for the world. You and I make a great team," she answered with a smile. She had counted on him to ask that question. "I'd be with you every step of the way."

She watched him as he got out of the car and walked toward the airport. He seemed to swagger, as he entered the building.

"*Arrogant little bastard,*" she thought. "*I bet he thinks he is in control of his destiny. What a fool he is. All you had to do was play to his ego a little and you could get him to agree to almost anything. He had a typical short man's complex. I'll see what he says on Thursday.*"

After returning to her apartment, Valda gives Leo a call at his office.

"Leo, can you talk?"

"Yes, just for a few minutes."

"I told Edward Tuckwell about the offer for him to run for president, and he stated that he needed two days to think about it. If I know him, I believe he will jump at it."

"Good. When he calls you, contact me immediately and let me know his decision. We have to get moving on this or the Committee will not be happy."

"Okay, I understand. I'll be in touch", Valda replied.

****

Two days later, at 8:30 in the morning, Valda received a phone call from Edward in her apartment.

"Valda, this is Edward. I have given the offer that you made me, a great deal of thought, and I have decided that I can't pass it up. I am ready to run for the presidency."

"That's great news, Edward. We don't have time to waste, and we need to get a campaign organization up and running. Luckily, your backers will take care of this, so all you need to do is to get yourself prepared for a grueling primary season and to hone your basic message."

"I have some great ideas, for the campaign and the messaging, which I will tell you about when we meet."

"Edward, I'll be in touch with you in a few days, as soon as I get everything organized. I already have a potential campaign manager who comes highly recommended, and we will set up your headquarters in Chicago. As soon as this accomplished, I will let you know where the office is and when we will meet there. Talk to you soon, Edward." Valda said, as she hung up thinking *"I've got to phone Leo and let him know the news."*

Valda dialed Leo on his private cell number.

"Leo, we have a candidate for the presidency. He fell for it hook, line and sinker", she said.

"Good," Leo replied. "Did he ask you to be on his campaign team?"

"Oh, yes," she laughed. "He thinks I'm his good luck charm. What do you want me to do next?" Valda asked.

"Resign from your job and get back here to Chicago as soon as possible. I'll get the campaign headquarters set up and activate the bank account for the funding. When you get here, call me and I'll give you all the information. By the way, I've booked you into the penthouse suite at The Palmer House, all expenses paid for the next year." Leo said, smiling to himself. He thought, *"I just may visit her a few times while she's here; just for old times' sake."*

Valda prepared her letter of resignation and turned it in. Her boss was taken by surprise, but accepted it. He knew how strong willed she was, and it would be a waste of time to try to get her to stay.

"How soon do you plan to leave?" he asked.

"I plan to leave by the end of the week," she said. "I'll finish up what I can and turn the rest over to Guy, my assistant; he should be able to handle things. I'll be available by phone to help, if he needs me."

"We'll miss you and, of course, your job will always be open, if you change your mind."

"Thanks, I'll keep that in mind," she said, as she left his office.

When Valda sat down at her desk, she tried to concentrate on her work, but it was useless. She thought of the upcoming campaign and the possibility that she would be a presidential advisor with all that power, made it difficult to tend to the paperwork at hand.

"I'll make myself indispensable to Edward Tuckwell and play his game, with so much finesse, that he'll believe he can't make a decision without my advice. If I know him, like I think I do, he hates to make decisions. It will be his indecisiveness that will put me in control," she mused.

6

Old History

She checked to see if the movers had taken all her belongings to storage. Everything seemed to be in good order. She'd miss this place she had to admit, but she consoled herself, with the thought of what the next few years could bring. She picked up the phone and called for a taxi to take her to the Boston Logan airport; she was on her way.

Valda's flight arrived at Chicago O'Hare around one o'clock in the afternoon. It was busy as usual, but as she walked out of the airport arrival area, down to the baggage claim on the lower level, she noticed a uniformed man holding a sign, bearing her name. Valda went up to him and told him, "That's me."

The driver told her he had been sent by the Atlas Transportation Company to help her. She pointed out her bags as they came down the baggage chute and he picked them up. He then led her outside to the black, stretched limo, parked close by and opened the door for her to get in.

"How thoughtful of Leo," she mused.

When she got into the back seat of the vehicle, there was a box of red roses on the seat and an envelope addressed to her.

It read, *"Welcome back. I've missed you,* Leo."

To tell the truth, she'd missed him also. They had been an item once, and she felt warm thinking of the nights they had spent, making love in her bed. Maybe they would get together while she was here. She knew that she'd be pretty busy with Edward Tuckwell's campaign, but maybe they could sneak a few nights alone. *"Just for old times' sake,"* she thought, as she smiled to herself.

Valda hadn't dated much in college; she had been too busy with her studies. She had graduated with honors and was on the Dean's List at the Harvard's School Of Law. There was no end to job offers she had received, when she graduated. She had taken one with a prestigious law firm in Chicago, by the name of Baker, Howard and Bell. After she had worked there a few months, the company gave a party for its most important clients.

That's where she had met Leo. She felt him, before she saw him, and when she looked up, he was staring at her intently. Valda thought he was the sexiest man she had ever seen, and when he walked over to her, her knees went weak. She had never felt like that before, with any man; it was overwhelming. They left the party together and ended up in bed at her apartment. It was like the world exploded, being with him. Each time he left her, she couldn't wait for their next rendezvous. Since Leo was married, they always met at her place. She didn't care, as long as she could be with him. It wasn't until a couple of years had gone by that she found out, what Leo did for a living. He was being groomed to take over one of the largest mafia organizations in Illinois, by his wife's father. But, by that time, she was so entrenched in the affair that she didn't care.

Their affair had lasted almost five years until, by chance one day, she met Leo's wife, LeAnna, while having lunch at Leonardo's restaurant, in downtown Chicago.

The law firm that Valda worked for represented the Atlas Group and a luncheon meeting was set up, in a private room, to discuss certain legal matters, which Atlas wanted to clear up. The Atlas Group of companies was owned by a Salvatore (Sal) Maneri and consisted of the following organizations:

> Atlas Movie Company
> Atlas Communications Company
> Atlas Security Company
> Atlas Construction Company
> Atlas Transportation Company

Valda was asked by her boss to accompany him to the meeting, and it was here that she met LeAnna DiMaggio. Sal could not attend the meeting due to his poor health, and he sent his daughter, LeAnna, to represent him.

It was a day Valda would never forget. Leo's wife was not only beautiful, but seemed quite sure of her position in Leo's life, since she referred to her husband glowingly. It was then Valda realized that, if she was to have a life of her own, she'd have to leave Chicago and Leo.

She submitted her resume to several firms, on the east and west coasts. Almost immediately, a large firm in Boston, Overseas Transit, offered her a job, as head of their legal department. Valda accepted their offer, packed her bags and left Chicago, without telling Leo goodbye. She knew that she'd never be able to leave, if he knew. He eventually found out where she'd gone and called one evening. She explained why she had left, and Leo knew she was right. They stayed friends over the years, keeping in contact by phone, never in person.

Later, when Sal died, LeAnna inherited the Group and Leo ended up managing the organization for his wife. In one way or another, Leo became involved in gambling, prostitution, drugs, casinos and money laundering. As a result, he became a very powerful and wealthy man in his own right. Chicago politicians often came to him, for advice and financial help, which indebted them to him.

7

Lovers Reunion

After Valda had settled into her suite at the Palmer House, she called Leo to let him know that she had arrived.

"Leo, I'm here in Chicago ready to go to work for the Tuckwell campaign. What do you want me to do?"

"I'm glad you're here in the Windy City, since I need to meet with you to go over some items concerning the campaign. I'll come to your suite around 6:00 pm for a discussion, if that's okay?"

Valda hesitated for a moment, and then said, "Yes, that will be fine. I'll see you here at 6:00."

As soon as she hung up the phone, she regretted that she had agreed to see Leo, in her suite alone. Valda knew that, if he wanted to make love to her, she could not resist him. Even when she talked to him on the phone, her heart beat faster and her pulse raced. There was too much at stake now, for her not to be in total control. Yet, she could not help, but feel that same old feeling she had, when she thought of him.

"*I'll call him back and make an excuse,*" she thought.

She picked up the phone to do just that, but she slowly put the receiver back down, with a sigh, and resigned herself to the fact that she needed to see him, as much as he needed to see her. There were lots of unresolved issues to be faced and taken care of.

He would be there in two hours and she made up her mind to enjoy the evening, however it turned out. Filling the bath tub with warm bubbly water, she slid her still beautiful, lithe body into the foam and relaxed. She had not gained an ounce since her college days. Despite the severe bun she wore her hair in at work; she was still a woman that received men's attention, when she walked into a room. She soaked for a good thirty minutes, and then after drying herself off, she put on a soft, terrycloth bath robe. She brushed her long auburn hair, until it shone. She decided to leave it down, because Leo liked her to wear it that way. She applied her make up and went to the closet, to choose what she'd wear. Valda had always had excellent taste in clothing and generally only wore clothes with a fancy label. All of her things were from a few famous designers, such as Versace or Hermès. She chose a long pair of black silk palazzo pants and a pure white silk blouse with pearl buttons, from The House of Wong. She took out the necklace with a long strand of perfectly matched pearls, and a set of identical earrings, and put them on. Leo had given them to her several years ago. Then she dabbed a bit of White Diamond perfume behind her ears, it was Leo's favorite.

As she looked in the mirror, she saw an attractive, sexy woman looking back at her. *"Not bad,"* she thought. She hoped Leo would also think so.

Going back into the living room, she decided to put on some soft music and make herself a drink, to calm her nerves. As she sat and sipped her drink, she thought of all the things she would say to him and what his response might be. She also thought, a little anxiously, what he might say to her. *"Had he forgiven her for leaving Chicago and*

40

going to Boston, without telling him goodbye?" He seemed to overlook her sudden departure, whenever they talked on the phone. However, Leo was good at disguising his true feelings, most of the time. Well, whatever their feelings were, they must remember the mission they were on, at all cost. The Committee would not tolerate less than success on their part. Their lives were on the line, and she knew it.

She was so deep in thought that, when the door bell rang, she jumped and almost dropped her drink. She got up unsteadily to her feet, and walked to the door, with her heart pounding.

As Valda looked through the security peep hole, she could see him standing there, and it took her breath away.

She opened the door, and they just looked at each other for a moment. Then he found his voice and said with a smile, "Aren't you going to ask me in?"

Startled, she said "Of course. I'm sorry, come on in."

She remembered his smile that she loved so much. It had been one of the main things that had attracted her to him, all those years ago. It made her knees weak.

As Leo handed her the flowers he had brought, (her favorite, Gardenias), he leaned over and gave her a slight kiss on her warm cheek. His lips felt hot on her face, as if the kiss had burned her skin. Valda turned away and, as they walked into the room, she said, "Thank you Leo, they are lovely."

"He remembered," she thought.

"Well," she said "It's great to see you again."

She thought to herself, *"He's just as handsome, or more so, than when I first met him, and just as sexy."*

"Have a seat Leo, while I put these into some water."

She left him, seated on the sofa, and went to the kitchen to get a vase to put the flowers in. When she placed the vase of flowers on the credenza, Leo handed her the champagne he had brought; it was a bottle of Bollinger Blanc de Noris Vieilles Francaises 1997.

"Nothing but the best for this night," Leo had thought, when he bought it.

As Valda took the bottle from him, their hands touched and it felt like electricity flowed through them. They quickly drew apart, and she poured some of the champagne into two etched flute glasses. She could not trust herself to sit on the sofa next to him, just yet, so she sat in the side chair, next to the sofa.

They sat and sipped silently, for a few minutes.

Then Leo said "Valda, I know we have been in contact by phone for some time, but I feel we never came to terms, with you leaving like you did, or at least I haven't."

"Oh, Leo, can't you see?" Valda said. "I had no other choice. If I had told you that I was leaving you, you would have persuaded me to stay and I needed, more than anything, to make a life for myself. If you hadn't been married to the daughter of one of Chicago's movers and shakers, I might have had some hope for us. Do you think LeAnna's father would have just let you divorce her and still be in the position you were in? I doubt we would both be alive today. I did it for both of us."

Valda's voice broke and tears were forming in her lovely green eyes. "I loved you too much, don't you see?" she said.

At that, the tears slid down her cheeks. Leo stood up, and before she could stop him, he took her in his arms and stroked her hair. "I've never stopped loving you either," he said. "And you're right; he would never have let it happen."

God, her scent was like honeysuckle, and he could feel her softness next to his body. He wanted to make love to her right then, but he knew she must be willing, for it to be as wonderful as it was before. He thought about the many nights and days they had laid in each others' arms touching, feeling and exploring each others' bodies. The joy they had felt with each climax and that wonderful feeling of excitement and expectation he felt, when he was on his way to see her. She was beautiful, but there was an intelligence and strength about her that heightened his feelings for her. His wife was beautiful also, but she had a way of clinging that always made him feel uncomfortable. To tell the truth, he probably would not have married her had he not worked for her father and was very ambitious. But that was before he met Valda. He felt he could be himself with her, he could forget about the side of his life he hated, when he was with her. He could lose himself in her love.

He felt her move away and immediately felt a void. She moved to the sofa and sat down, wiping the tears from her face.

"Leo," Valda said, "I'm glad we could talk and clear the air about us. However, we have to remember the task at hand; it is the most important thing we have to do right now. There are some pretty powerful people on the Committee, who would not look the other way, if we fail."

Leo knew she was right. They had to succeed, but it didn't make him to want her less; if anything he wanted her more. Her strength and determination turned him on, as much as her beauty.

They both sat down again and picked up their glasses of champagne.

"Leo, we're having a strategy meeting tomorrow at the Tuckwell campaign headquarters. Do you have anything that you want me to bring up or suggest at the meeting?" Valda said.

"Yes, as a matter of fact I do," replied Leo. "I've already got my own union men in place to influence the rank and file members, on how they should vote. We've also hired people to pack the town hall meetings in Tuckwell's favor, when he is scheduled to be speaking at them. The press has also been influenced to only ask him questions, acceptable to his campaign. Needless to say, Fox News has not been invited to cover the meetings."

Leo continued, "We have also put together a schedule for him to follow, including subject matter, dates and time.

The money's already in the Chicago branch of MB Financial, and only you, of course, will have access to the account. You will set up a separate account from which to draw money for his campaign, as needed. No one is to know of my involvement, except you and the Committee. It wouldn't look very good to have a man, in my business, openly supporting him. You and I will meet monthly to go over how things are going and make any changes necessary. We will also talk as often as necessary by phone. I'll have a private cell phone set up with a special number for you and myself, which no one else will have access to. I guess that's it for right now. Do you have any questions about anything I've just told you?"

"I don't believe so, not right now anyway," Valda replied.

"Good," Leo said. "Now let's have some more champagne and make a toast to our success."

They sat there and sipped their champagne in silence for a few minutes, barely looking at one another. When their eyes finally met, they both knew what they both so desperately wanted and needed from the other. They set their champagne glasses down and stood up. Leo took her in his arms and kissed her soft mouth; she responded with a low moan. He felt her firm breasts press against his chest, and he could feel his manhood rising. He picked her up in his arms and carried her to the bedroom. Here, he laid her down on the bed with her hair spread around her lovely face and unbuttoned her blouse. He undid her bra and kissed each breast; at which she gave a moan of pleasure. She sat up and slipped out of her clothing. *"God, she is beautiful,"* Leo thought. Then she reached for him and undid his belt, after which she unbuttoned his shirt and slid it off of his body, dropping it to the floor. He removed his pants and shorts and pulled her to him. With their passions rising, they fell onto the bed and he took her again and again, until they were both exhausted. They fell asleep in each other's arms. Just before dawn, he reached for her once more and she responded with as much passion, as she had the night before. If they had their way they would stay, just as they were, forever, but then reality set in. With a sigh, they both got up. Leo hurriedly got dressed, and Valda put on a dressing gown.

"I'll be back again as soon as I can." Leo promised.

They kissed a long kiss goodbye, and then he was gone.

"I wonder if this is a good idea for either of us, there is a lot at stake for both of us. We'll just have to be very careful, that's all," she thought. She needed him and his strength.

After Leo had gone, Valda made herself a cup of coffee and ate a slice of toast. As she sat at the table, she thought of the night before and the pleasure they had enjoyed. She wasn't sorry it had happened. But she was just a little apprehensive about the effect it would have on their mission, which she and Leo had undertaken. They must succeed at all costs.

With a sigh, she got up, went to the bathroom, took a shower and quickly dressed. Putting her hair up in the bun that she always wore to work, she looked nothing like the sexy woman of the night before. She needed to be all business, at the campaign planning session. Valda thought of the instructions Leo had given her last night, and mentally rehearsed the way she would present it to the campaign staff and Edward Tuckwell.

Valda picked up the hotel phone and dialed the number for her limo driver. The driver answered and Valda said, "I'm ready now. Can you pick me up immediately and take me to the Tuckwell campaign headquarters on Cicero?"

"Certainly Madame, I'll be there in less than five minutes and will be outside the hotel main entrance."

45

8

Running for President

Valda Lewis had called Edward Tuckwell Friday evening and asked him to meet her at the "Tuckwell for President" downtown Chicago office on Cicero, Monday, the 6th of August at 10:00 am, for a strategy meeting.

As he was driven in the limo, provided by Valda, from his house to downtown Chicago, Edward Tuckwell thought about his stroke of luck in being asked to run for president. He had gone to the University of California at Berkeley, where he studied law and political science. He had a mentor at the school, who was a confessed Marxist. Edward had absorbed this professor's socialist ranting, as a sponge would absorb water. He also thought about how he could put these Marxist principles into action, once he was president. He could change America, by appointing progressives to key posts in his administration. Back in the 1970's, they used to be called liberals and were generally members of the Americans for Democratic Action (ADA).

At that point, the limo pulled up outside his campaign headquarters.

"We're here, sir," said the limo driver, as they pulled up in front of a large office building, with the Tuckwell name shown prominently on a window. The driver got out and opened the door for Edward.

"Have a good day, sir", the driver said, as he tipped his hat.

Tuckwell walked toward the main office door. It suddenly opened, and there stood Valda Lewis to welcome him.

"Come on in," she said, "we're all waiting in the conference room to discuss the campaign."

They entered the conference room, and Valda introduced Edward to the Campaign Manager, William Hoare, and the Communications Director, Jeb Hudson. They all shook each others' hands, grabbed a cup of coffee and a bear claw pastry, and sat down around the conference table.

Valda Lewis started the meeting. "Our first goal is to make sure that Edward wins the nomination of his party. There're five other candidates, and Edward must win enough votes in the first few caucuses and primaries, to cause most of them to drop out, due to lack of campaign funds and momentum. Then, at the convention, we must persuade a majority of delegates that, if they want their party to win in November, they must go with Edward Tuckwell. Once he has the nomination, he must convince the independent middle class voters that he shares their values and concerns, and that he has plans for the government to help them, move up economically. We have the best campaign manager and the best communications manager, money can buy. Gentlemen, we depend on you to get Edward across the finish line, in first place."

After Valda had finished, William Hoare spoke directly to Edward. "As your campaign manager, I'm here to make sure you win, that is my task. Together with Jeb here, our job is to plan the strategy and tactics that will win the war. Yes, we're at war with the other candidates, and then with the candidate of the other party. What we need from you are the best speeches, you can deliver. We've heard your speeches as congressman, and they are excellent. You're a great communicator."

Valda turned to Edward and asked him, "Are you comfortable with allowing William to run your campaign? We must have your agreement on this to continue."

"Yes, I have the utmost confidence in him. I know how to communicate with people, but I'm not so good at planning. I believe that he and I will make a great team," replied Edward, looking at William and smiling.

"Good. First, we need a slogan. Do you have one, Jeb?" She asked looking at the communications director.

"We suggest: *Faith and Hope with Integrity"* replied Jeb

"That sounds good. What do you think Edward?" asked Valda.

"It sounds great to me, especially the *integrity* part."

Looking directly at Edward Tuckwell, William then said, "The first caucus is in Iowa, on the 3rd of January, which is only five months away. This is a must win for you, Edward, since you are fairly unknown across the nation. In order to get momentum and funds, it's critical to win this state. To do that, we must find volunteers to pack the caucuses and to overwhelm the opposition. We need you to go to Iowa for several speaking tours, so you can spread your message and for Iowans to get to know you. At the same time, Jeb will flood the airways, with ads that compliment your speeches."

"When do you want me to start?" asked Edward.

"How about in two weeks, you can start with a speech in Des Moines, two days later in Cedar Rapids and then two days after that in Waterloo. The speech can almost be the same, with some subtle, minor differences. We'll put the speech together for you. On the campaign staff, we've an excellent speech writer who will help to you to stay on message. The basic speech will be aimed at the middle class, minorities and disadvantaged poor. It'll include references, to taxing the rich and spreading the wealth. We'll also have a message for women and unions. The speech will include the desire for no more wars and foreign adventures, and that you will save the country from the fiscal mess, we are now in. In addition, we'll make reference to how the government can help the people of Iowa. The basic speech will end up with a pledge to keep an open government, instead of conducting business behind closed doors."

"I can deliver those messages without a doubt. The speech covers what I learned in school, with my progressive mentor." Edward responded.

The campaign manager outlined Edward's speech schedule for Iowa, New Hampshire, Nevada, South Carolina, California, New York, Illinois and New Jersey. All of these state primaries and caucuses would be in January and early February (Super Tuesday).

****

Edward Tuckwell launched into his speech schedule with vigor. Every stop was filled with people wanting to see this newcomer to national politics. The communications director filled the airways with ads, as planned, to reinforce Edward's message.

The congressman continued on the planned speech agenda until the 3rd of January, when the Iowa caucus took place. Edward Tuckwell confounded the political pundits by winning the State handily, even though he ran against five other candidates. Immediately after Iowa, two of the five other candidates dropped out, leaving just three, plus Edward.

The New Hampshire primary was held the following week, and Edward barely beat out the competition; but win he did. After this New England state's primary, a slew of contests came up with the Nevada caucus, South Carolina primary, and then Super Tuesday on the 5th of February. By this Super Tuesday date, half of the primaries were over, and Tuckwell was in the lead. The field of candidates dropped down to three; Congressman Tuckwell, Senator Rowe from Michigan and Senator Valpy from Arizona. These three went on to the end of the primary season that finished in June. The remaining candidates fought hard all the way to the finish line. None of them conceded that they were not going to win the nomination, although there was a lot of pressure on Arizona Senator Valpy to drop out of the race.

The vote tally, at the end of the primaries and going into the convention, on the 18th of August, was:

Congressman Tuckwell (Illinois) .... 2,176 delegates
Senator Rowe (Michigan)   .... 1,725 delegates
Senator Valpy (Arizona   ....518 delegates

Delegates to the Dallas convention, scheduled for the 18th to 21st of August, numbered 4,419 and the successful candidate for president had to get 2,210 votes to win.

The first two days of the convention were filled with writing the platform, and renowned past and present party leaders making speeches.

On the third night the voting began. The Party Chairman said, "Will the Madam Secretary please read the roll of the states?"

The Secretary walked up to the mike and started calling out the states for their votes. "Alabama. How do you vote?"

The Alabama State Chairman: "The great state of Alabama casts all fifty-eight votes for the next president of these United States - Edward Tuckwell."

The Convention Secretary echoed, "The great state of Alabama casts all fifty-eight votes for Edward Tuckwell."

The convention secretary then went down the list of states, and the final vote tallies on the first ballot were:

Tuckwell Congressman from Illinois 2,176

Rowe Senator from Michigan 1,725

Valpy Senator from Arizona 518

While the voting was going on, the campaign manager for Tuckwell and the campaign manager for Valpy had a secret meeting, behind closed doors. The result was on the next roll call vote, 301 Valpy votes went for Tuckwell and 217 Valpy votes went to the Michigan senator.

Edward Tuckwell ended up with 2,477 votes. This was 267 votes more than he needed to be nominated for president. The Michigan Senator then asked the delegates to select Tuckwell by acclamation. Edward Tuckwell had become his party's candidate for president of the United States, and he selected Senator Valpy as his vice presidential candidate. This was immediately approved by the convention.

The next night, Tuckwell and Valpy gave victory speeches to the delegates and the nation, as they were carried live by all the major networks. In their speeches, they thanked the delegates for their trust and would work hard during the next three months, to carry the party to victory. Tuckwell in his speech announced that his program would include taxing the rich and spreading the wealth. This was obviously aimed at the middle class and the poor.

The convention ended on a large dose of optimism.

Back in his hotel suite, Tuckwell had a meeting with Valda Lewis.

Tuckwell said, "I can't believe it. We actually made it. We conned them all. Now all we have to do is go on and win in November. I bet the Committee didn't think an Illinois congressman could get this far."

Valda responded, "We had faith in you. We knew you could make it, if you kept on message and did as William requested. He's the best campaign manager in the business. We still have plenty of work to do, as we need to beat the other party's candidate. The Committee will be willing to provide more funds now, as they see your chances of capturing the White House, and maybe Congress, rising."

After a short vacation, the campaign against the other party kicked into high gear. Tuckwell barnstormed the country making speech after speech, each one having basically the same format. Each of them included the slogan of "Faith and Hope with Integrity" and the following points from his party's platform:

> We will save the country from the financial mess
> No more foreign wars or adventures
> Shut down Guantanamo Base Cuba immediately
> Tax the Rich
> Government assistance for the poor and middle class
> Tax carbon output from polluters
> National Health Service operated by the government
> The other party is the party of the rich

What he didn't tell the people was that he believed in Lenin's six basic principles:

1. Ends justify the means
2. Firstest with the mostest (changing word meaning)
3. Never let a crisis go to waste
4. Call your opposition names and making them stick
5. Propaganda of Example
6. Blame your Predecessor

His method of making good speeches followed a familiar pattern while using the teleprompter.

1. Arrive a little late for the event to build up the suspense and frenzy of the crowd
2. Walk to the rostrum, stand and wait for the crowd to quiet down

3.   Speak softly initially and then get louder and louder. Use body language and facial expressions effectively.

4.   Pause now and again during the speech and look to the sky like he was waiting for "God" to speak.

5.   Speak about things in general but rarely give any specifics.

This method had worked before, and he followed it throughout the entire campaign. Tuckwell's other advantage was that he looked fairly young and fit, in comparison to his opponent who was older and always seemed tired. In addition, his rival was not a very effective speaker and could not excite the crowds.

****

The election took place on Tuesday, the 4th of November, and Tuckwell's party went all out to get their supporters to the polls. The unions were very effective in organizing the "Get out the Vote" campaign.

The polls continuously showed Tuckwell ahead. It helped a lot that the mainstream press was a supporter of his party. Only Fox News seemed to support the other candidate.

The polls opened at 8:00 am in most states and closed at 8:00 pm, both times were local time. Edward Tuckwell was in Chicago with his wife, children and Valda Lewis, at a hotel close to downtown.

When the vote count starting to come in, Valda Lewis was elated and said happily, "I think you're going to make it, since the results look very positive. The Committee will be glad to see that their money has been well spent. By this time tomorrow, everyone will be calling you President-elect Tuckwell."

Edward responded, "Let's be sure, before we get carried away and start celebrating."

However, one hour after all the polls closed, the networks were declaring Tuckwell as the winner. After most of the votes were counted, it appeared that he had won, with fifty-six percent of the popular vote. The elector count for the college showed a similar percentage.

After the opposition candidate made his concession speech, Tuckwell appeared downstairs in the hotel ballroom, where his supporters had been waiting.

He made a short speech. "I would like to thank all my supporters who have stayed with us throughout this campaign. In addition, I would like to thank my wife, children, campaign staff and Valda Lewis for sticking with me, all the way.

I'm going to be the best president this nation has seen in years. The government will now be used to help the poor and the disadvantaged, among you. You can finally have hope, after all these years of struggle.

Again, thank you all. We'll see you in Washington. Goodnight. God bless America."

With that, he went upstairs to his hotel suite with his family, Valda Lewis and senior campaign staff. There, they celebrated their victory with a party.

9

President's First Term

On the 20th of January, President Edward Tuckwell walked up to the podium with its shield of bullet proof glass, located in front of the U.S. Capitol building, and took the oath of office. His wife, Leslie, held the bible as Chief Justice Nash delivered the oath of office, before hundreds of thousands of people, assembled below.

Following the Chief Justice's prompts, Edward Tuckwell promised to faithfully execute the office of President to the best of his ability. In addition, he swore to preserve, protect and defend the Constitution of the United States. Following the swearing-in of the president, the Chief Justice delivered the oath of office to Vice President Valpy.

After the inauguration ceremony had taken place, President Tuckwell delivered his acceptance speech, which sounded much like another one of his campaign orations. Then, the president, vice president and their wives walked down Pennsylvania Avenue, waving to the cheering crowds of people lining the route. It was a chilly winter day in Washington, but the sky was clear and sunny. There wasn't a cloud to be seen anywhere. Once they had finished the stroll down the Avenue, the "beast" picked them up and took them back to the White House, where they got ready for the galas, which always take place on inauguration day.

President Tuckwell came into office with the well wishes of a majority of Americans. He had a great oratory skill and could uplift people, without committing to any position or policy. The president would stop periodically during his speeches and look to the heavens. He had learned his oratory techniques by watching films of Hitler and studying other great speakers in history; such as Napoleon, Lenin, Julius Caesar and Churchill. Hitler mesmerized his audiences and Tuckwell learned to follow the same mannerisms.

They were very effective for the German dictator. In a previous television interview an old, German man, who was in the Hitler Youth organization and attended a Nuremburg rally, stated, "It seemed like he was talking to me and me alone, when he talked about Germany depending on me." Hitler had five basic speech techniques that he followed all the time, and Edward Tuckwell had tended to follow some of these simple methods of captivating an audience.

The new American president also used, extensively and effectively, the teleprompter, so that he did not go off message. He followed the speech word for word as it appeared on the teleprompter, using both the left and right screens. The only problem with this technique was that he ended up very rarely looking straight ahead, where the television camera was often placed. Thus, he never seemed to be speaking to the television audience.

No matter, Tuckwell won the hearts and minds of a majority of the American people. By using body language and facial expressions, he gave the appearance of being the Messiah, who would lead the American people out of the wilderness, of the past few decades.

This approach, to speech making, was a key point in his election success. Even in Europe, they thought he was a new type of American president, but the enthusiasm faded in a few years, when they found out he was actually worse than previous presidents. They wanted a president in America who would lead from the front, not the rear, as he generally did. After Tuckwell became president, he continued to tour the country, making campaign like speeches. In fact, he was very uncomfortable trying to govern the country, as he disliked having to compromise or bargain with the other political party, and anyone for that matter. The president preferred to follow, rather than lead, the legislative process.

For the first two years in office, President Tuckwell and his party had control of both houses of Congress. It's easy to pass any legislation that you want, when you have the majority in the Senate and House. He, just like his predecessor, appointed over thirty czars, to control different areas of the economy and society. Tuckwell actually was a liberal, with a tax and spend philosophy. In order to make it more palatable to the broad American population, he and his fellow politicians used the word progressive, instead of liberal. It sounded better to the uneducated electorate.

Together with control of the House and Senate, the president was able to push through legislation affecting health care, education and renewable energy, some of which were detrimental to the overall welfare of the American people. He enacted a large stimulus package that rewarded his campaign supporters, but did very little to boost the economy. Even his vice president was embarrassed when he was put in charge of creating immediate jobs, even though no planning had been done in advance. President Tuckwell didn't need the support of anyone in the minority party to pass his legislation. So, during his first two years, legislation was basically passed, with no minority party votes. This first term president didn't care, because he won the election and they, the minority party, had lost it.

However, in the midterm election, Tuckwell's party lost control of the Senate. For the remaining two years of his first term, he had to govern with only the House of Representatives on his side. This made it very difficult for him to get any of his legislation into law. Thus, he had to use executive orders extensively, in order to keep his agenda proceeding. It didn't matter if the executive orders were constitutional, or not. He had more than enough votes in the Senate to block impeachment proceedings. He believed the Constitution, that had been written over two hundred years earlier, was old and obsolete. This was part of Edward Tuckwell's victim mentality.

He stacked the important positions in the government with friends and allies. It didn't matter whether they were qualified, as long as they would do his bidding. Many of the czars were political appointees, along with the cabinet positions, such as Attorney General, Energy Secretary, Health and Human Services and Labor. When needed, they all ran cover for him. Plausible Deniability was very important to Tuckwell, and his advisor Valda Lewis, so any scandal, which came along, did not involve him personally. He was willing to throw just about anyone under the bus, except Valda, but even she could be expendable, if it came to the worst situation. While Edward Tuckwell went around the country making post-election, campaign speeches, his chief advisor basically ran the White House.

During his first term, several scandals arose, but Tuckwell seemed to survive all of them, with the help of the mainstream media. There were at least twenty of them involving the Tuckwell administration, but none of them seemed to affect his approval rating among the general population. Tuckwell truly seemed to be a Teflon president. Most newspapers and cable news channels supported the Tuckwell administration. In the last two years of his first term, after Tuckwell's party lost control in the US Senate, the Senate started to investigate some of the scandals that had surfaced in one form or another.

These allegations involved the U.S. Department of Justice, the State Department, the Energy Department, the National Security Agency (NSA), the Internal Revenue Service, the Veterans Administration, the Health and Human Services Department and the General Services Administration. Most of the scandals were the result of abuse of power by individuals within the departments, which should have been caught and corrected by the management. However, it appeared, in some cases, that management itself may have been implicated, if a full investigation had been carried out.

President Tuckwell and his cabinet secretaries were able to deflect most of these scandals, or at least slow down the investigations, by stone walling requests for documents. However, the result of all these rumors and allegations was that they slowly reduced his credibility. It was like a slow death of cuts from a thousand knives. He had come in promising to change Washington, have an open administration and hold people accountable for their actions. As it turned out, his administration was far worse than the previous ones. In fact, the sheer magnitude of the scandals made his administration look a lot worse than prior ones; democratic or republican.

His previous statements about the national debt were embarrassing, but the main stream press saved him again, by not airing the videos taped, before he became president. When he was a congressman, he actually made some statements about how unpatriotic it was to rack up these huge debts, which would have to be paid off by the people's grandchildren. There was an actually some live video showing him talking about this, but only one television network replayed it. Valda Lewis was an expert in persuading the media to downplay any negatives about Tuckwell.

Most of the national newspapers and television networks supported Tuckwell. They had overwhelmingly supported him for president, so it was difficult for them to drop their support for him now. It would be an admission by them that they had made a mistake. It's similar to a manager in a company who pushes his boss to let them hire a particular person, only later to find out later they were unqualified. The manager could hardly go back to his boss and ask permission to fire them. It would make it appear he had bad judgment. So it was difficult for the mainstream media, which had originally supported Tuckwell without equivocation, to suddenly turn on him, without looking hypocritical.

It was difficult for Edward Tuckwell to make decisive decisions. When important issues came up, he often procrastinated long enough, until they resolved themselves or Valda Lewis made them for him. Other times he would create a diversion to take the spot light away from his inability to make decisions.

In foreign affairs, he was no different. Early in his first term, he went around the world on an appeasement tour. This policy was a result of his victim mentality he had formed early in life. He came from the wrong side of the tracks, and he blamed everyone else. He felt the general population was a victim too, and that is why he pushed through government entitlement programs, regardless of cost.

The main problem with President Tuckwell was he was great at making speeches, but couldn't govern. In fact he had no experience in governing anything. He lacked the depth of what it takes to lead, rather than follow.

Several months earlier, in an Oval Office meeting, Valda Lewis and the president had discussed the matter of him running for a second term.

"Edward. Most first term presidents win a second term, if they decide to run. It's difficult for an opposing candidate to defeat an incumbent. People tend to have short memories, and most scandals are forgotten, by the time the election rolls around. Your own party will support you because the members do not want to lose any more influence. It's power that counts most to congressmen and senators."

"Yes, you're probably correct as usual, Valda. Even though the odds are in my favor, I'll still need substantial financial support. Let me think about it and, before I can make a firm decision, I'll need to know if the Committee will be behind me."

Toward the end of his first term, he was having problems with the opposing party on some legislation. However, the unions, minorities, environmentalists, women, young voters and the media all supported him.

His first term was viewed by some people as being successful, and he was able to make the other party look worse than his administration was. The opposition helped in this view, since they weren't a cohesive force. His party would stick together regardless, while the members of the other political organization would bicker amongst themselves, and they had no strong leadership.

Edward Tuckwell was a disciple of Lenin and his six principles. Two of these principles he used all the time, during his first term in office.

The first tenet was to demonize the opposition. He called them names such as extremists, blackmailers, racists and bigots. It didn't matter what he called them, the mainstream press would help carry the "water" for him. The second axiom, which he used frequently, was to blame the previous administration, for all the problems he faced. Most of the time, he would blame the poor economic figures, such as unemployment, on the previous president and his party.

As he entered the fourth year of his first term, there was considerable talk around the country, and in the media, that he would not be reelected. However, it mainly depended on who the other party selected as his opponent. They didn't seem to have a front runner, and it appeared there would be a bruising primary fight among the candidates. Edward Tuckwell could therefore sit back and take it easy, until the fall campaign began, after the Labor Day holiday.

In June of the fourth year of his first term, he had another meeting in the Oval Office about running for reelection, with his trusted advisor Valda Lewis. All the recording equipment was turned off.

"Valda, I need to make a firm decision about running again for a second term. When will I know if I have the same support I had four years ago?" asked the president.

"I've been invited to attend the next Committee meeting in the Cayman Islands, later this month. Generally the members meet every four or five years, to discuss various global issues. You can rest assured that my prime objective will be to convince them, to come up with the funds to support you again. I was lucky to be invited, since this group is very secretive and obviously do not want to get any publicity."

Tuckwell replied, "Thanks for doing that. I believe this may be a tough campaign, and we'll need all the funds we can get. I assume the funds will not be visible to the FEC, as per last time. It would be very embarrassing to be caught with foreign money, supporting my campaign. How many people know about these foreign funds?"

"Only the Committee itself is aware of it, other than you and me. There is a member of the Committee who lives in Chicago and he is my main contact with the group. As for me, my star is tied to yours."

"When will you know for sure, if I have their support?" Edward asked.

"By the beginning of August, we should know for certain that they will fund your campaign," replied Valda.

With that, the meeting ended and the president went off to play a round of golf with his acquaintances.

10

Tennessee Governor

Martha Cartwright had come up through the political ranks the hard way, and it made her tough enough to handle just about any adversity, regardless of her personal views or values. She was very strong willed, which could have been the result of her being an only child. Born as Martha Vickers, she was from a small farming community, near the Tennessee capital of Nashville, and was raised by strict God fearing parents, who were conservative and loved their country. They owned a large profitable farm, and Martha enjoyed being among the animals, as a child. Her father had fought in World War Two and won the Medal of Honor for exceptional bravery, in the D-Day invasion on Omaha beach.

Martha was what was called Tennessee tough. Her copper-colored hair hung down to her shoulders, and her high cheek bones indicated that, somewhere in her heritage, there was probably Cherokee blood. She managed to keep her youthful figure, by regularly working out, at a local gym.

RICHARD AND BARBARA OSBORN

She and Richard Cartwright, whom she met at Vanderbilt University, got married in 1969, and he became her soul mate. At that time, Richard was in the United States Air Force in Vietnam, and he came home to marry Martha, during a break in the tour of duty. After the wedding and a short honeymoon, he had to return to Vietnam for three more years.

It was in Vietnam that Richard Cartwright became acquainted with Ian Black, who was also in the United States Air Force, as an intelligence officer. They became fast friends and remained in touch, over the years even though they were separated by twenty-five hundred miles.

When Martha's husband got out of the service, he returned to Tennessee, to be with the wife that he adored, and to run the plastics business, his father had built into a profitable venture. Richard and Martha became involved in politics and joined the Republican Party. Tennessee, like most of the southern states, was slowly turning from being a Democratic state to a Republican one, after the 1964 election, when Barry Goldwater was pitted against LBJ. By the end of the twentieth century, the South, including Tennessee, was almost solidly Republican.

Richard Cartwright, besides running his plastics company, was also a lobbyist for the American Plastic Manufacturers Association, and he travelled several times a year to Washington, D.C. Over the years, he developed many enemies, within the unions that wanted to unionize Tennessee, which was a right to work state. On one of these trips to Washington, the small plane, which Richard Cartwright was flying in, crashed, killing all four passengers and the pilot.

Martha had her suspicions about how the accident happened, but could never prove anything. The National Transportation Safety Board (NTSB), which investigated the crash, could not come up with any firm conclusion. The plane itself was smashed to smithereens, so there were not many clues, as to the cause of the accident.

At first, Martha was lost without her soul mate, and since she had no children, decided to become totally involved in politics. Making a better state out of her beloved Tennessee became her goal from then on. Maybe, she thought, in the long run, she could help make America develop into what it used to be; a government for the people and by the people, not just for the chosen few.

A few years after Richard's death, and almost two years after the election of Edward Tuckwell as U.S. president, she picked up the phone and called her old friend, Ian Black.

"Ian, this is Martha. I hope I haven't caught you too busy. I'd like to chat with you for a few minutes, about an idea I have."

"I always have time for you, Martha. How can I help?"

"What would you say if I told you, that I'm thinking of running for governor of Tennessee next year?"

"Martha, that's great news. You'd be an excellent governor, and goodness knows we need someone to fix all the problems that we've got in this State. What can I do to assist you?"

"There are two ways you can help me, Ian. First, I'm looking for an outstanding campaign manager to aid me, in carrying this off. Secondly, I would like you to be an advisor and a sounding board; if you know what I mean? You've been in the military and lived in other countries, so you would bring an international prospective to my team. Even though the governor is responsible for running the affairs of the state, there are times when the chief executive has to get involved in international matters."

"I'll be glad to be one of your advisors on any matters you bring up. Right now, I don't know of anyone who is a seasoned campaign manager, but let me check into it."

"Please don't publicize that I'll be running for governor, until I make it official. I would like to have the basis of my team in place, before making a public announcement."

"You can count on my absolute discretion, Martha. I will try and get back to you shortly, with the names of candidates for your campaign manager."

Over the next few days, Ian made contact with some very savvy politicians in Tennessee and across the nation. From them, he managed to come up with a list of about ten potential campaign managers, which he reduced to three, after checking into their backgrounds, experience and successes.

After developing the list, Ian called Martha.

"Martha, I have three potential and very qualified potential campaign managers, for you to consider. I am sending the names over to you, with their backgrounds, by special courier. I don't want to give them to you over the phone, in case our phone communications are being monitored. One never knows in today's environment."

"Thanks, Ian. I look forward to receiving your list. I have also come up with a couple of names and hope to select one in short order. Again, thanks for your assistance in this matter."

After receiving Ian's list and combining it with hers, she had five names to select from. Martha went over the backgrounds of all five very carefully and then selected two to be interviewed. Over the next week she interviewed both candidates and had Ian sit in on the discussions. After reviewing both candidates very carefully and seeking Ian's advice, she selected a man from California to be her campaign manager.

****

For the next few months, right up until the 2nd of November election day, Martha pressed as hard she could to win the Republican nomination and then the general election for governor. When all the votes were counted, she had won in almost a landslide. Martha Cartwright, who was well versed in politics, became the first female governor of Tennessee, with over fifty-eight percent of the votes.

She became one of the most successful governors the State had ever had. There was no corruption in her office that she was aware of. If she did suspect something wasn't right, it was swiftly taken care of, without favoritism. You either did your job honestly and correctly, or you were out. She was a no nonsense, strictly by the book, governor.

She initiated many new programs to bring new business into the State, with well paying jobs that allowed Tennesseans to support their families. She increased the international advertising budget, so the State could attract new companies, from outside the United States. Companies from Canada, Japan, Britain and Germany started to view Tennessee, as the place to enter the U.S. markets.

Even though funds were tight, Martha Cartwright managed to find the money to help deserving students go to college. She realized that the educational level of the State's citizens had to be raised, in order to keep attracting companies to the area. In this regard, she fought tooth and nail to prevent unions from entering the State, as her deceased husband had done.

In the background, her chief advisor, Ian Black, was always keeping an eye on her safety. Besides, advising her on several official matters, he was also her unofficial bodyguard. He still had the 1911 Colt 45 pistol, which he had purchased back in 1964, when he came to the United States from England. Since he was a citizen, it was perfectly legal for him to purchase the weapon.

11

Cayman Islands Revisited

Four years after the last meeting, the Committee assembled on the Grand Cayman Island, for the scheduled 25th to 29th of July meeting. As occurred before the previous get together, luxury yachts, registered in Panama, cruised into the Grand Cayman Island Harbour and anchored. Private jets, with just aircraft registration numbers, landed at Owen Robertson International Airport and taxied to the General Aviation Terminal. All of the occupants were whisked away, by a limo, to Harry Thornton's walled and gated estate, located on a bluff overlooking the ocean. Leo DeMaggio was accompanied by Valda Lewis because, as President Tuckwell's chief advisor, she made many decisions for him. They all settled in early for the night, as the meeting was scheduled to commence promptly, the next morning at 9:00 am. Some of the participants would probably have minor jet lag that had to be taken into account, when the actual agenda was set.

After talking with the meeting attendees individually, Harry Thornton came up with three major issues that needed to be discussed, and each one would be tackled on a separate day.

Tuesday, July 26 .... US president and election coming up
Wednesday, July 27.... European Crisis and French debt
Thursday, July 28 .... Indian inflation crisis

The main issue, that all of the participants were concerned about, was the U.S. election scheduled for the following year. The mental stability of President Edward Tuckwell was of major concern, since he had shown some erratic behaviors, to his closest associates.

Promptly the next morning at nine, Harry Thornton called the meeting to order.

"Thank you all for coming to this important meeting. As you have probably noticed, we have a non-member in our midst, Valda Lewis. If you will recall, she was appointed to assist Tuckwell in running for president and also be his advisor, once elected. Leo DeMagglio would be her contact with the Committee.

The main subject, for today's discussion, is the issue of next year's U.S. presidential election and the current president, whom we supported last time. Four years ago, we decided to endorse and fund Edward Tuckwell, and the results, so far, have been beyond our wildest dreams.

Since being elected, he has pushed through socialist programs and appointed progressives to key positions. The president has followed the six Lenin principles of power that can lead to a one party, socialist state, and he has removed military leaders that have spoken out against the administration's policies. Tuckwell has installed a government run National Health Service, similar to the British NHS, for all Americans, and he got Congress to raise some of the taxes, needed to pay for it. He has proved that a sitting U.S. president can ignore some laws and change others, with impunity. His administration has greatly expanded the national debt in order to increase the entitlement payments to the disadvantaged and disabled Americans. The number of people in the United States that are now receiving a government hand out, of some kind, is approaching fifty percent. However, on the other hand, he has not shown any ability to lead and may be locked into a victim mentality syndrome.

Does anyone else have any comments to make? Later this morning we must decide whether to support him for a second term."

The other participants then gave their opinions, individually. Some were positive and some were not so complimentary. Valda Lewis and Leo DiMaggio were the last to speak to the Committee.

"I have worked with him for several years and, from experience, I know I can control him," Valda Lewis said. "He will hardly make a decision without involving me and, in fact, generally I make the decisions for him. He deserves a second term and, if we can make certain things happen, he might be able to serve beyond the second term. You would then have a politician who owes everything to the Committee. I recommend a "yes" vote for supporting him for a second term. Please remember that if you vote no, you will need to find another candidate that will be easier to control than Edward and start the process all over again. That may not be easy."

Leo DiMaggio then spoke to the group. "So far Edward Tuckwell has done an excellent job in changing the U.S. to a socialist state. There is still work to be done, and he would be the best candidate to continue this work. If we ditched him now, it would move our goal for the U.S. back several years. He is attempting to increase the number of minority voters, by giving amnesty to the millions of undocumented citizens. Therefore, I recommend a "Yes" vote on funding Edward Tuckwell's second term run against the other party's candidate, whoever he or she is."

There was a momentary hush in the room that was finally broken by Harry Thornton, when he announced, "Let's have a fifteen minute coffee break. When we return we will continue the discussion and then take a vote."

Twenty minutes later, the meeting on the U.S. election, and the president, reconvened.

"I see everyone who wanted one has a cup of coffee," Harry Thornton said. "Is there anyone who wants to speak further on the subject at hand?"

"Yes, I do," said Andras Nagy: "As a financier, I'm concerned about the funds we will be spending to support Edward Tuckwell. How much did we spend last time, and how do we hide it from the U.S. Federal Election Commission?"

Thornton responded, "I believe the amount was in the area of $100 million for the primaries and the same amount for the general election. We know ways to funnel and use it, without the FEC finding out. Leo can fill you in on that, if you want more details. Unless there are any more questions or any of you want to make further comments, let's take a vote. All those in favor of supporting Edward Tuckwell for a second term, please raise your right hand."

Seven hands went up.

"All those against, please raise your left hand."

Four hands were raised.

"According to my count, the motion carries seven to four. Thank you for your participation in this matter. We will now adjourn for lunch. This afternoon is your chance to enjoy the Cayman Islands, and we will all meet again tomorrow morning at 9:00 am."

With that, they all went to lunch served on the veranda. As they walked out of the conference room, Thornton called Valda and Leo aside and said, "If Edward Tuckwell gets out of control, he'll have to be eliminated and Leo, you will be the one to make that decision. I hope you understand that."

Leo replied, "I understand the situation completely."

Valda responded, "I'll make sure he's under control, and he tries to overcome his victim mentality."

With that they joined the others for lunch.

The next day, the meeting covered the problems in Europe and the French debt. Karl Schiller and Andras Nagy both contributed greatly to the lively debate. No decision was made other than to keep a detailed watch on the matter, especially the situation in Greece.

The following morning, they discussed the Indian inflation crisis. Wei Chan and Jun Matsui provided a good review of this situation. Again, it was decided that the inflation was of concern, but the Committee had no direct control over the Indian Government, at this time. Maybe this was a matter to be considered at a later date.

Finally on Thursday evening, Harry Thornton hosted a grand dinner for the Committee. He ended the dinner with a short closing speech. "Thank you all for coming. I believe it has been a productive meeting, and we will assemble here again in four years, unless an emergency arises that requires immediate attention."

The next day, after being served a leisurely breakfast, all the guests were driven down to the airport or harbour, so that they could embark for their journey to their respective homes.

However, Valda's scheduled flight, for Miami and Washington, did not take off until 4:40 pm, so she used the opportunity to wander around George Town, doing some shopping, until it was time to leave. She visited the Boutique Cartier store at the Bayshore Mall in the capital of Grand Cayman, to purchase some jewelry and other personal items. Grand Cayman is great for shopping, since there is no sales tax and little or no duty.

She also stopped at a couple of other stores, and then went to the Café de Sol for some refreshment. Finally at 2:00 pm, Valda found a taxi and went out to the airport, three miles east of downtown.

12

Another Campaign

Valda Lewis caught the American Airlines 4:40 pm flight from Owen Robertson International Airport on Grand Cayman Island, and arrived at Miami International Airport, on schedule. There, Valda had a two hour layover, before her next flight to the Washington area. She therefore decided to make a phone call to President Tuckwell.

She dialed his private number, and after a few rings, he answered.

"President Tuckwell here, is that you Valda?"

"Yes. Edward. I'm at Miami International on my way back from the Cayman Islands."

"Did you have a good vacation?" Edward asked jovially.

"Yes. I did. I need to see you tomorrow. It's very important. Do you have any spare time?"

"Sure." Edward replied. "As far as I know, I'll be free at 3:00 pm tomorrow afternoon. If I'm wrong, and have a previously planned engagement, I'll let you know."

Valda responded, "I'll be there at 3:00 pm, unless I hear back from you. Bye for now."

With that, she turned her phone off and hurried to her departure gate, for the American Airline flight to Reagan Washington National Airport.

The plane landed on time, and after Valda retrieved her bags and found the taxi rank, it was almost midnight. She found a cab right away and ended up at her house by 12:30 am. She went straight to bed and slept through until nine o'clock.

The next afternoon, having had a light lunch at home, Valda drove to the White House and made it to the west wing lobby area, outside the Oval Office in time for her scheduled meeting. President Tuckwell's secretary knocked on the door promptly at 3:00 pm and showed Valda into the Office. President Tuckwell was behind his desk, reading a brief. As she entered the room, he looked up, smiled and then rose to his feet.

He approached Valda, holding out his hand. "Thanks for coming" he said, as he shook her hand. "What do you have to tell me?"

Valda responded, "As you know I went to the Cayman Islands to meet with the Committee. The result of this secret conclave was that they are prepared to support your campaign, for a second term as president."

"That's great news. Now I can continue my program of changing the basic structure of the United States. I enjoy being president, because I can spread the wealth to every citizen. All those that have been victimized in the past, by the moneyed people, will now be rewarded by the government."

Valda reminded Edward, "Don't forget the people on the Committee need to be rewarded again with government contracts. The stimulus program, you created in your first term, did give contracts to many organizations including unions, environmentalists, progressives and the Committee."

"Sure. No problem. We will absolutely reward the people who support us."

Valda ended the meeting with some good campaign news.

"William Hoare, your campaign manager, and Jeb Hudson, your communications director, have signed on again, to run your campaign for a second term. They're the best in the business, as you know. We'll set up a meeting in the near future, in Chicago, to discuss the strategy and tactics for winning."

"That sounds great," President Tuckwell replied. "Let my scheduling secretary know when the meeting will be, so she can put it on my calendar. I have to run now, to a meeting with a union boss. See you soon."

With that, Valda left the Oval Office and went to her own office in the White House. She felt good that everything seemed to be turning out alright. She always worried a little about Edward Tuckwell. He was so into himself and thought he knew everything.

The next day Valda called President Tuckwell's secretary and set up a campaign meeting for Monday, the 19th of September. It would take place in Chicago, at the Cicero **Tuckwell for President** office, which had just been set up again, after it was reopened from a three year hiatus. She then called William Hoare and Jeb Hudson and told them that the president and she would be at the campaign headquarters at 10:00 am on the nineteenth. Valda knew that Tuckwell did not like early meetings, if he could avoid it.

On Friday, the 16th of September, President Tuckwell flew into Chicago on Air Force One with Valda Lewis. The government paid for the trip, since President Tuckwell was going to do some government business while he was there.

On the trip from Washington to Chicago, Valda Lewis and President Tuckwell discussed the upcoming presidential election and the strategies for defeating any potential opposition candidate.

Valda suggested to the president, "We ought to start early so as to prevent any potential candidate, from even your own party, challenging you. It's not very likely, but one never knows."

"I'll dispose of them immediately, if anyone dares to challenge me. I have information on every potential rival. I also have information on the opposition's potential candidates. If any one of them seems to be getting a substantial lead, I'll destroy them. As president, I have access to all kinds of financial or salacious information that they could only dream of."

Valda responded, "Mr. President, we still have to be careful not to implicate you in any way in campaign snafus. Don't forget *plausible deniability* are the two key words."

At that point, the pilot came on announcing they would be landing in twenty minutes. Valda and the president talked about a few minor problems in the Middle East and then got ready for the landing.

At the Chicago O'Hare International Airport, the president was driven away in the presidential limo, also known as the "Beast", to a friend's mansion, where he was going to stay for the next few days. Valda took a taxi to the Palmer House, as she planned to remain in Chicago for a week, to visit some former colleagues. On Saturday, President Tuckwell was scheduled to speak to the Chicago Teachers Union and later to the Service Employees International Union.

On Monday morning, the president and Valda arrived at the Tuckwell campaign headquarters on Cicero, almost at the same time. There they met with the campaign manager, and the communications director, to plan the basic strategies for winning the caucuses and primaries, leading up to the convention being held in Atlanta the next August.

It was decided that the campaign would be active in all fifty states, and President Tuckwell would spend a great deal of his time touring the country, making speeches. This was his forte. He would extol the virtues of his administration and the need for a big government, in helping the poor and middle class, to survive. The opposition party, as usual, would be labeled the party of the rich and anti-immigration.

William Hoare would organize a campaign of disinformation whenever a candidate of the other party became too strong in their primaries. By the time the opposing party's convention came along, hopefully their candidate would be skewered by this misinformation. He or she would never be able to recover.

Jeb Hudson would work with his contacts in the mainstream media, to make sure only positive articles about President Tuckwell are published, but negative stories on the opposing candidate are highlighted.

As the meeting closed, Valda said, "We must make sure that the president is a winner before the campaign starts. The opposition must never be allowed to get traction. The debates must be on the turf we decide and the moderators are on our side."

William replied, "Don't worry. We Chicago people know how to win elections. This will be my last campaign that I'll be working on, and I want to go out a winner."

With that President Tuckwell left and went back to Washington, on Air Force One. Valda Lewis stayed around a few days to finish the planning, with the campaign staff.

****

President Tuckwell squashed the opposition in the November election and he went on to win a second term. He could now continue with his progressive programs to transform the United States into a socialist type of nation. It did not matter so much what type of jobs people had. The government would be there to hand out "goodies" and take care of them.

President Tuckwell was beginning to enjoy the job if only he could get rid of that irritant – the U.S. Congress. The lifestyle and perks of being president had become enjoyable.

Even his wife and children were becoming used to the life of luxury, at the government's expense.

13

President's Second Term

On the 20th of January, President Edward Tuckwell was sworn in by Chief Justice Andrew Nash at the top of the steps leading to the Capitol building, with his wife, Leslie, holding a bible. It was a cold blustery day, with large clouds blocking out the sun. All government officials and visitors were wearing heavy overcoats to protect them, from the harsh, freezing wind.

After Tuckwell had promised to uphold the Constitution, the Chief Justice then gave the oath of office to Vice President Valpy. After they had both vowed to protect and defend the United States, they were congratulated by all the well-wishers standing around them.

Then President Tuckwell walked up to the microphone and delivered a speech, which magically appeared on the teleprompter, and was basically a repeat from four years before. The speech was purposely kept short, because of the weather that had been predicted earlier by forecasters; a wind of over twenty miles per hour and snow flurries, for most of the day.

After the president's speech, both President Tuckwell and Vice President Valpy walked, together with their wives, a short distance down Pennsylvania Avenue. They then got into the presidential limo that had been following them and rode back to the White House. The crowds lining the route were small due to the weather, plus President Tuckwell was not as popular as he was at the beginning of his first term.

That evening they attended the presidential galas and balls commemorating the inauguration. The president was not much of a dancer, but he enjoyed meeting with the few friends and acquaintances he had.

The next day he met with some of his aides including, of course, Valda Lewis his chief advisor. The purpose of the meeting was to plan for the next two years of his administration, so his party could reclaim the U.S. Senate. This would make governing a lot easier without the opposition party putting up roadblocks, at every "turn".

President Tuckwell still planned to continue following Lenin's six basic principles, as he had done in his first term. They had worked well for Lenin and other rulers who had used modified versions of them down through history, and so far had worked well for Tuckwell.

First, you want to make the opposition look worse than you are.

Second, cast blame, for any failures or problems, on your predecessor or opponents.

Third, if a crisis appears, use it to your advantage. This had worked well for Tuckwell during his first term, when the economic problems enabled him to get Congress to pass a huge stimulus program.

Fourth, the principle of the "Ends justify the Means" has been followed by many leaders, in the past around the world. In other words, anything goes as long as it helps you meet your goals. Tuckwell would be able to use this principle toward the end of his fourth year to his advantage.

Lenin's fifth principle was to use propaganda of making examples to "terrorize" your opposition. Get people thrown in jail for committing economic crimes and making sure it is well publicized.

Lastly, the principle of the "firstest with the moistest" means taking the high road intellectually. If you create a meaning to a new word to describe a fact or problem before the opposition, you have an advantage.

One major problem, he was having during his second term, was getting Congress to pass new tax legislation, which was required to pay for the National Health System. If he couldn't get the new taxes through Congress his medical plan would probably collapse.

Congress was being pushed by the voters to reject any new taxes. The price of gasoline had already doubled in the past four years, due to a considerable increase in the federal excise tax. Other taxes had also gone up, including the introduction of a Value Added Tax (VAT). The U.S. was becoming like many other socialized countries, with high taxes and low growth. The citizens in all states had seen their tax bills go up under President Tuckwell's administration.

Tuckwell's plan for his second term was to pass an immigration bill, which would give the undocumented resident the basic rights of a U.S. citizen and a quick path to citizenship. This would give his party many more voters and supporters. He wanted to downsize the military so that there would be more money to give out as entitlements to the masses who, in their opinion, had been victimized over the years.

During his second term, he was able to down size the military, but he didn't get everything he wanted on the immigration bill. He was determined to try again even though he did not capture the Senate back in the mid terms. It was close. The opposition had fifty-one seats and Tuckwell's party had forty-nine seats. If he could get one of the opposition senators to crossover and also have the vice president's vote counted, he would have a majority of one in favor. Tuckwell planned to bring up the bill one last time, in September of his last year in office.

In the midterm elections, the House of Representatives turned slightly Republican, with two hundred and twenty Republican congressmen versus the Democrats two hundred and fifteen. With this slim majority, the Republicans in the House were able to elect the Speaker. This presented another problem for President Tuckwell.

However, in the back of his mind, he was often thinking the unthinkable. He liked being president with all its perks – the presidential plane, the foreign trips, everyone doing what he said. The only problem was he had to deal with Congress.

"*How could he get around all that? Hitler and Stalin did it by stacking their Reichstag or Duma with supporters. Other tyrants did away with parliament altogether. The U.S. Congress is a nuisance,*" he thought.

This problem kept coming back to him every so often, during his second term. His deepest thought was that he wanted to be president for life, like a dictator.

14

Governor Cartwright Encore

In the fourth year of her first term as governor of Tennessee, Martha Cartwright decided to run for reelection, as she and others believed that she had done an excellent job for Tennesseans. Again, Ian Black was one of her principal advisors during the campaign, and her campaign staff was almost identical to four years before. Her record on budget issues, trade incentives, education and health made her reelection almost a foregone conclusion. Also, since she did not look her sixty-five years of age, most voters thought she was in her late fifties, and therefore not too old for a second term.

On election night, the 4th of November, the results started to come in, as soon as the polls closed at 8.00 pm EST in East Tennessee and 7:00 pm CST in West Tennessee.

It was soon very obvious that Martha Cartwright had won a second term, and that she was going to do better than the last election, four years ago. When the results were finally tabulated, she had received sixty-one percent of the votes, which was one of the better showings by any governor, in the past fifty years.

Ian called Martha the next day, after her victory for the governor's office.

"Congratulations on your win, Martha. I thought your speech yesterday evening, after the results for the governor's race came in, was excellent and had just the right touch. If you don't have any plans for tonight, how about a victory dinner, just the two of us, at the Stock-Yard. I'll make sure that we get a corner table downstairs, with some privacy."

"That would be nice, Ian. How about 7:00 pm? I should be finished with my meetings by then. I'll meet you there."

"That sounds great, I'm glad you can make it. I'll see you then."

Ian arrived at the Stock-Yard a few minutes early and went downstairs, where the maitre d' was standing by a desk. The man recognized him immediately, as Ian had been to this restaurant many times.

"Mr. Black, I'm glad you are joining us this evening. The table you reserved is ready for you and your guest. Please follow me."

Ian nodded and followed the maitre d' to a corner table that was half hidden by some colorful screens.

"The governor will be joining me in a few minutes so I would appreciate it, if you could avoid seating other guests too close to our table, unless you absolutely have to."

"I'll do the best I can," the maitre d' responded.

In a short time, the man reappeared, followed by Martha Cartwright, the newly reelected governor of the Volunteer State. Ian rose and greeted her and then they both sat down.

"I'm glad you could find time to have dinner here with me so soon after your victory. I'm so proud of the way you carried the day. All political races should be run so cleanly. In order to celebrate, would red wine be okay?"

"That sounds great, Ian. I'll let you select it."

The waiter came over and they both ordered their food.

"We would also like a bottle of Archery Summit Premiere Cuvee Pinot Noir and two glasses. I assume you have it." Ian said.

"Yes, sir, we do. I'll bring it right away."

"Martha, I ordered an Oregon Pinot Noir which even the French think is as good, as any that one can get. I hope you like it."

"I'm sure I will," Martha said, smiling.

Just then, the waiter reappeared with the wine and two glasses. He poured some in a glass and gave it to Ian to taste.

"This is excellent. Thanks." Ian said to the waiter.

The waiter poured some wine in both glasses and left to get their meal.

Ian raised his glass and said, "Here's to you, Martha, on your magnificent election victory. It's great to know that Tennessee will be in your hands for another four years."

"Thank you for those kind words, Ian," she said, as they clinked their glasses together.

Pretty soon, the waiter appeared with their meals and they both started to eat, while discussing the election campaign and the upcoming four years in Martha's governorship.

After they had finished their meal and had drunk some more wine, the discussion drifted into a more personal nature.

"Ian, I'm not trying to get involved in your life, but how are you and Giselle getting along, after your separation, years ago? I haven't seen her lately."

Before responding to Martha's question, Ian started to think back in time to about forty years ago, when he was in Vietnam and married Giselle. Later, toward the end of his military service in the United States Air Force, he had been stationed in Washington, D.C. and was the White House liaison to the British, during the Falklands War. Ronald Reagan was president at the time and he wanted to assist his great friend the British Prime Minister, Margaret Thatcher, in retaking the island from the Argentineans.

"We're doing great now. As you're aware, we had a rough spot when I was called upon by the White House to be a liaison with the British military, during the Grenada invasion and the Falklands war. I was away a lot and Giselle figured that it would be best if we separated, since I was never around anyway. After I left the Air Force and went to work at Boeing, things changed for the better, and we got back together. When I retired from the aerospace company in Seattle, we moved into the Franklin house, which I had inherited from my mother, when she died. Giselle always seems to be busy doing volunteer work, now that our two children are grown up and have gone out into the world."

"Well, I'm glad to hear that everything is going okay."

"Would you like some more wine, Martha?"

"No, I don't think I will. I want to walk out of here without any stagger. It wouldn't be good for the other guests here to see their Governor on an uneven keel. I would like a cup of black coffee, however."

Ian beckoned the waiter over."Two black coffees please."

He soon appeared with the coffee and they drank it, while discussing old times.

"I think I'd better be going. I have an early morning meeting with the State's attorney general and I need the sleep in order to be wide awake for it. I've really enjoyed this evening. Thanks, Ian."

"You're welcome Martha. Let me escort you to your limo."

As they walked out of the Stock-Yard, Ian told the maitre d' to send the bill to his office and he would take care of it.

A few weeks after her reelection, Governor Cartwright was nominated and elected, at the next National Governors Association (NGA) meeting, to the Vice Chair position for the next year. The Chair (D) and Vice Chair (R) positions are held by governors from different parties and alternate each year, so as not to allow the association becoming a political arena. The next year, Governor Cartwright (R) will automatically become the Chair of the Association, unless she declines the position.

As Vice Chair and then Chair of the NGA, Martha will be on the Executive Committee overseeing the five major committees, developing programs for Education, Health and Human Services, Economic Development and Commerce, Homeland Security and Public Safety and National Resource.

In her home state of Tennessee, Governor Cartwright was determined to make life better for all citizens whether they were rich or poor, regardless of political affiliation, young or old. She wanted to end her second and final term in office, as a winner for everyone in the State.

Throughout the four years, Ian Black was by her side, advising her on key issues, along with her other two key advisors. Whenever issues concerning foreign trade or the military arose, such as the Tennessee National and Air Guards, he was there to offer advice, when called upon. He expected nothing in return, as he was in retirement. Whether this retirement would last, would depend on the state of the nation in the coming years.

15

Camp David

Early on Saturday morning, the presidential helicopter lifted off from the White House lawn and proceeded to the north-northwest from Washington. On board were the president, his wife and three children, a nanny, plus a couple of secret service agents. These agents were handpicked by President Tuckwell, and the sixty-two mile flight to Camp David near Thurmont, Maryland in the Marine helicopter, only took approximately thirty minutes. The Sikorsky aircraft, codenamed Marine One for the flight, landed on the grounds of Camp David, and the presidential family walked to their living quarters, for their weekend stay.

No major activities were planned, and no guests had been invited. Just a relaxing two days for the president, his wife and family, away from the pressures of Washington, D.C. The president of the United States, Edward Tuckwell, was in his second term and had less than a year to serve, before he would be out of office. He was spending the weekend, of the 27th and 28th of

February, at the presidential retreat contemplating his future and what he wanted to do, during his remaining time in office.

At noon, the Camp David staff served lunch to the president and his wife in the dining room.

Toward the end of the meal, Edward looked lovingly at his wife and said, "When we're finished, I believe that I'll go out onto the veranda, find a chair and survey the scenery. I need to relax after all the stress I've been under lately."

"That's sound like a good idea, Edward. Maybe I'll come and join you, after taking care of some correspondence that I've been neglecting."

As soon as they had finished their cup of coffee, Edward rose, went out to the veranda and sat down in the chilly afternoon sun.

He gave great thought on what had happened since his election seven years ago. He knew that, under the Constitution, he could not run for a third term.

He thought to himself, "*This document, called the Constitution, is outdated and needs to be changed, and brought up to date. Someone, such as myself, could do great things given time and power, eight years was just not enough time. Somehow I have to change this, but how*?"

He recalled that, in the past, he had disregarded federal laws, which he did not like, and had managed to get away with it. Even when there had been inquiries and hearings, nothing of any consequence happened. Given the fact that the attorney general was in his pocket, he had got by with just about anything he wanted to do. Even when an embassy in the Middle East had been ransacked and the American staff murdered, the main stream press gave him and the secretary of state a pass.

When the attorney general lied under oath and was subpoenaed, nothing came of it. He and the attorney general had just ignored the protest and went about their way. It had soon died down, or so it seemed.

As he remained sitting in the wicker chair, on the Camp David veranda, Tuckwell looked at the trees and shrubs and his mind wandered, pondering about his seven years in office.

"I persuaded the IRS to give me information on my opponents and the mainstream press basically ignored it. Oh, there was an outcry at first, mainly brought on by that rogue television network, Fox News. They are a pain in my side. Well, if everything works out as planned, they will feel my full fury.

If I managed to survive the first seven years, I can survive anything. I'm invincible," he thought smugly.

Tuckwell firmly believed, in his egotistical mind, that he was untouchable and could get away with anything. It had been easy to fool the needy and the have not's, the ones that thought they deserved more. They actually thought that he really wanted to help them. They were like lambs being led to slaughter. This did not matter, since it was the power he wanted. It seemed that they were mesmerized, when he spoke to them. Whatever he said they believed.

As his mind mulled over what had taken place since he took office, he thought, *"What fools they were. They placed their faith in me, even after I broke most of my campaign promises from the beginning of my administration. They still voted for me again. Of course, there had been a little juggling of vote counts in some states, which helped push me over the top. This vote fraud was brought on by the Committee. Since one of the group's members controlled most of the media publications and television stations, they always give me a bye. I fooled them all."*

UNBRIDLED POWER

The president had that singular ability to charm, cajole and place blame elsewhere that appealed to the uninformed masses, and seemingly the members of the Committee.

Tuckwell continued to reflect on the past few years. *"There is only that one television channel that won't give me any slack, and I'll take care of them once I have absolute power. There are some governors that bucked me and put their states above what I wanted them to do. Some governors and senators went so far as to ignore me, when I visited their states. They pleaded prior engagements, but I know the real reason. They have no respect for me, but I'll show them, when I become the supreme leader. They will regret the snub, and they'll pay for it."*

Tuckwell suddenly came out of the trance and back to the present, stood up and walked over to the railing, surrounding the veranda. Looking down on the lawn, he saw his wife walking down the stone steps into the garden. In the setting sun, her hair had a soft glow, and she looked as beautiful as the day they were married. She loved being the first lady and the power and money it gave her. When they first tied the knot, they didn't have much, and he had promised her that someday they would have everything they wanted; no matter what he had to do to get it? Now they did have everything anyone could want, and he had to figure out a way to continue to keep this status. He would do anything for her.

As they sat down to dinner that evening, she looked lovely in a soft peach sweater and matching skirt. He dismissed the servants, after they had served the dinner. He wanted to speak with her privately.

"Leslie, honey" he began, "I've been thinking about the next election. You know I can't run again, as the Constitution is now written."

"Yes, I know," she replied quietly. "It seems such a shame; you need more time to continue your work." *"Plus"*, she thought to herself, *"I like the role of being First Lady. I like being able to snub the ones who had snubbed me in the past."*

In fact, she relished the way she could rub their noses in it and get by with it.

"I saw you on the veranda this afternoon, but I didn't want to disturb you, you seemed to be deep in thought," she said. "What were you thinking about?"

He reached across the table and took her hand in his, it was soft and warm. "I was thinking about how I could continue doing my work. As things stand now, there's no way I could get the twenty-second amendment to the Constitution changed. I've too many opponents in the House and the Senate to do that easily," he said.

Most members of his own political party were even against it. They were fools too, most of them. When they backed him to run the first time they thought they could control him. They had only wanted their party to be in power again. They soon found out, however, that he would do as he pleased. After all, the Committee would take care of any dissenters.

"I have developed a plan that has been used before in history, and it will work for us this time," he told her. "However, I must have your full cooperation and approval, because it involves some risk to us and our family."

She sat quietly for a moment and digested what he had just said. "Well, I can't tell you how I feel until you tell me what you're planning."

"You know that I would never do anything which would put you and the children in grave danger, unless I thought I could control the situation," he said.

"I know that "she replied.

"Well, do you remember in our history class at college, about the 1930s in Germany and how Adolph Hitler took power?" he asked.

"I don't remember. What did he do?"

"He developed a plan whereby he supposedly had some men set fire to the Reichstag, and then blamed it on the Communist party. In the ensuing chaos, Hitler took control of the entire government, by getting the Reichstag to approve a "Decree for the Protection of the German People."

"Yes?" she said with a puzzled look. "I recall something about that. What about it, how can that help us?" she asked.

He then explained to her the plan he had thought up over the past few weeks. She sat quietly and listened to it, in awe of the audacity and brilliance of the plan. It would work, she knew it would. He could charm anyone and he could pull it off, she was sure.

She looked him in the eyes and said, "I'll back you all the way."

They retired to their bedroom and made passionate love. Then they slept peacefully in each other's arms, believing their plan would work, and they would be able to rule supreme for years to come.

On Sunday evening, President Tuckwell called Valda Lewis, his longtime advisor and trusted confidant.

"Valda, this is Edward. Please meet me in the Oval Office tomorrow morning at eight o'clock sharp. I need to discuss a very important matter with you."

Valda replied, "I'll be there exactly at 8:00 am. So I can be prepared, what is the subject to be discussed?"

The president responded, "It's too sensitive to mention over the phone. I'll see you tomorrow."

He had no time to waste, in initiating a start of the plan to ensure his victory. He felt Valda was extremely loyal, and valued her friendship and advice highly. She had been his advisor for many years.

After Tuckwell terminated the phone conversation, Valda called her Chicago contact, Leo, and reported the president's call.

"He sounded somewhat agitated and excited, and wants me to be at his office first thing in the morning."

"Just listen to what he has to say and report back to me," Leo responded.

"What did Edward Tuckwell have in mind?" she wondered.

He had become worrisome to the Committee as of late, she hoped she could keep him in check for just a while longer, until everything was in place. Then they would deal with him. She knew he was not part of the permanent plan the Committee had in mind. He was just a pawn and a useful tool, for the time being. Too bad she had come to like him and to somewhat admire his audacity, if not his ego.

"Well I'd better get some rest," she thought. *"It might prove to be a very long day tomorrow."*

16

Oval Office Meeting

On the 29th of February, at 8:00 am sharp, a half hour before the president's secretary generally came to work, Valda knocked on the Oval Office door.

"Come in," the president answered. He had come in earlier than normal, his mind racing with ideas.

As she entered the Office, he rose from his chair behind the large oak desk and said, "Have a seat, Valda."

After she sat down, he continued, "You know I trust you more than anyone, and I value your opinion. What I'm about to discuss with you, is between you and me, and can't go beyond this room. I've already talked it over with Leslie, and she is willing to go along with anything we decide."

"You know you can trust me. I've always been here for you," Valda replied

He then started to explain to her what he had been thinking about at Camp David.

"I need another four years, or more, to accomplish what we set out to achieve for the country. I recalled, the other day, how Hitler managed to declare a state of emergency in the 1930s, with the fire in the Reichstag. Perhaps we could have a similar situation in the United States, where some Islamic terrorists cause chaos, with a catastrophic attack."

As she usually did, Valda thought outside the box, and with a basic disregard for the Constitution. She played along with his dialogue, as if she didn't know the Committee already had some plans, for just what President Tuckwell was suggesting. In fact, a few members of the Committee had considered different methods, by which a president might be able to serve more than two terms.

"What if we can create a national emergency, citing a terrorist threat to the country? We could then declare a state of emergency, cancel the election and you could just stay in office. Who would come and remove the sitting president?" she asked.

Valda continued, "This problem has never arisen before, so it would catch everyone by surprise. It would take time for the politicians to figure out a solution. By the time they did, you would be firmly entrenched in power for life. The only thing the dissenters could do would be to declare war on you and the government. Would they dare to do such a thing to save democracy, or would they bow to your will, as they have done in the past? I doubt many of them would have the guts or power to challenge you."

"Of course, she was right" he thought. *"This idea had never been raised before, so it would take the Nation by surprise and paralyze the political system. He would be basically without much opposition. Of course, there might be some, but the Committee would take care of them or, if they didn't, he would. He would become the first dictator of the United States of America."*

"You know, you're right," Tuckwell said to Valda. "The only thing, my opponents might be able to do, would be to start a civil war, which, as you know, has only happened once before, in 1860. Do you think they would they risk that to save the Nation? Who do you think could actually force me out of office: members of my own party, the FBI, the

Armed Forces or the Supreme Court? Our party wants to keep power in Congress. The FBI and the Federal troops are under my appointees. The Supreme Court couldn't do anything, since they have only an internal security force.

As you know, I've placed key supporters in position of power: the U.S. Attorney General, the FBI director, the Chairman of the Joint Chief of Staff and the commissioner of the IRS. They would all support me, so they could keep their own positions of authority. Perhaps we could create a crisis here in the U.S. that would be an excuse, to cancel the election and stay in office. There would be a few noisy dissenters, but I don't believe they would be strong enough to oust me. They would be too late, as the fools would wait too long, before they could figure out what action to take."

Playing along with his train of thought, Valda suggested several scenarios to create a national emergency.

"Well" she said "maybe there could be a fire in the Capitol, or terrorist threats at the voting booth locations, or maybe another attack on several of our embassies."

"No," the president said, "it has to be something bigger than that. We need something that will cause panic; like a massive earthquake."

Pacing the floor, deep in thought, the president suddenly stopped and walked over to the desk, and sat down. Valda looked at him expectantly. He said nothing. Now is the time she thought to plant the idea, but she needed to make it look like he was the one to think it up.

Valda replied, "Well, if some of the leading senators and congressmen in Congress were unable to perform their duties, it would be up to you to take control, for the good of the country, of course."

"*There* "she thought," *I've planted the seeds, will he take the bait?"*

"Yes" he said, jumping up from his chair and almost knocking it over. "I know exactly what needs to happen." With a faint smile, he continued, "We could blow up the

97

Capitol. We just need to figure out how to do it without being implicated." They both looked at each other for a short time.

Then Valda said, "I know someone who could be very useful to us and help set our plan into action. He's a retired military man from the Air Force, who was passed over by the past administration for promotion to general. He's very bitter about that situation and might be willing to do a little pay back; for the right price; his name is Colonel Alan Burgess."

Valda had met Alan Burgess in Boston a few years ago when he came several times to her company, Overseas Transit, to set up and inspect a security system. He worked for Teknow Security Systems, out of Roanoke, Virginia. They had developed a friendship, and he had told her in confidence his feelings about the high up military brass and the Federal Government in general.

"Could you arrange a secret meeting with him and see if he is willing to do what we ask?" the president said.

"I believe so" she replied.

She breathed a sigh of relief; he had fallen for it hook, line and sinker. It would make Nixon's Watergate look like child's play. It would be the modern day version of Guy Fawkes and his group of fanatical Catholics, trying to blow up the Palace of Westminster and the English Parliament, in 1605. However, this time the operation would be successful. They would make sure of it.

In order to create a large enough crisis it had to be massive, with a big loss of life and a symbol of America that all citizens could relate to.

The six main ideas to create the need for a state of emergency that the Committee had come up with were:

1. Blow up the Capitol with explosives hidden in the basement. This would require sneaking the explosives past security. There were tunnels, but they were monitored very closely. The risk factor was high.

2. Sneak suicide bombers into the Capitol. They would surely be detected by security.

3. Fly missiles/planes into the Capitol. Planes would be a problem, since the USAF would shoot them down. Missiles would be better, if fast enough and available.

4. Suicide bombers would blow themselves up in polling booths in Boston, Miami, Chicago, Denver and Los Angeles on Election Day. This would reduce turn out, but the election would still go on.

5. Blow up the White House. Big symbol, but not a lot of life lost, plus the president and his family would be at risk.

6. Create an emergency overseas would not be justification enough, to create state of emergency. Most Americans would not feel that was a great threat to them.

After much thought, however, Leo and Valda had decided that the crisis had to take place on American soil. A fast missile attack on the U.S. Capitol would certainly achieve it. Ideas numbered four through six were discarded, because they would not create an environment dire enough for declaring a state of emergency.

Valda advised President Tuckwell. "In order to provide a cover for the attack, it must be conducted by people who resemble Islamic terrorists. In addition, to support this false flag operation idea, a news item has to be fed to Al Jazeera, the Arabic news service, that the attack was organized and carried out by Al Qaeda terrorists. I know a man in Chicago who has contacts in the news business. I'll ask him to make arrangements to have a news item leaked to Al Jazeera, at the appropriate time."

17

Former USAF Colonel Recruited

On Wednesday, the 2nd of March at 8:30 am, Valda picked up the phone and placed a call to Colonel Burgess in Roanoke. After three rings, Alan picked up the phone. She had caught him just in time. He was getting ready to drive to work at an electronics company, Teknow Security Systems, where he was the vice president of engineering.

"Colonel Burgess. How are you doing? This is Valda Lewis. If you remember, we met briefly a few years ago, when I was the lawyer, for a Boston firm, called Overseas Transit. I'm now in the White House, as the senior advisor to President Tuckwell. "

"Yes. I remember you Valda. You were that good looking lawyer that didn't look like a lawyer," he said with a laugh. "What can I do for you?"

"We're looking for a bright, ex-officer who has no qualms about doing a "dirty" job. By the way, what actually happened when you were in the Air Force, in line for that first star, and then you suddenly retired?"

"Well. Let's say I said something, I shouldn't have, about the Chairman of the Joint Chiefs of Staff, under a previous administration. It didn't go down well, even though it was the truth. The next thing I knew I was being asked to resign or retire. Oh well, that story is in the past. Although, I'm still bitter about the whole situation and would like to get even, one of these days."

"I can understand that. Are you ready to get even now? We've a job to be done and we're looking for a leader, who can accomplish an unpleasant task. We would pay you well, and you could retire in a lot better situation, than the general who had you fired. That would be revenge, yes? It would also be in the best interest of America?"

"What's the job you want done?" Burgess asked.

"We can't talk about it on the phone; the NSA could be listening even though, at my end, I'm on a secure line. Can you meet me at Roanoke airport this afternoon at two o'clock? I'll fly in on a government plane, and we can talk about it then."

"It sounds good to me. I'll meet you at the Roanoke private jet reception area at 2:00 pm."

"See you then, Alan. Goodbye."

With that they both hung up the phone and Alan headed for work in Roanoke. As he drove, he wondered what all this was about. Retiring now sounded good and getting even, with the top military brass, sounded best of all.

***** ******************

At 2:00 pm sharp, an unmarked government Gulfstream G-3 jet taxied to the Roanoke Regional Airport corporate jet reception area and out stepped Valda Lewis. Alan thought *"She still looks as good as she did when I last saw her, a few years ago. She hasn't aged a bit."*

Alan walked over to her and shook her hand. "Glad to see you again, Valda. It's been a while, since we last met. We can go and sit in my car, if you like. My company has it checked for bugs regularly and our conversation will be completely safe and secure."

"That's a good idea, and after our talk, maybe we can go and get a stiff drink at early happy hour. Yes?"

"Sounds good to me," Alan said as they walked to his car, not far from the private jet terminal.

Alan opened the passenger door for Valda, and then he went around to the driver's side and climbed in.

As she sat beside him, she knew what she was about to tell him could be used against her and the president. However, she also knew that, if Alan didn't agree and go along with their plan, he would be disposed of quickly by the Committee.

She took a deep breath and began, "First I want you to understand Alan that this conversation is completely off the record and never took place. Is that totally clear?"

"Yes. You have my word on that and I can assure you I have no hidden tape recorder or bug."

"The United States is at a critical point in its 250 year history. We have to make some major changes. Unless we do, the country as we know it may not survive. We need to create a crisis so huge that it will be possible for the president to make the needed changes to the American society and the Constitution. Therefore, we propose to hit the U.S. Capitol with explosives, so that there will be major devastation and casualties. This will allow the president to declare a state of emergency and cancel the presidential election. Then he can make the necessary changes to the political make up of the country. We have to succeed in this or the country will not survive. Are you with me so far?"

"I'm with you up to now and understand what you're saying."

"We've come up with three basic ideas on how to accomplish this attack on the Capitol. We would like you to come up with the details on how to accomplish these three ideas. We need to know the pros and cons, cost, difficulties, etc. of each idea. Do you think you can do this?"

"Yes. I believe I can. Of course, there will be assumptions built into the three scenarios, which will require more research. When do you plan to have this attack take place?"

"The goal is to attack the Capitol in the beginning of September. The exact date is still to be determined. This will give you about six months to prepare and carry out the attack, assuming you agree to lead the effort?

"What are the three ideas?"

"The first is to sneak explosives under the Senate and House wings and detonate them remotely at a given time. The second is to have suicide bombers wears explosive vests or belts and obtain entry to the wings of the Capitol. The last method would be to launch two missiles from a base located near Camp Lejeune that would be programmed to hit the Capitol wings, a couple of minutes apart."

"Are you talking about launching the Bomarc missiles from Camp Warrior, in North Carolina?"

"Yes. We understand you were involved in the planning and building of the eight Bomarc C bases a few years ago."

"Yes, that's true. The previous president wanted the Bomarc bases to be available, in order to shoot down any incoming planes launched by our terrorist enemies."

"Are you willing to prepare the scenarios, hire team members and lead the operation? We would need the scenarios to be submitted by the 9th of March."

"Valda, let me ask you a basic question. To accomplish what you are requesting, it will take a lot of money, in the millions of dollars. Specifically, you would have to reward the team members well, so that they have no qualms in attacking a major symbol of the country."

"How much do you estimate?" Valda asked.

"Doing a very rough calculation in my head, it would take anywhere from forty to eighty million dollars, depending on the scenario selected. Will this be a problem?"

"No problem at all. We have access to funds that are not accounted for in the normal way. If you are willing to go ahead, we will meet back here on the 9th of March same time, same place."

"I'm willing to go ahead so far. However, before I give my final answer, I reserve the right to step down, if I believe the scenario selected is not a good one."

"Good. I agree", said Valda, "it's settled then. I'll see you back here, same time, next week. Let's now go and get that drink. I need it."

With that, Alan started the car and drove to a nearby secluded bar. Valda wore sunglasses, just in case someone recognized her. After the drink, Alan drove her back to the airport where the pilot was waiting for her. Valda quickly climbed up the aircraft's stairs and entered the plane. The door closed and the aircraft taxied out onto the runway. After the pilot revved the engines for a few seconds and received take-off clearance, the jet sped down the runway, lifted off and headed back to Washington.

18

Attack Scenarios

During the week of the 3rd to the 9th of March, Alan Burgess took a week's leave from the electronics company, where he worked as a vice president, in order to think about the task presented to him, by Valda Lewis. He sat down in his Roanoke, Virginia home and developed three possible proposals for attacking the Capitol building in Washington, D.C. Each scenario had its advantages and disadvantages and, depending on the desired result, the best plan would need to incorporate surprise and swiftness of attack.

The first proposal analyzed was the use of plastic explosives, such as Semtex and C-4. They would need to be smuggled through security at the Capitol and there were utility tunnels which might be useful for this purpose. The entire complex would have to be investigated between now and CE (Capitol Explosion) day.

The quantity of explosives, needed to blow up both the Senate and House wings of the Capitol, would have to be calculated. In order to obtain the damage and casualties needed to justify a state of emergency, a large amount of explosives would probably be needed. As Burgess looked at this problem, he felt like Guy Fawkes of 410 years ago, who planned to blow up the British Parliament building, along with King James. Back then gun powder was the explosive of choice, and there were cellars under the building where Guy Fawkes hid it. He was luckily caught by soldiers, just as he was about to light the fuse.

The following is a layout of some of the tunnels connecting the Supreme Court and the Library of Congress with the Capitol.

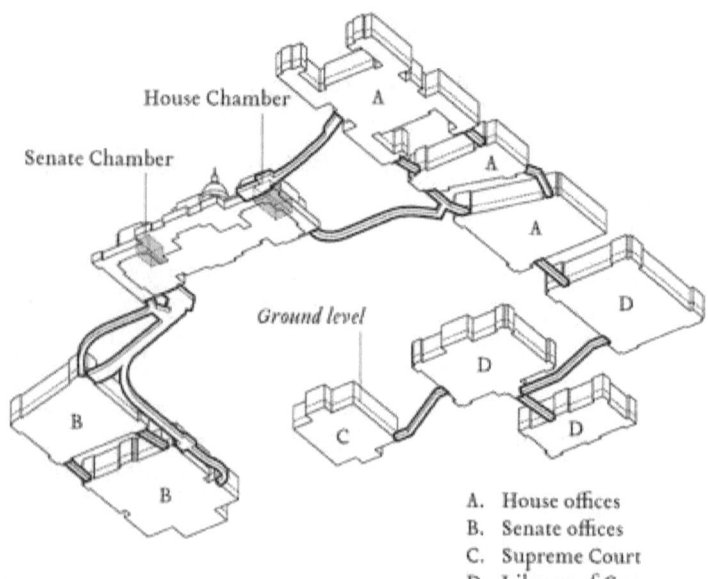

A. House offices
B. Senate offices
C. Supreme Court
D. Library of Congress

It appeared to Burgess the best approach for scenario one would be to smuggle the explosives in through the utility tunnels. The amount of explosives and the tunnel usage would have to be calculated between April and September. Experts on explosives would also be required. Overall, this would be a tough scenario, but could be facilitated by bribing a few Capitol Police. Anyone can be bought, if one has enough money. Alan estimated thirty to forty senators and sixty to ninety congressmen would be killed, or wounded, under this scenario. It would require placing the explosives at just the right spot under the floors of the wings. There were two additional questions that would need to be answered; how thick the floors were and how much explosive would be needed to break through them.

****

The second proposal, Alan explored, was the use of suicide bombers, with explosives strapped to their bodies. Here, it would require volunteers to blow themselves up. Ideally, women and children would be the best bombers, since they would receive the least scrutiny going through security check points. However, the suicide vests would have to be smaller than those that a man would wear. Most suicide vests contain anywhere from eleven to forty-four pounds of explosive. Thus with two bombers per wing, the maximum explosive charge would be eighty-eight pounds. Compared to the other methods, the damage and casualties would be lower.

Initially, the bombers would go to the visitors' gallery and then, at the appointed time, rush down to the main floor and blow themselves up. If this was not feasible, they would jump over the balcony down to the main floor below, as they pulled the explosive charge cord.

There were many questions that needed to be answered before this method could be used on CE day.

Burgess thought to himself, "*Who would build these vests, belts, shoes or underwear? What were the best explosives to use? How to obtain the explosives for use in the vests? How would you go about finding volunteer suicide bombers? Could they build vests that would get past security? Would two suicide bombers per Capitol wing be enough to cause significant damage and casualties? There were so many issues to resolve.*"

If the attack succeeded, Alan's best guess was that twenty to thirty senators and forty to sixty congressmen would be killed, or wounded. Under this scenario, there would be fewer casualties than the first method.

The overall question, for this attack, is whether the death and destruction would be enough, to justify a state of emergency to the general population. The idea of suicide bombers was simple enough, but Alan Burgess had doubts about its success. If he enlisted the help of more suicide bombers, the probability of destruction and deaths would go up, but the probability of an information leak also goes up. The more people involved in the plot, the less secretive it would be and surprise might be compromised.

****

The third proposal seemed the one with the best chance of overall success to Burgess. It offered the opportunity to deliver five hundred pounds of high explosives through the roof/ceiling of the Senate and House wings of the Capitol. The Bomarc C missiles were equipped with a contact fuze that could be set for the explosives to be detonated from one-half second to five seconds after contact. If set for about one second, this would allow the missile, and its explosive charge, to travel down toward the Capitol wing floors and thus cause maximum casualties and damage.

The latest version of the Bomarc could be programmed with the coordinates of the target and then guided by GPS. Just in case, the GPS satellite is shut down, the missile can still be guided by the TERCOM (Terrain Contour Matching) using the onboard radar system in the nose of the missile. The highly accurate GPS system would allow each individual missile to target the Senate or House wings of the Capitol.

Since the missiles travel at 3,000 mph, once they are cruising at their assigned altitude, the chance of them being intercepted and shot down would be very small. It would not be like World War II, where the German V1s were upended by Spitfires, which flew alongside and, using their wing, were able to flip the missile over. The flight time to the target would be only about ten minutes from Camp Warrior, North Carolina. The minimum time to detect the missile, make a decision and scramble jet fighters is a minimum of eight minutes. In fact during some questionable flights with security issues into the US, it has taken up to fifty-five minutes to scramble and intercept the possible threatening airliner.

The third scenario was the most challenging, as far as also being technically feasible. However, to be successful, the element of surprise would be critical. Would anyone ask questions when two practice missiles are sent to the old Chanute base, with test equipment? "Perhaps," Alan thought, "but we could claim that we're making a documentary, for the television History Channel, about the Bomarc missile and how it protected the United States from Russian bombers in the 1960's and 1970's."

Alan came to the conclusion that the third scenario had the best chance of success, and it would also cause enough panic in Washington, to allow the president to declare a state of emergency.

PROPOSAL #1

Overall Objective	Create an atmosphere that allows for declaring a state of emergency
Tactic	Destroy all or parts of the Capitol. Maximize casualties among Senators and Congressmen
Method	Sneak explosives into the Capitol and explode them with a remote control device
Personnel Requirement	Four. Team leader plus three members
Equipment Requirement	Plastic explosives that are hard to detect with bomb sniffing equipment. Probably C-4 or Semtex
Cost	$43 million payment to team plus cost of explosives
Advantages	Simple low technology solution. High chance of success after explosives are smuggled in.
Disadvantages	Hard to smuggle in explosives. Capitol police will have to be bribed, if possible.
Probability of Success	30%
% Capitol Destroyed	40%
# Dead Senators	35
# Wounded Senators	25
# Dead Congressmen	80
# Wounded Congressmen	75

PROPOSAL #2

Overall Objective	Create an atmosphere that allows for declaring a state of emergency
Tactic	Destroy all or parts of the Capitol. Maximize casualties among Senators and Congressmen
Method	Suicide bombers enter Senate and House public galleries. Then rush floor and blow themselves up.
Personnel Requirement	Five. Two per Senate and two per House plus team leader.
Equipment Requirement	Sophisticated suicide belts and/or vests that cannot be detected by Capitol security.
Cost	$35 million including possible bribery payments to Capitol guards.
Advantages	Simplicity of attack. No technical advantages
Disadvantages	Danger of being caught high before detonation. Finding four suicide bombers a problem.
Probability of Success	60%
% Capitol Destroyed	10%
# Dead Senators	25
# Wounded Senators	25
# Dead Congressmen	75
# Wounded Congressmen	50

PROPOSAL #3

Overall Objective	Create an atmosphere that allows for declaring a state of emergency
Tactic	Destroy all or parts of the Capitol. Maximize casualties among Senators and Congressmen
Method	Launch two Bomarc missiles from Camp Warrior aimed at Senate and House Chambers of Capitol
Personnel Requirement	Six consisting of a team leader and five team members
Equipment Requirement	Two practice CIM-10C missiles, associated test equipment and two buildings at old Chanute AFB
Cost	$75 million total including team payments plus equipment and facility rental
Advantages	High probability of success. Hard to shoot down due to speed/surprise. 10 minutes launch to impact.
Disadvantages	Technically difficult. Missiles miss target. Missiles intercepted. Incorrect GPS coordinates programmed..
Probability of Success	95%
% Capitol Destroyed	60%
# Dead Senators	50
# Wounded Senators	15
# Dead Congressmen	150
# Wounded Congressmen	100

19

Colonel Meets W.H. Advisor

On Thursday, the 10th of March, Valda Lewis flew back to Roanoke, as planned, to meet with Alan Burgess. Her government provided jet taxied up to the Roanoke private plane reception area exactly at 2:00 pm, as agreed to previously. Alan was there waiting for her and waved at her, as she stepped off the plane. She walked over to him and gave him a slight smile and shook her hand.

"Glad to see you again Alan," she said warmly. "Do you have something for me?"

"Yes, I do. We can discuss the matter under consideration, as before in my car. Is that okay?"

"That will be fine," Valda replied.

Alan walked her to his "bug" free car, as it was the best place to have their meeting. The necessity for secrecy made it imperative that their conversation be completely private. However, what he didn't tell her was that, for this meeting, he had a hidden audio recording device so that, if he needed evidence of the meeting for protection, he would have it.

"I've developed the three proposals as you requested. I have them here with me."

Alan then handed her a sealed envelope containing the three reports.

Alan continued, "I must inform you however, after much consideration, that proposal number three is the only method that has a good chance of success. The first two scenarios are much more risky and may be difficult to achieve positive results."

"Why do you say that?" Valda asked.

"With the security checks and sniffing equipment they have today, it would be extremely difficult to smuggle explosives into an area underneath the floor of each wing. In addition, getting people to wear suicide vests would probably be even harder."

"Couldn't you bribe a few guards to let you enter with a minimal check?" asked Valda.

"Yes, maybe, but even so, to get enough explosives in, to create the damage and casualties you need, would be extremely difficult."

"Isn't there a danger that the missiles, in scenario three, could be shot down before reaching the Capitol?" Valda queried.

"The danger is minimal, because we'd have the element of surprise. The missile travels at close to Mach 4.0 and, by the time the decision is made to try and intercept it, the missile will have reached the target. Proposal number three, the missile approach, is the only one with a high degree of probability for success. Again, it's the one scenario that will provide the required damage and casualties you require. I'm willing to take the lead in the missile attack, but for the other two scenarios, you'll have to find someone else to lead them."

"I'll have to get back to you on the final decision. I don't have the authority to make it on my own," Valda responded.

"One more item that must be discussed" Alan said. "It's the question of compensation for the team and me. This must be agreed to, along with the plan we use.

Specifically, for the five member team, the following payment shall be:

Three thousand dollars per month during the training period, deposited in personal bank account

Fifty thousand dollars cash, on the day of the attack

Ten million dollars deposited three months after attack, in the Swiss Bank UBS

For myself, to lead this team and take the risks inherent in this plot, I'll need the following:

Five thousand dollars per month during the training period, deposited in personal bank account

One hundred thousand dollars cash, on the day of the attack

Twenty-five million dollars deposited two months after the attack, in the Swiss Bank UBS

In addition, each of us will need a new car registered, insured and parked at a safe house in Wilmington, North Carolina."

"Hum. That's an awful lot of money. I'll have to clear it with Washington," Valda replied.

"It'll be well worth it to you and Washington, I can guarantee it. By the way, if this approach is upheld, we'll need a few more details approved and delivered on. First, Jackson Hall, at the decommissioned Chanute Air Force Base in Illinois, must be rented for six months, along with the Bomarc building next door to it. In addition, we'll need two Bomarc C missiles brought to Chanute from a storage base near Wichita, Kansas, together with the associated test equipment and spare guidance system modules. These modules will have to be modified and they'll not be returned. We'll need to dispose of the old modules. We'll need all of this, so we can practice programming the missiles and making the necessary modifications to the guidance systems. Once the buildings are rented, they'll have to be cleaned and made ready for a six month stay."

"Alan. You're very demanding, but I can understand why. I'll bring all this up with Washington. I'll try to get a decision as soon as possible; maybe within forty-eight hours. In the meantime, please make a list of your requirements in writing for the payments, equipment, buildings, etc. so there'll be no confusions or delays. Well, I'd better get back to Washington. We don't have time to waste. We'll have to bypass the drinks today."

With that, Valda and Alan exited his vehicle. Alan walked with her back to the government jet. The pilot came to open the cabin door to let Valda in.

Before she climbed the steps, she turned and gave Alan a quick handshake.

"See you soon", she said, as she turned and entered the jet.

The cabin door closed and the engines started up. A minute later, the Gulfstream taxied out to the runway and took off. Alan climbed into his car, retrieved the audio tape from the recorder and stored it for safe keeping. He then went back to work at Teknow Security.

20

President and Advisor Huddle

Early in the morning of Friday, the 11th of March, Valda met with the president in a closed door meeting, in the Oval Office. The president's recording machines were all turned off and the office had been checked for bugs before the meeting began. Cell phones were left outside the office, in case the NSA turned one of them on, unbeknownst to Valda or Tuckwell. Absolute security was vital.

Plausible deniability for the president had to be maintained, especially on the matter to be discussed.

He would never meet Alan Burgess or talk with him on the phone. Valda Lewis, Tuckwell's trusted advisor, would be the only contact between the administration and the former colonel.

Valda presented to President Tuckwell the three proposals that Burgess had prepared. They then discussed the briefs in detail. The major question, on the table, was which scenario would provide the maximum panic, casualties and destruction that would allow Tuckwell to declare a state of emergency, by executive order. Another concern was how much the various scenarios would cost and where the funds would come from.

President Tuckwell asked Valda, "Can we trust this Alan Burgess? Exactly what is his background, and how do we know he has the knowledge and capability, to carry out any of these scenarios, especially the expensive one?"

Valda responded, "As I believe I mentioned to you the other day, Alan Burgess is a retired USAF colonel who had been passed over for promotion to general by the previous administration, after making some derogatory statements to the press about the Chairman of the Joint Chiefs of Staff. He is very bitter about that and will be happy to get retribution. He is very bright and has a background in missiles, including the Bomarc. He was involved with the building of the eight Bomarc bases under the previous president. We can be sure that he is competent and can carry out proposal number three; the one involving the use of the Bomarc missile. He did tell me that as far as the first two scenarios were concerned, he did not want to be involved, since he believed the chance for success was minimal."

Tuckwell replied, "If you're convinced, Valda, that he can be trusted and accomplish the mission, then I'll go along with your decision. It sounds like we go with the missile scenario. Can we obtain the seventy-five million dollars he's asking for? There must be no trail of where the money came from."

Valda responded, "Yes, the Committee is willing to supply the funds, since they see it in their best interest to keep you in office. In order to accomplish the mission, Burgess says he needs two Bomarc missiles with associated test equipment and spare guidance modules for training purposes. They will need to be shipped from the storage base near Wichita, to the old Chanute AFB. You would need to sign a requisition order for this equipment. I'll make sure that the paperwork is destroyed once the mission is over. There'll be no trace of it. After the training has been completed, the equipment will be picked up and returned to the Wichita storage depot. Colonel Burgess assures me that the equipment will be returned in the condition it was, when it arrived. It would be best that it arrives in the middle of the night, so there should be few witnesses. If there are any, the Atlas Group will take care of them."

"Good." said the president. "Then we'll go with the missile scenario and I'll sign that requisition. I believe that the best date for the launch of the missiles will probably be Friday, the 9th of September. The Congress will be back in session from the summer recess. However, don't communicate this date yet to Burgess. Just tell him that the launch date, he should aim for, is in the early part of September. We can't take a chance of a leak on the actual date. We can confirm that date as we get closer to it."

Valda replied, "I believe you've made the correct decision, Mr. President. I'll contact my liaison with the Committee and make arrangements for the funds and vehicles that Burgess has requested. I'll contact the colonel immediately, so we can get this mission rolling. Good Day, Mr. President."

"Thank you for your help," said Tuckwell.

As Valda walked out of the office, he thought *"I'm lucky to have her on my side."*

She went down the hallway to her White House office and sat down at her desk to call Alan Burgess.

She dialed his number, and the colonel answered almost immediately.

"This is Alan Burgess speaking."

"Alan. This is Valda Lewis. I need you to come to Washington on Monday, the 14th of March, to meet with me. I have some important news."

Alan replied, "There's a daily US Air flight at 8:00 am from Roanoke Airport that I can catch and be at the Washington National Airport around 9:30 am. Where do you want me to meet you?"

Valda responded, "That flight sounds good. I'll have a car pick you up, outside the baggage area. The driver will be in a white Ford Fusion, with a sign in the passenger window reading "Deep Silver". Your code name for this driver is Mr. Lamb, and he'll bring you to our meeting place. Please don't bring any cell phone, camera or recording device with you. See you on Monday." With that they both hung up.

21

The Go Ahead

On Monday morning, the 14th of March, Alan drove to Roanoke Airport and caught the 8:00 am American Airline flight to the Washington National Airport. While in the air, he went to the toilet, took a miniature audio recording device out of his briefcase and strapped it onto his body. The plane was right on time and landed at approximately 9:25 am and taxied to the gate. He went out through the baggage area and looked for a white Ford Fusion with a sign in the passenger window reading "Deep Silver". He spotted it almost immediately and went up to the driver.

"I'm Mr. Lamb and I believe you're here to pick me up. Is that correct?"

The neatly dressed driver replied "Good morning Mr. Lamb. Yes, I've been ordered to pick you up and take you to Pershing Park." With that he drove away from the airport, with Alan in the back seat. As the car departed the airport grounds, Alan reached inside his coat and switched on the recording device.

It wasn't long before they were near Pershing Park. The driver stopped, went around to the other side of the car and opened up the rear door.

He said, "Mr. Lamb. This is Pershing Park. I've been asked to tell you to wait here. Another vehicle will be by here, momentarily, to pick you up."

Alan got out of the car and stood on the curb. The white Fusion drove off. Luckily it was a warm, dry day and the birds were singing. In about thirty seconds, a black Buick pulled up right behind him. He heard the engine and turned around. There, in the car, was Valda Lewis with a smile on her face.

"Jump in," she said. "We're going for a ride Alan. Good to see you. I'm glad you could make it."

Alan climbed into the passenger front seat and said, "Nice to see you again Valda."

With that, she drove off. "We're going to a spot where we can talk and also make sure nobody is watching or listening to us."

Alan replied, "That'll be great. On the way, could we quickly drive through a fast food restaurant and get a sausage egg biscuit. I haven't had anything to eat yet this morning."

"Sure." Valda replied and in a couple of minutes drove through a Burger King restaurant.

"Thanks," Alan said as she handed him the food.

Valda kept driving, as he snacked on the sandwich. In about fifteen minutes, she parked in a fairly deserted parking lot, turned toward Alan and started to speak.

"Alan. We've agreed that your proposal number three is the best and the only viable solution, for achieving the desired results. Therefore, we want to proceed with that plan. You should immediately start the search for the five ex-servicemen, with the correct credentials, to join your team. The president has signed the requisition for the transfer of the two Bomarc C missiles, test equipment and spare guidance modules from the Wichita storage base to the decommissioned Chanute AFB. The Atlas Movie Company out of Chicago will handle all arrangements in

122

renting Jackson Hall, and the Bomarc missile shelter at Chanute. They'll also provide security and transportation, while you're there. The buildings will be renovated, and your team will be able to move in on Sunday, the 17th of April. The missiles and equipment will be there at Chanute, when you arrive. You'll have from the middle of April until the end of August, to train your team. You should be prepared to launch the missiles by the early part of September. No firm date has been decided yet but, when it is, it will be communicated to you immediately. Do you understand all this so far?"

"Yes," Alan replied. "However, I've one major question. You haven't made any mention about the payments I asked for and the vehicles. Will they be available on the dates I requested, in our last meeting?"

"Yes, they will," responded Valda. "We have approved the monthly payment, the cash on completion of the task and the funds in the Swiss bank. The vehicles will be provided as per your request. We can't guarantee the team's first choice of vehicle and color, but we'll do our best to provide them.

Alan replied, "Great, I'd better get busy, since I have a lot of work to do. How do I contact you, if we run into a problem or need something?"

"You can call this special phone number that I'm giving you now, on this card, and leave a message. However, the preferred way will be to use the management at Atlas Movie Company. They'll be able to provide almost immediate action, regardless of the need. Is there anything else you require at the moment?"

"No. I don't think so." said Alan. "I'd better get home and start to work on hiring the team. My plane leaves in just over an hour."

"Alright, I'll drop you off back at Pershing Park, and "Deep Silver" will pick you up and take you back to the airport," Valda responded.

With that, she started the car and headed back to Pershing Park. There she let Alan out and said "Good luck Alan. Please don't let us down. We're counting on you. Don't forget to send me progress reports of your training at Chanute."

"I'll do that," said Alan and shook her hand, as got out of the car.

He stood on the sidewalk for about a minute and then along came "Deep Silver". The driver got out of the car and opened the rear door.

"Hope you had a productive meeting here in Washington Mr. Lamb," said the driver, as he closed the rear passenger door.

Soon they were back at Washington National Airport, and "Deep Silver" let Alan out at the departure terminal. "Have a good trip," the driver said, as he got into the car and drove off.

Before going through the airport security, Alan Burgess went to the men's restroom, entered a stall, removed the recording device and placed it in his briefcase. He then flew back to Roanoke, to start a new chapter in his life. The immediate task was to find and hire five technically competent volunteers that had a bone to pick with their country.

22

Red Moon Team Recruited

Alan Burgess set about hiring a team to work on the Bomarc C missile. He decided he would only use his first name, when talking to the applicants, so they would have a problem identifying him at some future time. He figured that he needed five skilled people, besides himself, to accomplish the task of modifying and launching the missiles. He had about six months in which to hire and train the team.

He thought to himself, *"Where can I find five experts who will be willing to sell their souls for ten million dollars each? I need to find engineers and/or technicians, who have a grudge against the U.S. Government and need money."*

After giving it much thought, Alan decided to take a two pronged approach, to locating the right people. First, he would visit veterans groups and subtly ask veterans about colleagues who are in trouble or bitter about their military experience. Second, he would advertise in various newspapers, without giving too much information. The advertisements would be as follows and placed in the personal column:

Wanted: Experienced veterans, knowledgeable of weapon systems and unsatisfied in your present position. Do you have financial problems that you need to correct? Are you unhappy with the way that the VA/Government has handled your situation? Any branch of service will be acceptable and considered. Send your resume outlining service qualifications in complete confidence to the Email address saveamericanow@ntintl.com

This advertisement was published in newspapers in the major cities of the U.S.

For the next two weeks, Alan also travelled to Phoenix and Miami, where veterans groups were holding annual meetings. At these two meetings, he attended the dinners and talked with several attendees, about their service and their colleagues. He discovered two potential candidates for the Red Moon team.

At an Iraq Veterans group meeting in Phoenix, Alan sat and surveyed the group of men attending the meeting. They all wore name tags with their branch of service and rank. His gaze came across a man named Mike Thornburn. He looked down on his luck, so Alan decided to approach him after the meeting. As they were leaving, he went up to him and introduced himself.

"Hi Mike. My name is Alan. I used to be in the Air Force before I was forced out into retirement. Is this your first meeting?"

"It's nice to meet you, Alan. No, I've been a couple of times before. I was in the Army and got out after twelve years. I served in Iraq during Operation Desert Storm and was a tank gunner.

"Who do you work for now?" Alan asked.

"To be honest, since I got out of the Army, I've had trouble finding steady work. The Veterans Administration has not been helpful at all. This is one reason I come to these veteran meetings, hoping to find somebody who will provide me with some work."

"What did you actually do in Operation Desert Storm?"

"I was involved in the tank pincer movement that went far behind the enemy lines in the Iraq desert, hit the Republican Guard and ended up at the backdoor of Kuwait."

"That sounds as though it was exciting," Burgess said.

"Yes, it was exciting, but also a little scary. I live in Prescott now, with my girlfriend. She works with the local school district. My parents live in Phoenix, and I try to help them out financially, whenever I can. They're not in the best of health."

"Say Mike; would you like to join me for a drink? I may have something you'd be interested in" Burgess offered.

"Sure" Mike said, "If you're buying."

They walked to the hotel bar and sat at a table in the back of the room. The place was almost empty and offered a measure of privacy for their conversation. When the waiter came, Mike ordered a whisky, neat and Alan ordered a vodka martini. When the drinks were served and the waiter left, Alan turned to Mike and said, "How are you with a rifle? Are you a good shot, if need be?"

"You bet I am. I was the best shot in the unit when we went to the range. The other guys in my unit were a little envious of my accuracy."

"Well, how you would like a one time job that will pay you enough to be financially independent and also help out your parents. This job will last about six months and would involve some risk, but no more than Operation Desert Storm."

"Given my financial situation, I certainly would be interested. What would I actually be doing?" Mike asked.

"At the moment, that's confidential, but you'll be informed in due course and given the chance to back out. I can assure you that you'll be well paid. Initially, at the end of the job, you would receive fifty thousand dollars and, then three months later, you would receive a large amount from a bank holding it in trust for you. Are you interested?"

"You bet I am," Mike said.

"You understand that this conversation is confidential and can't be mentioned to anyone. It would put them, you and the operation in grave danger," Burgess warned.

"I understand," Mike said. "You can count on my discretion."

"Okay. I'll put you on the list and I'll be in contact with you, in the next few days. The job will start in about a week. Get your affairs in order, because you'll be going to another part of the country and be out of contact for a while."

"Thanks, for this opportunity Alan. I'll wait for your call," replied Mike.

Alan paid their tab and then they left the bar and went their separate ways.

****

Two days later, Alan was in Miami at another annual veterans' gathering, where several of the attendees were from the Navy. He talked with a few of the former sailors during the social hour, before the meeting was called to order. Much of the discussion between the Vets was about jobs or the lack thereof.

Alan listened, more than he talked, and he met a man named Pasco Martinez, who was in the Navy for eight years. He seemed very troubled about his financial affairs, since he had a wife and kids, and his job prospects were not very good.

During a coffee break in the middle of the meeting, Alan got Pasco to one side and started talking to him.

"Pasco, my name is Alan and I used to be in the Air Force. I understand from what you said earlier that you're having trouble getting steady work?"

"You heard right. I've a wife and three children, and things are getting pretty desperate, financially. I haven't seen you before at this meeting. Are you from this area?" Pasco asked.

"No. I'm from Virginia and I'm just visiting Miami for a few days, trying to round up some help for a project of mine."

Immediately, Pasco's ears perked up.

"What kind of help are you looking for?" he asked.

"What experience did you have in the Navy and what have you been doing since you got out?" Alan inquired.

"I was working for a cable company until a couple of years ago. The company had some cut backs and I was laid off. Since then, jobs have been hard to find, even with my communication experience. The slowdown in the economy has been murder, on the job market. In the Navy, I was involved with operating and maintaining satellite communications equipment. This was both on board ship and land based facilities. To be exact, I was a Communications Cryptologic Technician or CTO, for short. The government agencies that are supposed to help veterans, including the Veterans Administration, haven't been very helpful."

"Did you have a security clearance?" asked Alan.

"Sure did. I had to have a top secret clearance, since the communications traffic was highly confidential." Pasco answered.

"That must have been very interesting work." Alan responded.

"Yes it was. What did you do in the Air Force, Alan?"

"I was involved with missiles, until I ended up in a desk job. How would you like to have a one time job that lasts about six months and, a year from now, will make you independently wealthy; no more financial worries? You would have more than enough money, to take care of all your family needs," responded Alan.

"The money sounds good, but what kind of job is it? What would I have to do?"

"At the moment, that is confidential, but you will be informed in due course and given the chance to back out. I can assure you that you will be well paid. Initially, at the end of the job, you would receive fifty thousand dollars and, then three months later, you would receive a large lump sum, from a bank holding it in trust for you. Are you interested?"

"I certainly am. When would I start? Will I make some money each month, so my wife and children can eat?"

"You'll be paid three thousand dollars a month until the task is complete, when you'll receive the fifty thousand dollars. I'll call you in a few days, with more details. In the meantime, since you'll be away from home for a while, make sure all your affairs are in order. It's been nice meeting you. I'll be in touch soon.

"Thanks Alan. It's been great talking with you. I'll be waiting for your call."

With that, they went back to the meeting. After it started up again, Alan slipped out and caught a flight back to Roanoke.

****

Once home in Roanoke, he reviewed his special email account that contained dozens of messages from veterans, who had seen his ad in the various newspapers. Of the dozens of messages in his mail box, three of them were of special interest to Alan.

The first one was from a John Norman who lived in Franklin Tennessee, with his wife and two children. He had been in the Air Force and retired, after his wife had enough of the frequent moves. The most interesting part of his resume was that he worked on the old Bomarc B program, and then on the later Bomarc C. Alan decided to give him a call. He dialed the number John had listed in the Email.

"Hello, this is John speaking."

"Hi John, this is Alan. I have the email you sent me in response to my ad in the Nashville paper. I too was in the Air Force and I think I may have met you once, a few years ago. I gather that you worked on the Bomarc C, the same as I did. I see that you enlisted back in the early 1970's and spent three years working with the old Bomarc B. Did you happen to go to Chanute AFB for the training?"

"Yes. I went there for my training on the B version, and then was assigned to McGuire AFB, until the program was discontinued, in 1972."

"What section of the missile did you work on?"

"I was involved with the entire guidance system, including the data link and active target seeker." answered John.

"What did you do after they shut down the Bomarc program?"

"I worked on several missile systems, until they called on me to work on the Bomarc C, after a major Islamic terrorist attack."

"Maybe that's where I met you. I was involved with the start up of the Bomarc C, when the president felt it was important to have the capability of a fast air defense system, in case terrorists decided to attack the US mainland."

"I worked on the Bomarc C for three years until I was given a desk job. I retired from the Air Force with the rank of Tech Sergeant, after thirty five years of service."

"What have you been doing since retiring from the Air Force?" asked Alan.

"Not much, I've had a few odd jobs here and there. It's hard to find a good paying job, when you're over fifty."

"How would you like to make enough money so that you or your family would never have to worry again?"

"That sounds great, but what would I have to do for that money?"

"Well, you would have to work on the Bomarc C."

"That sounds right up my alley. Exactly what will we be doing with the Bomarc C? More importantly, how much will I get paid?

"At the moment, the exact job is confidential, but you'll be informed in due course and given the chance to back out. I can assure you that you'll be well paid. Initially, at the end of the job, you would receive fifty thousand dollars, and then three months later, you would receive a large amount from a bank, holding it in trust for you. In addition, you'll receive three thousand dollars a month, until the task is complete. Are you interested?"

"Yes, count me in. I need the money for my family, and I'd like to be able to really retire."

"I'll put you on the roster and call you in a few days with instructions. You'll be away from home, for a few months, and out of contact.   So it would be best if you get your affairs in order. By the way you'll be seeing Chanute again. You'll hear from me soon."

"Okay," John said.   "I'll wait for your call", said John Norman as he hung up the phone.

"*It sounded great*," he thought. "*Maybe this is the break I've been looking for.*"

Alan Burgess had two more calls to make in response to the emails.

The first one was to a Chris Smith, of Atlanta, Georgia. He dialed the number, and a man answered, "Hello!"

"I'm calling for a Chris Smith."

"This is Chris speaking. What can I do for you?"

"I'm calling about your reply to my advertisement in the Atlanta paper."

"Yes, what further information do you need?"

"I just want to confirm some of the details," said Alan. "I understand you were in the Air Force for over twenty years and served in both Operation Desert Storm and the Iraq War. Is that correct?"

"Yes. That's right. I decided to get out and retire, after I'd put in twenty-five years. Unfortunately, I found out that it wasn't so easy to find a good job, after you've been out of the civilian job market that long, even with my computer programming skills."

"What did you exactly do in the Air Force?" asked the colonel.

"Well mainly I started out as a computer programmer and worked on various missile and weapon systems. I ended up my career as a Senior Master Sergeant.

"That work, you did, sounds very interesting. What are you doing now?"

"I work for a computer company in Atlanta, but the future prospects are not too good. So far, I haven't been laid off, but they're cutting back and the older employees are usually the first to go." replied Chris.

"Did you have a security clearance in the Air Force?"

"Yes I did. I needed a secret security clearance to do the computer programming, I was performing."

"Good. How would you like to go to work on my team and earn enough money, so that in one year you would be independently wealthy? You wouldn't have to work anymore."

"That sounds almost too good to be true. What would I have to do to get this money? How much will that be, by the way?" asked Chris.

"Your task would be to do some programming on a missile system. All I can tell you at this point is that the exact job is confidential, but you'll be informed in due course and given the chance to back out. I can assure you that you'll be well paid."

Alan then explained the same compensation package that he had given to the previous three men.

"Are you interested?" asked Alan.

"You bet I am. The money would make all my financial problems go away. You said I could withdraw, if I don't like the exact job. Is that correct?"

"Yes, you'll be given the chance to back out. Once on board though and you have agreed to do the work, you'll have to complete the mission assigned."

"That sounds fair enough. When will I start?"

"I've one more team member to locate. As soon as I have done that, I'll be in touch with you. By the way, you'll be gone from your home for a few months, so it will be wise to get your affairs in order."

"Okay. I'll wait for your call. Thanks for the opportunity Mr. Burgess."

"You're welcome. This project is top secret, so do not tell anyone about it. If it gets out, it could put us all in danger. Goodbye for now."

With that, they both hung up the phone and Alan reached for the last resume he had that looked interesting. He read the resume again and then reached for the phone, to call the man who answered the advertisement, Gerry Davies. Alan dialed the number listed and a woman answered."Hello."

"I'm looking for a Gerry Davies." Alan said.

"May I ask who is calling?" the woman replied.

"Yes, this is Alan and Gerry sent me his resume. I would like to discuss some of the details with him."

"Hold on a minute and I'll go and get him."

Alan heard the woman, on the other end of the line, shout in the background "Gerry. There's a phone call for you."

"Who is it? Gerry asked.

"It's some guy named Alan. He said you sent him a resume."

"Okay," Gerry shouted. "I'm coming."

A few seconds later, he picked up the receiver. "Hello. This is Gerry Davies."

"Hi Gerry, this is Alan calling about the resume you emailed to me the other day in response to the advertisement in the Philadelphia paper."

"Gerry. I understand you were in the Marine Corps for twelve years and served in Iraq and Afghanistan. Is that correct?"

"Yes", replied Gerry. "After the twelve years, I had enough of military life and got out."

"What did you actually do in the Marines?" asked Alan

"Well, I was a Satellite Communications (SATCOM) technician for a few years and then I worked in Tactical Remote Sensor System Maintenance (TRSS). All the duties were very challenging."

"Did your work assignments require you to hold a security clearance?"

"Yes, they did," replied Gerry. "I had to have a secret security clearance and I had one the entire time I was in the Marines.

"Your jobs in the Marines required you to be good at electronics, I assume," inquired Alan.

"They sure did. I aced all the electronics courses, offered in the Marines."

"That's good. How are you with a rifle?"

"Excellent, I was the second best shot in the entire squad."

"What are you doing now?"

"I work a few odd jobs," said Gerry. "It's hard to get full time employment out of the Marines and the VA does not help much. I'm also trying to help my mother financially. Life is pretty hard. I survive thanks to my girlfriend, who you spoke to briefly."

"How would you like a job that lasts about six months and, at the end, you would be independently wealthy, with no more financial problems?" asked Alan.

"This isn't a scam, is it? It almost sounds too good to be true. What would I have to do to earn this money? Invade Syria, by myself," laughed Gerry into the phone.

"No. This is for real," replied Alan. "Your task would be to do some electronics work on a missile system and also stand guard at the site. All I can tell you at this point is that the exact job is confidential, but you'll be informed in due course and given the chance to back out. I can assure you that you'll be well paid."

As he did with the other four candidates, Alan described the compensation package in detail, giving the amounts and when it would be paid.

"Are you interested?" Alan asked.

"Of course, I am. It sounds interesting and not too dangerous. Also, the pay sounds very attractive. You can count me in," said Gerry.

"Good. I'll put you on the team roster and I'll call you in a few days with the travel instructions. You'll be on the job and out of contact with your home, for a few months. It would be best if you put your affairs in order." instructed Alan.

"Okay. I'll wait for your call. Thanks for the opportunity Alan."

"You're welcome. This project is top secret so do not tell anyone including your girlfriend about it. Goodbye for now."

After they hung up the phone, Gerry went and got a beer out of the fridge, and Alan put a check mark by his name.

****

"Finally I have a full team that, with training, should be able to launch the surprise missile attack, on time and on target," Alan thought.

He called the phone number Valda Lewis had given him earlier and left a message, telling her that the team was now hired.

Later that day, he called the Atlas Film Company office in Chicago and gave them the names of the five team members. Atlas placed them on the Red Moon team roster and, as Alan requested, they made plans to obtain five airline tickets for Sunday, the 17th of April. They would arrange for the tickets to be picked up at the airline counter, closest to their home. Alan also asked them to provide five limos, to transport the team members to Chanute, after they arrived at Chicago O'Hare.

Colonel Burgess's plan was that an Atlas Movie Company employee would meet each flight, with a sign listing the team member code name, and escort him to a waiting car. They would then be driven to Rantoul, Illinois and Chanute AFB, about one hundred and twenty miles south of Chicago. He planned to greet each member, as they arrived at Chanute, and escort them into Jackson Hall.

After the flight and pick up plan had been scheduled by Atlas, Alan called each member of his team, and gave them the details.

"This is Alan with instructions about what to tell your families and on how to travel to Chanute. First, you must inform your families that you are on a secret government mission, and it will not be easy for you to contact them, over the next few months. Second, arrangements have been made for the monthly deposit of three thousand dollars to your personal, family bank account for living expenses. Third, you will go to your local airport, pick up the airline ticket for travel to Chicago O'Hare, on the 17th of April, and bring enough clothes to last for the approximate six months. There will be opportunities to use a washer and dryer, where you will be staying. Someone from the Atlas Movie Company will call you within the next twenty-four hours and give you a code name. You must remember this name, since when you arrive at Chicago O'Hare, you will be met by a man holding a sign, with your code name on it. You will then be driven to Chanute, where I will greet you and show you to your room, any questions?"

All that the colonel could do, now, was to await the mid-April date and commence the Bomarc missile training mission on the eighteenth. In the meantime, he would set up a schedule that would fulfill the required training.

23

National Police Force

During the third week of March, President Tuckwell had a meeting in the Oval Office, with Valda Lewis and the Attorney General, Robert McIntyre, to discuss an idea he had.

"Bob, as you are well aware, the crime rates, in the major cities, are rising at an alarming rate."

"Yes, that's true, Mr. President. We can do only so much about it, since we don't control the local police forces, except by denying federal funds. Does the administration have any firm plans to reduce the violence?"

The president looked at Valda Lewis, who nodded in agreement, as to what the he was about to say.

Tuckwell then turned to the attorney general, and said, "Our plan is to create a National Police Force, or NPF for short, and it would be under your control, Bob, along with the FBI. We see the NPF having arrest and enforcement powers, while the FBI would become mainly an investigative and crime solving department. This NPF organization would be akin to the NCA (National Crime Agency) that was recently formed in Great Britain. We believe having a strong NPF would help reduce the violence in the major urban areas and control the discriminatory tactics of the local police forces."

"Mr. President, the NPF sounds like a great idea and I'll be glad to have it in my department. However, my major concern is whether my budget will be increased to pay for this force?"

"Your budget will be increased accordingly, so you don't need to worry about the funding issue. In order to assemble the force quickly, we plan to transfer about thirty thousand officers, who have arrest powers, from other government agencies, as soon as possible. Actually, there are forty federal government agencies that have approximately one hundred and twenty thousand officers, who are authorized to carry weapons and make arrests."

"From what agencies will these officers be transferred?" asked the attorney general.

"I think I can answer that," said Valda Lewis. "They will be reassigned from the Environmental Protection Agency, Bureau of Prisons, Drug Enforcement Agency, Interior Department, Department of the Homeland Security, to name just a few."

"When will the formation of the NPF actually take place?"

"In about a week, the president will announce the formation of the organization, with the signing of an executive order," Valda replied.

"Bob. Thank you for coming, at such short notice. We'll keep you informed, as to the exact date of the announcement," the president said.

****

Less than a week later, on the evening of Friday, the 25th of March, President Edward Tuckwell signed an executive order creating the National Police Force (NPF).

Friday evenings were always a good time to announce a controversial news item, since many editors and reporters in the mainstream press have gone home for the weekend. The average American did not pay much attention to the news channels on the weekend, but they preferred to watch ESPN, or some other sports network.

Since a Friday evening was generally a slow time for news, the NPF executive order did go largely unnoticed, as they had planned.   Edward Tuckwell's friends and allies were in favor of it, since they saw an opportunity to maybe shut down Fox News and other unfriendly news stations. On the weekend talk shows, Valda Lewis had some friendly politicians go on the air and, if they were asked about the NPF, they would state the "party" line, about how it was necessary to control corrupt elements in the population and reduce the rising crime rates in urban areas. They would also state that the president had no choice, but to create this department.

President Tuckwell and Valda Lewis visualized the NPF as being an important tool in controlling the news and population in the next nine months.   With the coming events, he would need broad executive and enforcement powers.   If they let events get out of hand, it could be dangerous for them.

The NPF would supersede any state, county or city law enforcement organizations.   President Tuckwell, with his control over the NPF through the attorney general, could intimidate news, political or educational organizations, so they would not be a threat to him when he clamped down further, in the coming months. This was necessary in the broader scheme of things. The president would be able to use it, as a force, to silence his enemies and detractors, when the actual attack on the Capitol took place.

24

Rantoul, Illinois

One day in early April, a neatly dressed man walked into the Rantoul, Illinois mayor's office at 10:00 am and offered his business card to the secretary, "guarding" the mayor's door. He glanced at the name on the desk block. Carol Woolcott.

"Good morning, Ms. Woolcott" said the man, "I would like to speak to the mayor, about a confidential matter that will be of great benefit to Rantoul."

Carol looked at the man for a moment, sizing him up, and then speaking in a soft Midwest accent, said, "He's a very busy man, but let me see if he can spare you a few minutes."

She walked into the mayor's office and closed the door behind her. He looked up. "What is it?" said the mayor, as he sank a golf ball into a target cup. Carol gave him the business card and repeated what the man told her.

"Okay. Give me a minute to tidy up and then show him in. After five minutes, give me a call on the phone, so that if I want to get rid of him, I will have an easy excuse." The mayor started to tidy up the office and put his putter and ball away.

Carol went out and said to the visitor, "The mayor will see you shortly. He's just finishing up some important paperwork"

In about a minute, Carol's buzzer sounded and she picked up the phone, listened and then replaced it on the cradle. She looked at the man and said, "He'll see you now."

The man walked up to the closed door and knocked gently. The mayor inside said, "Come in."

The man entered the office, walked up to the mayor's desk and held out his hand. My name is Arnold Pridham and I represent the Atlas Movie Company," he said. The mayor shook his hand, as he glanced at the business card. The name matched the card, and he noticed the company was out of Denver, Colorado.

"It's nice to meet you. What can I do for you?" said Mayor Blanchard.

Mr. Pridham then proceeded to make his proposition. "My company would like to rent one block of the former Chanute AFB for six months. This block contains Jackson Hall and the old Bomarc training building with the high roof. We need it to make a documentary about the 1960's and the Air Force. That's all I can tell you, as the project is confidential, at this time. We're prepared to pay fifty thousand dollars a month, for the six months, plus we have made arrangements for the U.S. Government to release some funds to help you clean up the toxic sites on the base. I believe you have a few sites containing asbestos and chemicals, and the city of Rantoul doesn't have the money to clean it up."

Mayor Blanchard thought for a minute and then gambled. "How about rent of seventy-five thousand dollars a month?"

Mr. Pridham looked at him, hesitated purposely, for a few seconds and said with a smile, "Atlas is willing to go as high as seventy thousand dollars. Will you accept that?"

The mayor jumped at the counter offer. "Yes, I believe we can agree to that. Seventy thousand dollars for six months it is, starting immediately. Also don't forget the toxic funds."

Right then the phone rang. It was his secretary with the five minute call. "Not now" said the mayor into the receiver. "I'm very busy right at the moment," and then he hung up the phone.

Arnold Pridham took an envelope out of his pocket and gave it to the mayor. "You can count it. I believe you will find it contains seventy thousand dollars cash, for the first month's rent. I would like a receipt for legal and tax purposes. By the way, we'll be bringing in equipment for the documentary, but we'll do it at night, so as not to block your roads. Please talk to your police chief so that we will have no problems."

The mayor nodded, "I can guarantee the Rantoul police will not hassle you."

"Good, and it's been a pleasure doing business with you," replied Arnold Pridham. "Atlas will draw up the contract and get it to you in a day or so for you to sign, if that's okay. That way you will have a minimal legal expense. I will get out of your way now, so you can get back to your city business."

Pridham smiled to himself as he said that. He knew what business the mayor was probably up to.

Two days later, Mayor Blanchard received a contract from a Chicago law firm. He quickly had the town lawyer look at it, signed it and sent it back to the Chicago law firm that worked for Atlas, headquartered in Colorado.

Pridham walked out of the mayor's office and nodded at Carol, as he left the outer office. He strolled to his car and drove off.

"That was easy", he thought, as he turned into the former base to have another look at the buildings. He called his office on an unregistered phone and gave the good news to the man who answered. The Atlas Movie Company had already arranged for security at the site. As soon as the Chicago Security manager received the call and heard that it was all arranged, he immediately sent a team to secure it.

Before Pridham's visit to the mayor's office, Colonel Burgess, the Red Moon team leader, had already looked the base over to make sure the facilities would be adequate, and the launcher equipment was still there. When the base was decommissioned in 1993, most of the equipment was stripped and sent to other bases. However, the Bomarc missile training building, with its strange looking roofline, and the launch boom were still there. Only the missiles and the test equipment were missing. Alan had not seen the base for several years and was disappointed at how run down it looked.

Less than a week later, a crew from The Atlas Movie Company arrived and set up shop in the main building, Jackson Hall. This building was close to the Bomarc shelter building. The movie crew all looked authentic with real lights, cameras, etc. There were only three motels in Rantoul, and they had been lodged at all three. The motels were only two or three star, but they were adequate.

The buildings needed some major updating and repair work. Jackson Hall would be home to the Red Moon team and some of The Atlas Movie Company crew, for the next few months. The whole building needed cleaning, since it had been abandoned for the past few years, when the base was decommissioned. Bedrooms and conference rooms needed to be installed. A kitchen was also necessary, since the Red Moon team would not be allowed unaccompanied off the base. The Atlas Movie Company brought in its own crew from Chicago to accomplish all the work; this way security could be maintained. They worked very feverishly, so that all the modifications would be completed, by the time the Red Moon team arrived on Sunday, the 17th of April.

The president had previously signed an order to move two unarmed missiles and associated test equipment from a storage base near Wichita, Kansas, to Chanute.   Three vehicles carrying this equipment would arrive late at night, in early April, so as not to cause any alarm to the residents. Those people, who were still awake at that late hour, would assume that it was for the historical documentary, being shot at the base.   However, if any of the citizens asked too many questions, they would be taken care of by the Atlas security force.

25

Missiles Arrive at Chanute AFB

Two CIM-10C Bomarc C missiles, along with associated test equipment and extra guidance system modules, arrived, as planned, at Chanute from the storage facility, near Wichita, in early April. The equipment arrived at around midnight in three large vehicles, so as not to arouse too much interest of the Rantoul citizens. If a few "night owls" heard the trucks with the loads, they would assume they were dummy missiles for the documentary, which was being shot on the base. The filming had been announced in the local newspaper. The Atlas Movie Company security team from Chicago was on hand to make sure no questions were asked or answered. The truck drivers had already been cleared for the transportation task.

The missiles were complete with guidance and automatic control pilot systems. Except for the lack of the solid fuel, rocket motor, the missiles were similar to the ones located at Camp Warrior and the other seven bases, around the American coast line.

The Atlas Movie Company personnel greeted the trucks and airmen. They informed the air force personnel what the tasks were and where to place the equipment. They also told them to be as quiet as possible, so as not to wake up the good people of Rantoul.

One missile was installed on the erector arm in the special Bomarc building, with its strange looking roofline. This allowed the missile to be raised and lowered, without being in the outside elements. Rantoul can sometimes receive a lot of snow in the winter, with some temperatures approaching -10 to -15 degrees F.

The other missile was placed on a special cradle in the Jackson Hall hangar. This is where the team would work on the guidance system and active radar set, to make sure everything was ready for the missile launch.

The test equipment racks were also placed in the building hangar, alongside the missile. In addition, two sets of guidance modules were placed on benches, where they would be modified and used in the mission.

The USAF airmen, who came with the trucks, were very qualified to move the missiles, without damaging them. They had been informed that this was a classified operation, and they were, under no circumstances, to discuss it with anyone. They would follow orders closely, since they did not want to be subject to a court martial. It would affect their career in the Air Force and their service pension.

After the vehicles were completely unloaded and the equipment installed, where the airmen were directed, by the Atlas Movie Company personnel, the leader of the Atlas group did a quick inventory count, to make sure everything was in order.

The lieutenant went up to the company manager and said, as he held out some papers, "Will you please sign these release forms for the missiles and equipment?"

The company manager looked over the papers and responded, "Okay. I think everything looks in order." He then signed the multipage document, gave it back to the lieutenant and said, "I guess you'll be the same crew that will pick up the equipment, at the end of August, right?"

"I believe that's correct, unless there's a change in orders," replied the lieutenant.

The officer returned to the vehicles, where the airmen were milling about. "Okay, let's go. We'll stop for chow down the road, on the way back to base," the lieutenant said to the airmen, as he walked to the lead vehicle and climbed into the cab.

The rest of the airmen climbed into the three vehicles. The drivers then proceeded to exit the base, drove through Rantoul and headed toward I-57, which led to St Louis.

26

Red Moon Team Arrives

Alan Burgess, the Red Moon team leader, arrived at Chicago O'Hare, from Roanoke, on Friday, the 15th of April. He was met by a driver from the Atlas Movie Company and driven to Rantoul, about one hundred and twenty miles south of Chicago on I-57. The drive took a little less than two hours. As they drove south, he placed a call to Valda Lewis's secret cell phone and, when she failed to answer, he left a message.

"Valda, this is Alan, I'm in Illinois, on the way to Chanute. The rest of the team will be arriving on Sunday, two days from now. As we agreed previously, I'll give you periodic updates on the training. I understand from Atlas that the two missiles and test equipment have already arrived at the base. Talk to you soon."

The Atlas driver left the freeway at the Rantoul exit, and quickly approached the former base from the west. They entered it through the main gate and drove to the rented buildings, located off the main street.

The driver dropped him off at Jackson Hall, and the security guard, on duty, welcomed him to the building. He went in and looked around. Atlas had done an excellent job in cleaning it up and most of the required modifications had been completed, with a few minor exceptions. He went to look for the building manager and found him in the kitchen area, having a cup of coffee.

Alan went up to him and said, "I'm Alan Burgess, the team leader of the group that will be arriving on Sunday. Is everything about ready? I've looked around and things seem neat and tidy."

"Yes. We're all ready for them. We just have to make a few more small modifications, and then the work is finished. I'll be here for your entire stay, so if I can be of service, or you need something done, please let me know."

"Great, can you show me to my room, so I can deposit my luggage?"

"Sure thing," replied the manager, as he proceeded to lead the way up the stairs, to the second story and took him to room #211.

"This is it. I hope it meets with your approval."

Alan nodded and responded, "Thanks, everything looks in order."

After the manager left, Alan placed his bags on the bed and unpacked. The room was not luxurious, but it certainly met his basic needs. After he finished emptying his suitcase and had freshened up, he went for a walk in downtown Rantoul. The small farm town had a population of about thirteen thousand and its economy had suffered severely, when the Air Force base was decommissioned in the early 1990's.

Alan found a coffee shop, located in the downtown strip, and ordered something to eat. He then returned to the base and went to bed.

The next day, he checked out Jackson Hall and the attached hangar area. There, he found one of the two

Bomarcs on a cradle cart and the test equipment. It all looked in excellent condition, and had obviously been installed properly. He then walked over to the special Bomarc building with its high roofline. It was actually built in the late 1950's, specifically for the purpose of allowing a missile to be raised and lowered, in case of inclement weather. It too had been cleaned up, and there was a Bomarc lying on the launch erector boom. Everything looked to be in order. The rest of the day, he spent planning the training to be carried out, over the next four and one-half months.

On Sunday, the seventeenth, the Red Moon team members flew into Chicago O'Hare, at different times as planned, and each of them was met by a driver from Atlas, who drove them to Rantoul. When they arrived at Jackson Hall, they were met by Alan Burgess and he showed them to the room that they would be occupying, for the next few months.

First to arrive was John Norman, who reached Chanute at around two o'clock. Subsequently, the team members, Chris Smith, Gerry Davies, Pasco Martinez and Mike Thornburn, arrived about one hour apart, and all of them were met by the colonel.

After he greeted them, he ushered them to their respective rooms. As he did so, he said, "Please give me your cell phone and it will be returned to you at the end of the mission. We need complete security here, because you never know who might be listening, like the NSA. Let's plan to meet in the kitchen-dining area, on the first floor, at 7:00 pm, for some food. Tonight, we're going to have TV dinners that can be micro-waved. In the future, for the rest of your time here, we'll have catered meals, which will be brought in, from town, by the Atlas security personnel."

At this first meal, Alan informed all of them that there would be a team meeting, the next day at 9:00 am, in conference room #105, on the main floor.

This would be a critical get together for the team, since Colonel Burgess would outline the task ahead and also get them to verify the bank information, which was required for them to get paid. In addition he needed to talk to them about what automobiles they wanted, at the end of the mission, and the Middle Eastern names, they would be known by.

27

Team Meeting

The next morning, Monday, the 18th of April, the team assembled in the main conference room at nine o'clock sharp. The colonel walked into the room and addressed the five team members:

"Good morning, as you all know my name is Alan Burgess and that is the last time you'll hear my real name, until the end of the mission. I'll give you my new Islamic name in a minute. First though, I want all of you to give us your real name and a few words of your background, to the rest of the team. When you're all finished, I'll then give you your new Islamic name, which will stay with you until the end. John, why don't we start with you and go clockwise around the room?""

"My name is John Norman and I was in the Air Force for over thirty years. My assignments included working on the Bomarc B and C, besides other missile programs."

"My name is Gerry Davies and I enlisted in the Marine Corps. I was in for twelve years and served in Iraq and Afghanistan, where I was a technician on satellite communications and Tactical Remote Sensor Systems."

"I'm Chris Smith from Atlanta and served in the Air Force as a computer programmer. I was posted to the Middle East for Operation Desert Storm and the second Iraq War, and I retired after twenty-five years."

"I'm Pasco Martinez from Miami and I served in the Navy for eight years, as a communications expert."

"My name is Mike Thornburn and I was in the Army for twelve years. During that time, I was involved in Operation Desert Storm, as a gunner in an Abrams tank."

"Thank you all for your brief introductions." Alan said. "In order to protect your identities, you have all been assigned a cover name and I'll read them out. First though, from now on, until the operation is concluded, my name is Hisham. Listen very carefully, as I give you your cover names.

John Norman, Anwar; Mike Thornburn, Gamel; Gerry Davies, Mohammed; Pasco Martinez, Qusay; Chris Smith, Ahmed.

Memorize these Arabic names and, from now on, you will address each other and me, by our alias. To assist you in this matter, you'll all be provided with a badge that bears your new identity, and you must wear it at all times, during the training sessions. This tag will also help your team members call you by your Arabic name, so that when you conduct the actual operation, there will be no slip ups. You may be wondering why you need a Middle Eastern title. Let me ask you a question. Do any of you know what a false flag operation is?"

None of the team members answered Hisham's question.

"Then, let me explain. The term "false flag operation" actually has its origins in naval warfare, where a ship would fly a flag other than their true colors, in order to fool their enemy. It is designed to deceive your opponent into thinking that they are being attacked by a specific group, who aren't, whom they seem to be. Our goal, with the names which you have just been given, is to pretend to be an Islamic terrorist group, and not a group of Americans.

Now then, I know you're all wondering what all this is about. Basically, the bottom line is that we're going to save the United States from the decay and rot, of the past few decades. Sometimes one has to destroy something, to save the future. We all consider that this is a great country, which has gone astray. Each of you believe that you've been let down by the Federal Government, over the way you were treated, upon leaving the service. We're going to help you correct this abuse and lack of appreciation.

As I mentioned when I signed you up a few weeks ago, you'll all be paid handsomely for the task ahead. Each of you will receive three thousand dollars a month, until the job is completed. At the end of this meeting, you'll confirm your bank account information, and the April payment will be transmitted electronically, to your bank, within twenty-four hours. In a few months, when the job is completed, you'll be given a lump sum of fifty thousand dollars, in cash, to tide you over for the following three months.

The exact date, for implementing the mission, is still being determined, but should not be more than seven months from now.

Three months after the mission is completed, you'll have access to the ten million dollars that is being held in trust at the Union Bank of Switzerland. You'll receive your specific account number at the bank and instructions on how to collect the money, when the mission is concluded. In addition, you'll given a new car paid for, registered and insured for sixty days. These cars, which will be yours to keep, will be parked at the safe house in North Carolina, when we reach there. You'll be given a list of five cars shortly, from which to choose. Select the make and model on the list, with a check mark. In addition, choose the exterior color you'd like to have. We'll do our best to give you your choice, but we can't guarantee it.

The task ahead is in two parts and the pay I just mentioned is your reward for taking part. For the next few months, we'll work with the Bomarc C missiles, right here in the hangar and also in the missile shelter building, next door. We must make sure we know how to launch a Bomarc manually and to program coordinates into the Global Positioning System and mapping coordinates into the TERCOM.

Now, I'm going to pass out the training schedule for the next few months, which will start tomorrow morning."

Hisham then proceeded to hand out a piece of paper with the following schedule on it.

DATES	SUBJECT MATTER
Apr 19-May 13	Basic Bomarc training, how it works, etc
May 16-Jun 10	Guidance system training
Jun 13 – Jul 8	Guidance system modification/program.
Jul 11- Aug 5	NORAD & SOCC cable override
Aug 8-Aug 31	Bomarc launch procedure
Sep 1 - Sep 2	Recap of training

SOCC= Special Operations Control Center

NORAD = North American Aerospace Defense Command

"When we leave here, there must be no doubt that we are able to complete the mission, once we arrive in North Carolina. Finally, the plan is to launch two Bomarc missiles from a base in North Carolina and destroy a section of the Pentagon. This action will give reform minded politicians the momentum to change things in Washington, and the country will return to its former glorious days. You'll be part of this reawakening of our country.

If there are any of you that feel this operation creates a moral or ethical problem, please speak up now and you can return home, without participating in this mission, and with no hard feelings."

No one spoke up. What Alan Burgess did not know, and would not have told them anyway, was that, if anyone did

157

speak up and stated they wanted out, they would never reach home. The Chicago outfit would arrange an accident on the way there.

"Okay, since none of you have opted out, we're all in on this until the end. You must speak to no one about this operation. Not even to security posted outside this building or to the Atlas Movie Company personnel. The documentary film making is just a cover, while we're here.

There are telephones here in the building, and you may make one call home per week, which will be monitored by security. In addition, there's a mail box at the front door of the building but, please note, all mail going out of this building, will be monitored by security. Remember, you can't tell anyone, you write to or call, your location, nature of the project, etc. In other words you must tell them nothing.

When we've launched the missiles, you'll be free to go home. The date has not been set yet, but will probably be sometime in September. That's all I can tell you at the moment.

In order for you to go home, you'll need a vehicle, as I mentioned a few minutes ago. This new car will be delivered to the safe house in North Carolina for each of you and it'll be yours to keep. Atlas needs to know what specific make and model you would like. I am now handing out a form for you to select your choice of vehicle and color. Please turn it in to me by the end of April.

Team Member Islamic Name:				
Model	**Choice**		**Color**	**Choice**
Ford Mustang			Black	
Ford Fusion			Red	
Toyota Camry			White	
Ford Explorer			Silver	
Honda Odyssey			Dark Blue	

If you want more information concerning this operation, I'll be in my office in room #115 and we can talk privately, if you wish. We'll all meet, in this conference room, tomorrow morning at eight o'clock sharp, to begin the basic Bomarc training.

Does anyone have any immediate questions?   If not, that's all for today."

28

Team Training

For the next four and a half months, the Red Moon team was trained on the theory and operation of the Bomarc. Since Hisham and Anwar had been involved with the missile in the past and were extremely familiar with its operation, they conducted the sessions.

During the first four weeks, the training involved studying the guidance systems, auto pilot, pulse Doppler radar, the propulsion systems and fuze system. The fuze system consisted of a close proximity, side looking radar and a contact trigger with a timer, for the detonation of the explosive charge or nuclear warhead. They explained the total operation of the missile from before launch, until the end of flight, when the explosive charge was detonated. They watched videos, taken by the United States and Canadian Air Forces, of the Bomarc B being launched, back in the 1960's and 1970's. There were no videos available on the Bomarc C, but the missiles were almost identical, except for the guidance systems and the contact fuze capability. The possible threat to shooting down the missile was also discussed in length, and they studied the specifications of the various planes and their weapons. Throughout, Hisham and Anwar stressed the key element was going to be surprise. With no warning of the launch, the defense forces would have minimal opportunity to shoot them down, as the flight time would be in minutes.

At the end of the first four weeks of training, Hisham made arrangements for the group to go to Chicago, to watch a Chicago Blackhawks hockey game. They were in the NHL playoffs for the Stanley Cup. He made it clear that they had to stay together at all times and, although they didn't know it, they were monitored closely by security personnel, the entire time they were off the Chanute base. They went up in a van, driven by a member of the security team and came back in the same way. Atlas had to make sure there were no security leaks.

Before they started the next four weeks of training, Hisham asked them, "Do any of you have any questions concerning how the missile is launched and its subsequent flight profile, all of which was covered in the first four weeks?"

As Hisham looked around the room, the entire team shook their heads and responded, "No."

"Good. Before we start the next section of instruction, I need to collect the vehicle selection paper, which I handed out to you at our first meeting. As I pointed out then, these cars will be waiting for you at the safe house in Wilmington and will be for your use to return home."

Hisham compiled the list of their choices, from the papers they handed him and submitted it to the building manager, who in turn forwarded it to the Atlas Transportation Company.

Name	Vehicle	Color
Hisham	Ford Fushion	Dark Blue
Anwar	Honda Odyssey	White
Gamel	Ford Mustang	Red

Mohammed	Ford Mustang	Silver
Qusay	Honda Odyssey	Dark Blue
Ahmed	Ford Explorer	Black

During the following four weeks, they delved into the block diagrams and schematics covering the Bomarc's different guidance systems. The most critical one for this mission would be the GPS. This capability was not available on the Bomarc B, but was on the Bomarc C. The global positioning system would allow the programming of the target coordinates into the guidance modules and the missile would then hit with an accuracy of three foot, using the military GPS satellite.

Then, they reviewed the TERCOM (Terrain Contour Matching system) that used the radar in the nose of the missile. This would be a back up guidance method for it, in case the GPS failed or the signal was cut off by the U.S. Air Force.

Finally, they covered the Digital Scene Matching Area Correlation system or DSMAC, as it is known in the U.S. military. The DSMAC and the TERCOM were added to the Bomarc C, and were not, however, available on the Bomarc B. The only time they would come into use would be if the GPS failed, for whatever reason.

At the end of this second block of training, the team understood exactly how the missile would home in on the target, hit it and set off the explosive charge.

As a reward for completing the second training session on time, Hisham took the team back to Chicago. They went to watch a Chicago Cubs baseball game, at Wrigley field. As before, he made it clear to the team that they had to stay together at all times. They went up to the windy city in a van, as before, and were driven back the same way. They were all watched closely the entire trip, in order to make sure that there were no security leaks.

From the 13th of June until the 8th of July, they covered the required modifications to the guidance modules that would be needed to achieve success. As needed, they reconfigured the spare modules supplied with the missiles, from the base near Wichita. Using a lap top computer, they also learned how to program the GPS, with the correct supplied coordinates.

Bomarc Guidance System Modules

During the fourth block of training, they learned how NORAD and SOCC control the missiles in the shelters and launch a missile if necessary against an incoming terrorist threat. To perform the Red Moon mission, they had to learn how to bypass the cable coming into the missile shelter, from NORAD and SOCC. This had to be done in a way that the Federal Government military and civilian agencies thought they had control of the missiles in the shelters, at all times. This was extremely important in order to achieve complete surprise, when the Bomarcs were launched and guided to their targets.

After they had completed the fourth block of the training, which lasted another four weeks, Hisham took the team to a local picnic area called the "Lake in the Woods". It was about thirty minutes from the base and they were treated with a barbeque and beer. This area was somewhat isolated, so that the Atlas Movie Company did not have to worry too much about any security breech. A couple of the team went swimming in the lake, although the water was not very warm yet.

A few days later, a visitor came to Jackson Hall to see Hisham. It was Leo DiMaggio, who had disguised himself with a moustache, and identified himself as Peter Graziano, from the Atlas Management Group. He came to talk to Hisham about the training, and the ability of the group to perform the mission. He was met at the door by the head of the Atlas Movie security detail and escorted to Hisham's office. He entered the room and introduced himself to Hisham, as Peter Graziano.

After the door was closed, he asked Hisham. "Is the team ready to conduct the mission, without any problem or difficulty? We have a lot invested in this project and you, and my superiors want an assurance that everything will go as planned."

"The team is well trained and they know what they have to do," Hisham replied. "They don't know what the real target is and will not know, until they hear the news, after the fact. They still believe that the strike is going to be against the Pentagon, and all they care about is to be well paid to do the job."

Peter nodded and said, "That sounds good. For your information only, we expect the mission to take place sometime between the 7th and the 9th of September. You will receive the actual date and time in the near future. It all depends on when Congress will be in session, coming back off the Labor Day break, and what legislation will be scheduled, in both the House and the Senate."

Peter then handed Hisham six thick envelopes, with names printed on them, saying "Here is the money and UBS Swiss bank account information for the five team members, plus yourself. Guard them with your life. My superiors will be extremely upset, if the envelopes get lost. Also, in your envelope, there is an address for the safe house, which is in an isolated area near Wilmington, together with the code to open the front door. The cars that you all ordered will be parked there, and the keys will be on the kitchen counter. My phone number is on the paper, with the safe house address. If you have any problems from now on, until the mission is complete, don't hesitate to call."

With that, they took a quick tour of the facility and then Peter got into his car and drove back to Chicago, satisfied that everything was going to plan. On the way, he placed a telephone call to Harry Thornton on the Grand Cayman Island.

"Harry, this is Leo. I just visited Chanute AFB and the Red Moon team leader, Alan Burgess. He told me that the team training was on schedule and everything was going forward as planned. I also looked around and couldn't observe any problems."

"That's good, Leo. Keep me informed if anything changes. Talk to you soon."

Finally, the Red Moon Team reached the last three weeks of the training, which involved the procedure to actually launch a Bomarc missile manually. Since the cable from NORAD and SOCC would be bypassed, the Red Moon team would launch both missiles by hand from the control room at the Camp. Cameras had been installed when the shelters were built, so that the missile firings could be monitored safely, from the blockhouse.

The final two days of training were spent reviewing what had to be done at Camp Warrior and how they would break into the Camp. Hisham told them they would be leaving Chanute on September the 6th for good, and they would be driving to Wilmington, North Carolina. There they would be at a safe house, a few miles outside the city.

He believed they were ready to modify the guidance systems, program them and launch the missiles, without a hitch.

A team meeting was called on the 5th of September for three o'clock in the afternoon, in the main conference room.

"I commend you all for your diligent work in achieving the training results necessary to accomplish our mission." Hisham said. "We'll be leaving here tomorrow morning at 5:00 am and will drive to a safe house near Wilmington. In order to make it in one day, we'll be driving nonstop, except for food and other necessities. This will require one, or two of you, to help me with the driving. So pack your bags and get to bed early, as we'll have to get up at around 4:30 am, so we can leave here by 5:00 am. Again, I thank you all for accomplishing the required training, on time. I'll see you tomorrow morning early."

They all turned in by around 8:30 pm, so they could get a good night's rest. It would be a long trip the next day.

29

Election Year Maneuvering

While President Tuckwell and Valda Lewis were planning the missile attack on the Capitol, the two major political parties were going through the motions of selecting a candidate for president. The national organizations of both parties were totally unaware of what the White House was planning.

Candidates from each party entered the various state caucuses and primaries, held in the first six months of the year. No candidate in either party garnered enough delegates, to become a clear winner. Each went into the conventions with more than one voting round required to select a candidate. They were both being held in August; with the Democratic convention being located in Boston and the Republican one in Seattle.

On day two of the Democratic convention, President Tuckwell came to the hall to make a speech. He walked up to the microphone and gave one of his best speeches yet. The crowd gave him a standing ovation, and afterward he walked through the hall, shaking hands with many of them. The delegates believed the president would be gone from office in six months and that he would be an elder statesman, like previous presidents. He gave no hint of his plans for the following month.

On day three, the Democratic convention delegates had a choice of three candidates to pick as their presidential nominee. They were: Vice President James Valpy, Senator Greg Craven from Minnesota and Delaware Governor Hedley Dodd.

James Valpy was the leading candidate, simply because he was the vice president. However, President Tuckwell had not endorsed him. In fact, the president didn't endorse any candidate. Why should he? He was planning to stay in office.

In the end, after two rounds of voting, the Democratic convention selected the current Vice President James Valpy and Governor Hedley Dodd, as their candidates for president and vice president respectively. Senator Greg Craven dropped out, after the first round of voting by the delegates, and threw his support to the vice president.

When the Republicans held their convention, a few days later in Seattle, both Governor Cartwright of Tennessee and Governor Chuck Prince of Texas were scheduled to speak. Neither had decided to run for the Republican candidacy. Governor Cartwright gave a rousing speech, about the need for people to take personal responsibility in their lives, instead of looking to the Federal Government for handouts.

Governor Prince's speech highlighted how the State of Texas had greatly improved the financial lot of Texans, in the past six years. He had reduced unemployment to three percent, below the national average of almost five percent, and workers were making more money than ever. Both speakers received standing ovations.

Balloting for the candidates proceeded on the third day of the convention. There were five candidates running for the office of President. They were: Ohio Governor Vincent Brown, Utah Governor Clarence Smith, Senator Brian Phillips from North Carolina, Senator John Wills from Oregon and Congresswoman Jane Taylor from Kansas.

The primaries did not provide any one of them with a clear majority and so there wasn't a leading candidate going into the convention.

There was a lot of horse trading, in smoke filled rooms, by all the candidates, trying to garner the necessary votes. After three rounds of voting, Senator Wills dropped out of contention. Then, after the next round, Governor Smith dropped out, and finally Governor Brown, leaving only Senator Phillips and Congresswoman Taylor, in the running. After a total of seven rounds of voting, going late into the night, the Republicans finally selected Senator Brian Phillips and Congresswoman Jane Taylor, as their candidates for president and vice president, respectively.   Martha Cartwright, the governor of Tennessee, tried to facilitate the differences between all the candidates, so that they went out of the convention united.

The presidential candidates in both parties thought they had an excellent chance of winning, since President Tuckwell could not run again, for a third term.   They didn't understand that no matter what they thought, it wouldn't make any difference?

There was a third candidate for president: Edward Tuckwell!

Both the Republican and Democratic presidential candidates planned to campaign heavily, immediately after Labor Day, since the early national polls showed the election could be close to a dead heat.

They both started campaigning on Labor Day, by going to picnics, pressing the flesh and kissing babies. Heavy television, radio and social media advertising started immediately, after the conventions.

169

30

Wilmington Safe House

On Tuesday morning, the 6th of September, at 5:00 am, the Red Moon team climbed into a large SUV, with Hisham at the wheel. The vehicle had been provided by Atlas Transportation and, unbeknownst to any of them, it had a tracking chip installed. This way Atlas would know at any particular time, where the vehicle was located.

They had a long eight hundred and ninety mile, fourteen plus hour drive to the safe house, located just north of Wilmington, North Carolina. With stops for breakfast, lunch and dinner they probably would not arrive, until around 11:00 pm. Since Rantoul was on Central Daylight Time and Wilmington was on Eastern Daylight Time, the trip would actually "lose" them one hour.

The route chosen would take them via Dayton, Ohio, Charleston, West Virginia and Rayleigh, North Carolina. They stopped for a quick breakfast at a local diner, two hours after leaving Rantoul. Hisham, Anwar and Qusay took turns driving, so no one got tired, and they used the cruise control as much as possible, in order to avoid being stopped by police, for speeding. Most of them slept a good part of the trip or played cards in the rear.

Around 1:00 pm they stopped for lunch and at 6:00 pm for dinner. They picked restaurants where they would not attract a lot of attention. None of them really talked much during the trip. They were all thinking about the mission ahead, and their personal responsibilities for launching a missile attack on the Pentagon.

They finally arrived at the safe house close to Wilmington around 11:00 pm. The first thing the team members noticed was that there were six shiny new vehicles, either parked in the garage or in the driveway. Exactly as they had ordered, all received the submitted choice. What they didn't know was that a tracking chip had been installed in each vehicle, so Atlas Transportation in Chicago would know where the vehicle was at any time.

They got out of the SUV, stretched their legs and entered the safe house. On the kitchen counter were the keys for the new vehicles, parked outside. They all grabbed a cold beer from the refrigerator, drank it quickly and then each found a bed, or sofa, and dropped off to sleep.

Next day, Thursday, the 8th of September, they all got up late and made breakfast, with the groceries stocked in the kitchen. Atlas had filled the refrigerator and pantry, with plenty of food to last their short visit. Hisham called a meeting for 2:00 pm that afternoon in the family room of the house, to go over the schedule for the next day, September the 9th.

When the meeting started, Hisham addressed the team members and said, "Tomorrow, our mission will commence. We've spent the last few months training for this day. We must not and cannot fail. America depends on us to create an atmosphere, where real change can take place and the country can stand tall again. As I have said previously, our politicians need our help in making it easier for them to make the changes needed to fix our fiscal chaos. What we accomplish tomorrow will shake America to its core, and help it return to its true roots of individualism. People will have the responsibility to handle their own affairs and not depend on the government.

The alarm clock will go off at 3:00 am and we'll leave here at 3:30 am. So, go to bed early and get plenty of sleep. I'll wake you all up at the appointed time. Do you have any questions?"

"Yes. I have a question," said Gamel. "How do we obtain the ten million dollars from the Swiss bank, we've been promised?"

Hisham replied, "You'll need to fly to Zurich, Switzerland and, on or after the 9th of December, go to the main UBS AG office at Bahnhofstrasse 45. Make sure you take your account number with you. You can then get access to your money."

Gamel responded, "So I have to go to Switzerland to obtain the funds, I can't get it here?"

Hisham said, "That's correct. You have to go to Zurich, that's how it's been set up. It's a nice city and, with all that money, you should be able to have a great vacation. Are there any other questions? If not, I'll see you all tomorrow at 3:00 am."

31

Operation Red Moon

Precisely at 3:00 am, Hisham's alarm clock rang. He rose quickly and went to wake the other five team members.

Knocking on their doors, he shouted, "Rise and shine, it's time to get up. Don't forget to put on your black clothes with the Arabic labels inside. We can't leave anything to chance."

A quarter of an hour later, they assembled in the kitchen for a quick bite to eat, and Hisham spoke to them one last time. "This is the day we've been training for, these past few months. In addition, it will be huge payday for all of us, after we return here in a few hours. Don't forget to bring all the equipment, including the modified guidance systems and the rocket-propelled grenades."

It was the morning of Friday, the 9th of September, and they walked out of the safe house toward the large SUV, at exactly 3:30 am. The entire mission had been timed to the exact minute, to insure there was no hitch. Since the vehicle had Illinois plates on it, when they drove Chanute, they had installed North Carolina plates, which had been provided by Atlas. This way, if they were seen by the

State Police, they would not attract attention. Along with the plates, they had been given a registration slip, in case they were stopped.

As they pulled away from the house, Hisham, who was behind the wheel, said," Put on your ski masks and don't forget to call each other by your Arabic name and in your Middle Eastern pseudo accent."

As they drove on route 77 toward Jacksonville and Camp Warrior, Hisham thought about all the practice drills that they had conducted at the Chanute Bomarc site, using the old training program of the 1970's. No one in Rantoul had paid any attention to the activities on the base, because of the documentary story given and publicized in the local paper.

On the way to the Camp, Hisham said, "Okay men; remember our practice drills and what your responsibilities are, when we get to our destination. We must have no slip ups. After the first missile is sent on its way, a second one will be launched, two minutes later, to another part of the target. If for some reason, either one of the shots is not successful; we must be prepared to quickly fire a third one."

The overall plan called for a look out near the Capitol, with an unregistered cell phone, to be talking with Hisham and letting him know whether the hits were on target. With the speed of the missiles, they could easily get two launches off, before security could determine where the shots were coming from. Plus, it would take at least fifteen to twenty minutes for Camp Lejeune security to realize something was wrong and send a patrol out, to see what was going on at Camp Warrior. The blast of two missiles would be seen from the any of the Marine bases in the area. Besides Camp Lejeune, there was Camp Geiger and the Marine Corps Air Station. This Air Station was the base for helicopters and V-22 Bell Boeing Osprey tiltrotor aircraft. The missiles would also "light up" the radar scopes, up and down the East Coast.

At around 4:15 am, still under the cover of darkness, Hisham parked the SUV in the tall trees surrounding Camp Warrior, and the men camouflaged it, for good measure. The six team members approached stealthily on foot the Bomarc missile site, Camp Warrior. They were all wearing the black clothes Hisham had provided them and they had put on ski masks on cover their faces and identity. They were well versed in using their Arabic names and each carried a copy of the Koran in their backpacks. In addition, some also carried Arabic books and missile plans. In fact, they were Americans planning to launch the greatest disaster to befall America, since the Maine, Pearl Harbor and 9/11.

The seven building, missile site was guarded by one armed Marine from a nearby base and a high security fence with infrared sensors. Since it was close to Camp Lejeune and had never been publicized, officials believed that it was secure. It was a moonless night and the base was guarded twenty-four hours a day. The Marine on duty was not scheduled to be relieved until noon, and no one was expected to come by the missile site, until then.

Before infiltrating the missile base, Hisham whispered to the team, as they crowded round him, "We must leave enough evidence so that any investigators will believe that we really are Islamist terrorists," Anwar, you drop a Koran on the ground in a knapsack, and Qusay, you drop the attack plans, written in Arabic. Just make sure you make it look like an accidental drop of the material. Don't forget, it's important to talk with an accent and call each other by our assumed names. This way, the guard, when debriefed, will be certain to inform investigators that terrorists invaded the camp and launched the Bomarcs."

The team followed Hisham to the east side of the camp behind building #7, where the infrared security system had a small blind spot. He knew this problem with the base defenses, since he was involved in its design and set. It was a mistake that had never been corrected. The main blockhouse housed the control room and the camp facilities, in addition to the guardroom.

Hisham whispered, "Okay men, be as quiet as you can until we gain access to the camp and overpower the guard." He went over to Anwar and said, "Okay, cut a hole in the fence right there" as he pointed out the area of the security fence that was not covered by the infrared monitoring system.

Anwar crawled over to the fence and took a pair of heavy clippers out of his knapsack. Quietly, he started to cut away at the fence material, pausing now and again, to listen in case the alarm went off. He heard nothing, so he realized Hisham knew what he was talking about, when he mentioned the security system had a defect. Sweating profusely, Anwar kept cutting away, until the hole was large enough for one man, at a time, to crawl through.

He crept back to Hisham and whispered, "Okay, it's done."

Hisham quietly moved toward the hole, followed by the other five men in single file. Four of the men made it through the fence, and the fifth one passed the guidance modules and equipment, to the men already in the Camp. After each of the men and the equipment were inside the fence, they went and stood by the blockhouse wall.

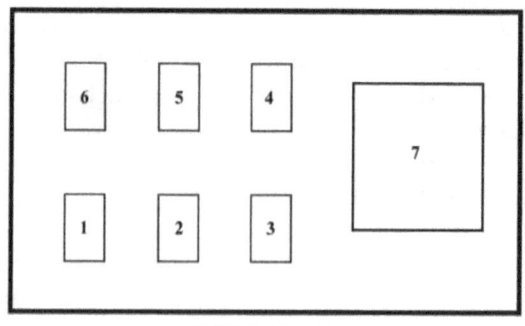

CAMP WARRIOR

One of the sharp shooters, Gamel, went to the door of the building and, after oiling the hinges, slowly opened it. The guardroom door was ajar, but no noise came from it. Gamel silently crossed the floor to the entrance and peered inside. The Marine had fallen asleep, in the chair. Gamel crept into the room and placed the barrel of his rifle against the chest of the sentry. The man awoke with a start. Gamel placed a finger to his mouth, to signal to the guard that he had better not make a sound.

He softly said, with a foreign accent, to Hisham who was standing outside the room, "Okay Hisham. Everything is under control in here."

Hisham and the other four men came into the guardroom. Two of them tied up and blindfolded the sentry.

Hisham spoke to the Marine, in a fake foreign accent.

"What's your name and rank?" he asked.

"Corporal Josh Jones, sir," the Marine said, with a wavering voice.

"Okay. Listen Corporal Jones," said Hisham. "We'll not harm you, as long as you do exactly as we say. If you try to escape, shout out or doing anything, other than what we tell you, you will die. Do you have a wife and any children?"

"Yes, I do," the corporal said, shaking with fear.

"How often do you have to report in and when is the next time?" Hisham asked.

"I have to call in every two hours and my last report was at 0400," said the sentry.

"Okay good," said Hisham. "You'll report in at 0600 and 0800, on time. This man, guarding you, will hand you the telephone receiver, and you'll report in as usual. Any mistake and you will die. You will leave your widow, and any children, to fend for themselves. Allah will not be good to them. Do you understand?"

"Yes," the corporal replied.

32

Missile Programming

Hisham then sent the sharpshooter, Mohammed, with his sniper rifle and a couple of rocket-propelled grenades, outside to watch for any approaching Marines. He and the other three men, Anwar, Qusay and Ahmed, entered the Control Room, located in the blockhouse.

After he found the keys to the missile shelter side doors, hanging on a board in the control room, Hisham said to the three Islamic terrorists, "Let's go to the shelters #1 and #2 and make the necessary modifications, so we can launch the missiles"

As they exited building #7, Hisham spoke, in a foreign accent, to Gamel, who was guarding the tied up sentry, "Make sure he doesn't move, or get loose. If he causes you any problem, take care of him."

As planned in the mission schedule, the four men arrived outside shelter #1 at 5:00 am, and Hisham opened the door with the key that he had found in the blockhouse. They entered the building with the guidance modules and other necessary equipment.

Using his flashlight, Hisham found the light switch close to the door, turned the shelter lights on and said, "Okay, let's get to work."

First, they attached a special circuit and wiring to bypass the incoming NORAD/SOCC cable. Once they had completed this, they disconnected the connection to NORAD and SOCC, so that the missile could only be launched manually from the control room. Next, they removed some of the missile shroud panels from around the guidance system bay, so the existing modules could be replaced with the modified ones they had brought with them. This was Anwar's task, since he was the expert on the Bomarc guidance systems. These modules were the ones that been modified at Chanute, to permit the missile to use the GPS for guidance to the target.

Hisham checked Anwar's work and said, "Be as quiet as you can. We don't want to wake up the Marines at Camp Lejeune."

After he replaced the guidance modules with the modified ones, he and Hisham went and set the contact timer to detonate the explosive charge one second after the missile slammed into target A. They wanted to make sure the missile actually penetrated the target before exploding, which actually should not be much of a problem, since it would be travelling at close to Mach 4.0

Ahmed, the computer expert, attached his laptop to the umbilical cord within the guidance system bay. He then asked Hisham, "Is it okay now to download the longitude and latitude coordinates of the Pentagon East Section, into the GPS? Also, I need to enter the mapping information into the TERCOM."

"Yes, go ahead" said Hisham. "Here are the target coordinates. Don't forget to also set the missile cruise altitude for twenty thousand feet, as planned."

Hisham handed him a piece of paper with the following coordinates printed on it.

Target A

	Degrees	Minutes	Seconds
Latitude	38	53	26 4042
Longitude	-77	0	32 6118

In actuality, Hisham handed him the coordinates for the Senate Chamber of the Capitol, but Ahmed didn't know it.

In the meantime, Qusay, the communications expert, was checking out the satellite tracking system on the missile, to make sure it was operational and working correctly. In flight, the missile would send a position signal which could then be picked up in the control room. This would allow Hisham to send the necessary flight correction data to the missile, in case it was required.

At 6:00 am, while all this was going on in shelter #1, in the guard room of building #7, Gamel, who was watching the tied up sentry, held the phone receiver up to Corporal Jones' ear and told him to report to Camp Lejeune.

The corporal spoke into the phone that had been answered by the Marine duty officer. "Sir, this is Camp Warrior and everything is quiet and okay. Nothing unusual to report." said Jones.

"Very good, corporal", said the officer. "Report back in at 0800."

"Yes, sir," said Jones. Gamel hung up the phone and said, "Well done corporal."

By 7:00 am, the men in shelter #1 had finished their tasks and the missile was ready to be launched. They then moved on to shelter #2.

As they had done in shelter #1, they disconnected the connection to NORAD and SOCC, so that they could fire the missile locally. In doing this, they attached a special circuit to the NORAD/SOCC cable so that it looked like the missile had never been disconnected to SOCC. However, if SOCC tried to fire the missile to shoot down a terrorist aircraft, they would not be able to do so.

They repeated the task of removing some of the missile shroud panels from the left side, so they could replace a couple of the guidance modules. Again, this was Anwar's responsibility, since he had the expertise to do this task.

Hisham checked Anwar's work and nodded his approval, saying, "Great job, Anwar. I don't know what we would do without you."

When the guidance modules had been replaced, Anwar and Hisham then went and set the explosive charge to detonate one second after the missile hit target B. Just as they did with the first missile, they wanted to make sure the missile actually penetrated the roof before exploding.

While all this was going on in shelter #2, Gamel was in the building #7 guard room, with the tied up corporal. He picked up the phone receiver and held it to the sentry's ear, at precisely 0800, and told him to report to the Camp Lejeune duty officer.

The corporal spoke into the phone that was answered by the duty officer. "This is Camp Warrior and everything is quiet and okay. Nothing to report, sir," said Jones.

"Very good", said the Marine officer. "Report back in at 1000."

"Yes, sir," replied Jones. Gamel hung up the phone and said, "You did well, corporal."

In shelter #2, Ahmed, the computer expert, attached his laptop to an umbilical cord within the guidance system bay.

He then asked Hisham, "Can I now download the longitude and latitude coordinates for the Pentagon West section, into the GPS? In addition, as previously I need to enter the mapping information into the TERCOM. Is that okay?"

"Yes, go ahead," said Hisham. "Here are the other Pentagon coordinates and, as before, don't forget to program the missile to fly at an altitude of twenty thousand feet."

Hisham handed him a piece of paper with the following coordinates printed on it.

Target B

	Degrees	Minutes	Seconds
Latitude	38	53	20 5116
Longitude	-77	0	32 7666

In actuality, Hisham handed him the coordinates for the House of Representatives Chamber of the Capitol, but Ahmed didn't know it. All along, Hisham hated to deceive the team members about the real targets, but he thought it was a necessary precaution, just in case one of them got cold feet.

After the second missile was programmed, they turned out the lights and closed the doors on both shelters.

As they did so, Hisham said, "I'm going back to the control room now. You two go to shelter #3 and prepare the missile for launch. Here is the key you will need to get in. We must be prepared, just in case one of the first two doesn't hit the intended target. Program missile #3 with the same coordinates as for Target B and then join me in the blockhouse."

The two men did as ordered, and then later they joined Hisham in the control room.

33

The Launch

Precisely, at 9:18 am, on Friday, the 9th of September, Hisham pushed the "open roof" buttons for shelters #1 and #2, on the launch display console in the blockhouse control room. The roof sections slowly slid open, driven by the powerful motors contained within the shelters. Actually, there were two fifteen foot roof sections, for each missile shelter. The total thirty foot gap was wide enough, for the missiles to be raised and launched.

"The roofs are moving and should be completely open, in less than thirty seconds," Hisham reported quietly to the other occupants of the control room, as he watched, on the closed circuit television system, the roof sections slowly moving apart.

After the sections were fully open, the roof lights for shelters #1 and #2 turned green. "The shelter roofs are now open and we're ready to erect the first missile," Hisham said loudly in his foreign accent, so the tied up Marine in the guard room could hear it. "Allah is good."

At 9:19 am, he pushed the erector button for missile #1 and then similarly, the button for #2. The missiles were slowly raised into a vertical launch position, by their respective booms. In thirty seconds, both missiles were fully erected, clamped to their exhaust deflectors and ready for launch. Once the missile was vertical, the erector arm lowered itself, so as not to impede the actual launch.

"Are we ready for the launch?" Hisham asked the other three men, in the blockhouse. They all nodded and said, "Yes."

The sharpshooter, with the rocket-propelled grenades, was outside the building, watching for anyone approaching the camp. From his location, he could see the shelters with their open roofs and the missiles sitting vertical, ready for go.

All five of them thought to themselves, *"This is zero hour. Now we're going to earn our ten million dollars."*

Hisham glanced at his watch briefly, and then said to the men in the control room, with his fake Arab accent, "Get ready. It's the moment all of us have been preparing for. We're going to launch #1 now and, then in two minutes, we'll launch #2." The time was exactly 9:20 am.

He pushed the red launch button for #1 on the control room launch display console, which started the ignition process for the solid booster rocket in the missile. It wasn't long before flames and smoke spewed out of shelter. After the missile booster had built up enough thrust, the deflector clamps released and the missile rose slowly and majestically into the North Carolina, bright, morning sky. Hisham was able to watch the ignition of the rocket and the initial launch, on the closed circuit television.

It was a typical clear sky for that part of the country, without a cloud in sight. The unmanned weapon gathered speed and, as it climbed, appeared out of the smoke, billowing from the shelter. The ground at Camp Warrior shook from the vibration, caused by the solid booster. It was actually an extremely impressive sight, seeing the missile rise into the September sky.

184

The Bomarc accelerated rapidly, at an ever increasing speed, until it reached the programmed twenty thousand foot altitude and then leveled out. As soon as the ramjets had enough air rushing through them, they ignited and provided the propulsion for the remainder of the flight. It wasn't long before the missile was flying straight and true at Mach 4.0 and headed for target A, in Washington, D.C. The missile looked like a plane without a cockpit or a pilot, and, at about three thousand miles per hour, it would only take about ten minutes to reach the target.

Hisham turned and said to the men in the control room, "Okay, get ready. We'll launch the second missile shortly."

Precisely at 9:22 am, Hisham pushed the red launch button on the launch display console, for #2. Just like the previous missile, in a couple of seconds, flames and smoke spewed out of the shelter. After the missile booster had built up enough thrust pressure, the deflector clamps released and the missile slowly rose into the morning sky. It was soon headed for target B, in the Washington, D.C. area, which was only a distance of about three hundred miles.

Hisham looked at the display monitor, mounted in the launch test equipment rack for a few minutes and determined that both missiles were on the correct track for their targets; the House of Representatives and the Senate located in the Capitol. He could confirm this information, since the missiles were sending back real time data, via satellite, their current latitude and longitude coordinates. Hisham determined, based on the console display, that no midcourse correction was required.

In ten minutes, an Atlas Communications observer, who was near the Capitol building, called Hisham to confirm that Red Moon was a complete success. As planned, both targets had been hit with the high explosive Bomarcs, two minutes apart. The launch of another missile was not required.

34

Detection

The first Bomarc was launched at 9:20 am, and soon attained a height of five thousand feet, with the use of the solid fuel engine.   It wasn't long before military and commercial airport radars started to detect the unidentified, flying object.   The missile continued climbing up to the twenty thousand foot programmed altitude, where it leveled out and continued on its flight path to Washington, D.C., using the ramjets for propulsion.

The initial Terminal Radar Approach Control and Air Traffic Control Tower location, to pick it up, was at Wilmington International Airport.   Later, it was also tracked by the radar at Raleigh-Durham International Airport. The data, from these two sites, was automatically and continuously fed into the Special Operations Control Center (SOCC) located in Rome, New York.

Since the Wilmington airport was closest to Camp Warrior, an air traffic controller, located in the control facility below the cab, was the first to see the blip on his twenty inch monitor. He noted that the target wasn't moving horizontally, but only vertically. This was very strange, since only a few planes could climb vertically; mainly military jet fighters and the V-22 Osprey tiltrotor aircraft. Also, the object seemed to be coming from a location, close to Camp Lejeune, in North Carolina.

"What the F--- is that?" the Wilmington controller exclaimed. He called his supervisor over, so he could also look at the radar scope.

"How long has it been on your screen?" he asked the radar operator.

"It only appeared a few seconds ago. It now seems to be leveling out at twenty thousand feet and heading toward the Washington, D.C. area."

"I'd better call SOCC in Rome." He picked up the phone, which had a direct line to them.

"Do you see the contact we have detected and appears to be headed north?" he asked Colonel Jackson, the Air Defense Liaison Officer (ADLO).

"Yes. We've just had confirmation, from a couple of other radar sites. In addition, the Washington Air Route Traffic Control Center has also called in a similar report. The object looks like it's travelling at a high rate of speed and is heading straight toward the Washington, D.C. area."

Just about then, the Wilmington air traffic controller spotted another object on his radar, acting just like the first one. The time was just past 9:22 am.

A few seconds later, the copilot of a United Airlines flight that had just taken off from Norfolk and was flying west to Chicago, said to the captain. "Geese, did you see that? It looked like a plane with no cockpit. We should call it in. It passed very close in front of us. I've never seen anything like that object before. Maybe it was a UFO."

The captain replied, "Yes. I saw it also, for a second or two. It was very close and dangerous. I'll call it in immediately."

With that, he picked up his mike and called air traffic control. "This is United 751 heavy climbing out of Norfolk heading west toward Chicago, and I wish to report that a fast plane, a missile or a UFO, flew across our nose, a few seconds ago. We'd been cleared to climb to thirty thousand feet, and weren't warned, in advance, of any flight that would cross our path. What the heck is going on?" the pilot asked.

The controller replied, "Thanks for the report. We understand your concern. We'll have to get back to you on that. We've something unusual going on, but we don't know what. We're trying to get clarification from the Special Operations Control Center."

"What the blazes is going on?" exclaimed the SOCC liaison officer.

He had received no advance notice of any U.S. Air Force operations for that day, which would involve high speed aircraft. He decided that he had better call his superior and inform him, as to what was going on. It had been almost five minutes, since the first launch, and three minutes since the second launch. By this time, all the radars up and down the East Coast were starting to "light up", since they had detected these objects and were feeding their data directly into SOCC. Reports were coming in from everywhere.

The liaison officer called his superior, General McLean, saying, "Sir, this is Colonel Jackson. We've detected two objects flying, two minutes apart, at close to Mach 4.0, toward Washington, D.C. This situation looks extremely serious, and it appears they came from an area, close to the Camp Lejeune Marine base. I recommend we launch four F-22 Raptors, armed with Sparrow missiles, from Langley AFB, in order to investigate, intercept and shoot them down, if necessary.

In a corner of the Special Operations Control Center, there sat a crusty old military man, who was an advisor to the colonel. He should have been retired a long time ago, but his knowledge was irreplaceable. Having heard all the commotion, he rose and went to stand by the Colonel Jackson.

Speaking softly, he said, "You know there is a Bomarc missile site, with six shelters, located at Camp Warrior, a few miles from Camp Lejeune. The latest Bomarc can fly at Mach 4.0. You'll have a major problem trying to intercept them, if that's what you're up against."

The general, at the other end of the phone, heard these remarks that were addressed to the ADLO.

The general said to the colonel, "Your recommendation sounds appropriate to me. Regardless of what your advisor just said, we must try and intercept them, before they destroy anything. Scramble the four F-22 Raptors from the 1st Fighter Wing 27th Fighter Squadron. Give them orders to shoot down the two unidentified objects."

By this time, 9:28 am, almost eight minutes had passed since the launch of the first missile.

The liaison officer made the call to the operations officer at Langley AFB, a joint air force/army base with Fort Eustis.

"This is Colonel Jackson calling from SOCC. You are hereby authorized to immediately scramble four Raptor F-22 fighters, armed with Sparrows. They are to intercept, identify and destroy, if necessary, the two targets that are flying at around twenty thousand feet, toward Washington, D.C. Their speed is estimated to be about Mach 4.0. We believe they are Bomarc missiles from a base near Camp Lejeune, North Carolina. We will feed the latest coordinates of the objects to you, once the F-22s have taken off."

"Orders understood. We're scrambling the jets as we speak, and they should be airborne in one minute," replied the Langley operations officer.

Four pilots raced from the ready room at Langley to their F-22 Raptors, started up the engines and taxied for takeoff.

The lead pilot, nicknamed Typhoon, contacted the control tower. "This is Colonel Seagraff in the lead Raptor, requesting permission for immediate take off."

The control tower operator replied, "Permission granted for you to take off on runway two six. Wind is out of the southeast, at five miles per hour."

At this time, a radar operator at Langley noticed that the first object was descending from the twenty thousand foot level and it finally vanished from the scope. The time was 9:30 am. He called his supervisor over to observe the descent and he, in turn, called the information into Rome. That was all he could do.

Two minutes later, the second object was observed on the radar screen descending and ultimately it vanished also. The time was 9:32 am.

The four Raptors took off and climbed to thirty thousand feet and headed toward Washington, D.C. The lead aircraft radar picked up the second Bomarc, as it started its descent to hit the Capitol. The pilot, Typhoon, had his hand on the fire button for the Sparrow, under his right wing. He reported to base that it looked like a fighter plane, without a cockpit. He was ready to release the missile, but then thought about what would happen, if the Sparrow missed the object and hit some building on the ground. At this point the second Bomarc was only about one thousand feet above the Senate wing.

The U.S. Air Force planes never had a chance to intercept and destroy either of the missiles.

At the same time, while all this confusion in the air was going on, a Secret Service agent on the roof of the White House heard all the communications traffic. He raised his shoulder launch Stinger missile ready for launch, but he never received the "lock on" signal, coming from the launcher. The agent didn't get an opportunity to launch the Stinger and down either of the Bomarcs.

At 9:30 am and 9:32 am, the missiles hit their planned targets, the House of Representatives and the Senate Chambers, in the U.S. Capitol building.

35

Mission Accomplished

On the 9th of September, at 9:00 am, the House of Representatives was called to order, for the purpose of debating the Federal Government budget for the next fiscal year, due to start the 1st of October. At the same time, the vice president instructed the clerk to call the roll, so that the Senate vote on the latest immigration bill could proceed. Since it was expected it might be close, Vice President James Valpy was present, in case he had to cast the deciding vote.

The first missile crashed through the United States Senate Chamber ceiling of the Capitol building, precisely on time at 9:30 am, as the senators were getting ready to vote on the bill. The Mach 4.0 Bomarc missile easily crashed through the roof and, one second later, exploded its five hundred pound warhead. Immediately, approximately half of the senators in the chamber lay dead and a considerable number of the others were wounded. Vice President Valpy was among those who were wounded in the attack. He didn't seem to be conscious, although he was still breathing.

Brian Phillips, Senator from North Carolina and Republican presidential candidate, was killed outright, when the missile exploded. There was absolute chaos.

"Oh God, what happened?" asked a security guard as he rushed into the chamber. "Who would do this?"

The scene was total pandemonium, and the smell of the exploded warhead hung in the air. There were fires burning everywhere and smoke filled the air of the once dignified Senate Chamber. Another member of the United States Capitol Police dialed 911 to request assistance, but before he was connected, a secondary blast, caused by the missile's remaining ramjet fuel, killed him.

Just two minutes after the first blast, at 9:32 am, the second Bomarc missile slammed into the roof of the United States House of Representatives wing, also at a high rate of speed. Again, one second later, the five hundred pound explosive charge went off, killing more than half of the congressmen and seriously wounded scores of others.

One of the casualties was Congresswoman Jane Taylor from Kansas. Just a month earlier, she had been selected as the Republican vice presidential candidate, at the Seattle convention. The explosion caused extensive damage to the chamber, and the air was filled with smoke and the pungent smell, emanating from the missile warhead explosion. Fires were burning throughout the chamber. Security rushed in to help save as many of the congressmen, as they could. After the second explosion, everyone realized that it was no accident.

By a stroke of luck, Speaker Clive Knight had called into his office that morning, stating he had a family emergency and would not be in, until later in the day. He called a fellow Republican congressman and asked him to act as speaker, with the result Knight was neither killed nor wounded, in the attack.

Another security guard rushed to a telephone and again tried to call for help. This time he was successful in connecting to 911.

"What's your emergency?" asked the 911 operator.

"The Capitol has been hit by two explosions, and we need ambulances, police and fire engines here immediately.

"What Capitol are you talking about?" asked the operator.

"The U.S. Capitol, you idiot, get help here immediately." shouted the security guard.

"Okay. I'm calling for assistance right now." With that, she placed calls to the Washington, D.C. police, ambulances and fire departments and warned the area hospitals to expect many casualties.

Fairly soon, the Washington, D.C. police, ambulances and fire engines were arriving to help out. A call was made to the White House, by the Capitol security chief, to inform them of the attack. Andrew Taylor, the White House Chief of Staff, knocked on the door and then burst into the Oval Office, to give the president the terrible news. He was followed by Secret Service personnel. Of course, the attack and blasts were of no surprise to President Tuckwell or Valda Lewis.

The Secret Service told the president he was to be moved to safety immediately, in case another missile hit the White House. They hustled him, and his family, into a tunnel leading from the White House to a secret location, from where they could be transported to safety.

36

Team Departs

In his phony Middle East accent, Hisham shouted to the Red Moon team, "I've received word that both missiles hit their targets. Let's get the heck out of here. We've got to make it to Charlotte as soon as possible, so we can catch our flights out of the country. Don't leave anything behind."

The tied up sentry heard this and remembered it, for his future debriefing at Camp Lejeune. Actually, Hisham said this, so any search party would go in the wrong direction. They were actually going back to their safe house, just north of Wilmington.

As soon as he finished speaking, the Red Moon team hurriedly exited Camp Warrior, using the same hole through which they had entered the compound. They ran to the parked SUV and removed the camouflage netting. Time was of the essence. It wouldn't be long before the Marines, at Camp Lejeune, would send a party to investigate what had happened at Camp Warrior.

"Everyone on board?" asked Hisham, as he started the vehicle.

"Yes, we're all here," replied Anwar who had been designated by Hisham, as the responsible team member to keep track of the men.

Hisham then put the vehicle into drive and drove back to the safe house, at the legal speed limit. He couldn't afford to be stopped by the police for speeding. All of them now dropped their Arabic names and returned to their real names.

At 10:15 am, right on schedule, they reached the safe house, where they immediately went inside and started to change their clothes. As planned ahead of time, they all placed their mission clothes, with the Arabic tag, in garbage bags to be deposited in a convenient dumpster on their way home.

After they had changed their clothes, they assembled in the family room of the house, for a final group meeting.

The colonel walked into the room and said, "Okay, listen up. I'm going to give you an envelope, containing the fifty thousand dollars, which was promised to you at the beginning of the mission, and the Swiss bank account number, for the ten million dollars. Don't forget you can't obtain the money at the Zurich main office, until the 9th of December. For security reasons, when you leave here, you must not travel together or contact each other. Furthermore, it's extremely important to remember not to tell anyone, including your girlfriend or wife, anything about this operation, since it could put them in danger. Finally, do not speed going home. The FBI, state police and other authorities will be on the lookout for anyone looking suspicious or dangerous. Under no circumstance are any of you to go to an airport, train station or bus terminal during the next three months, in case you are stopped and say something inappropriate."

Each one of the team walked up to the colonel and shook his hand. As they did so, he handed them the envelope containing the money, and the UBS bank form listing the account number, along with the address in Zurich, Switzerland. In addition, the colonel returned their cell phone and thanked them for all their hard work. Unbeknownst to any of them, the cell phones had been modified by the Atlas organization, so it could be tracked independently, by Atlas and by the phone company providing the communication service. This way Atlas would know where the phone and, more importantly, the owner were located, at any given time.

The team members then shook hands with each other and prepared to leave the safe house. So as not to attract attention from any neighbors of the safe house, the team members left separately two minutes apart. They climbed into their vehicles and drove off in different directions. As they did so, they could hear Marine helicopters racing overhead. They knew that the military and police would be on high alert, for foreigners or suspicious looking men.

In addition, none of them had any idea that their vehicles, which Atlas had given them, were modified to include a tracking transmitter. Atlas security wanted to be able to monitor the cars location at any time.

When all the men had departed, Alan Burgess parked the SUV, used in the raid, inside the garage. Even though all the men had taken the precaution to wear gloves, he wiped the inside of the vehicle and door handles clean. This was to make sure there were no fingerprints left behind. As an added precaution, Alan opened up the hood, and disconnected the battery, so that any tracking transmitter, which had been installed, would go dead. He then exited the house, locked the door, climbed into his new vehicle and drove toward Roanoke, Virginia.

37

Investigation

On the same day that the missiles lifted off, on their way to Washington, there was a scheduled security meeting at Camp Lejeune. The attendees consisted of top National Guard officials from several states, United States military personnel and a few civilians, from the Pentagon. The meeting was ostensibly held to discuss ways to combat terrorist actions, in each of their states. Among the meeting participants were the Commanders of the Texas and Tennessee National Guards, as well as Ian Black, the military advisor to Tennessee Governor Martha Cartwright.

The launching of the missiles, from Camp Warrior, did not go unnoticed at Camp Lejeune, as it was only a few miles from the Bomarc base. Captain Mitchell, the security duty officer, happened to be outside, when Hisham pushed the first launch button. The captain heard the missile exhaust noise and then he saw the smoke billowing above the pine trees. At first, he thought nothing of it. He assumed it was a new VTOL aircraft rising from the Marine Corps Air Station across Morgan Bay and New River. However, when the second Bomarc lifted off, he realized that they were not coming from the Air Station, but a little further north.

"Damn," he thought. *"There goes my coffee break".*

He was dumbfounded and froze for a few seconds, after seeing the smoke rise above the trees in the distance. He wasn't the only Marine at Camp Lejeune that noticed the missile smoke trails. Several other Marines heard the noise of the missile being launched and they rushed outside to see what was going on.

The security duty officer ran back inside the guard house and called the corporal on guard duty at Camp Warrior. Getting no answer from the sentry, he phoned his superior about the situation. After getting agreement that it could be serious, he gathered together a squad of men with rifles and commandeered two Humvees to go and investigate. He also contacted Camp Geiger and asked them to investigate the matter, since they were closer to the point of lift off. It took at least ten minutes to gather together all the men and the Humvees, with drivers. The duty officer and Marines then raced off toward Camp Warrior, which was about twenty minutes away from the main base at Camp Lejeune

Ian Black heard all the commotion and overheard the security officer saying they were going to check out Camp Warrior. He suggested to the National Guard Commanders that they should follow this convoy.

"Let's follow the Marines and see what's going on. It appears two missiles may have been fired from a base called Camp Warrior. Did any of you know that there was a missile base close by?" he asked the National Guard Commanders. "Does anyone know what type of missiles they were?"

One old guardsman said, "Based on the second missile launched, it looked like a Bomarc to me. I haven't seen one of those things for years".

The Marine Humvees, followed closely by the State National Guard men in two SUVs, arrived at Camp Warrior fifteen minutes after the Red Moon team had left the area.

When they arrived at the Camp, they could smell the exhaust fumes that had emanated from the booster rockets. Two of the shelter roofs were open and, from the Camp gate, it appeared the missiles were no longer on the shelter booms. They followed the Marine duty officer who drove into the Camp, after he opened the large gate, with the security code. He had the Humvee drivers' park the vehicles and the Marines jumped out, with their rifles drawn. The National Guardsmen followed them into the missile base. They parked close to the Humvees, and followed the Marines into the blockhouse.

There the duty security officer found the sentry, Corporal Jones, tied up, and realized why he didn't answer the call thirty minutes before. He ordered his men to untie him.

"Okay, corporal, tell me what happened," ordered the duty officer.

"Well, sir. These six men, wearing ski masks and speaking English with a foreign accent, invaded the Camp, but the infrared security alarm system didn't sound. In addition, they called each other an Arabic name. Anyway, the next thing I know is that there is a gun pointed at my head, and they tied me up. After they launched the missiles, they quickly left, after talking about going to Charlotte, in order to fly out of the country. That's about all I can tell you."

Ian Black heard all this and then looked around Camp and the two missile shelters. Since he had worked at Boeing when the president ordered the eight Bomarc missile sites to be built, he was somewhat familiar with the system. He discovered that the cable connecting the missile status to NORAD and SOCC had been bypassed.

On seeing this override, Ian thought to himself, *"The people who did this were no amateurs. They knew exactly how to conduct their mission."*

Also, he noticed the hole in the security fence was cut in the blind spot. He remembered hearing that this had been an issue during the time he had worked on the Bomarc project at Boeing. He now realized it had never been fixed. In addition, the guard said they spoke English with a foreign accent. Again, the whole operation bothered him and he thought that this appeared to be more of an "inside" job.

"How could a group of terrorists have carried this off, unless they had some help from the inside, or the team included someone who had in-depth knowledge of the missile system and the associated bases," he thought.

Ian had a lot of experience in military matters and was a retired colonel from the U.S. Air Force, with extensive intelligence experience. His intuition was generally correct and he thought all of this looked too neat and tidy, but he couldn't place a handle on why.

Then, he came up with a BFO (blinding flash of the obvious). *"Real Arab terrorists would have probably communicated in Arabic not English. Therefore, they were not Arab terrorists at all, but of some other nationality, probably from an English speaking country."*

His cell phone suddenly vibrated in his pocket, breaking his thought process. He retrieved it from inside his jacket, noticed the caller ID number listed was for the governor of Tennessee's office and turned it on.

Stepping outside the blockhouse, Ian answered the phone.

"This is Colonel Black."

"Hello Ian. This is Governor Cartwright. Do you have a few seconds to talk?"

"Yes, for you, of course governor. At the moment, I'm currently at Camp Warrior, near Camp Lejeune. We're investigating the launch of two Bomarc missiles. However, we don't yet know where they landed."

"Ian. That's why I'm calling you. There've been two explosions at the U.S. Capitol in Washington, D.C. It appears there've been numerous casualties. There may be up to fifty dead in the Senate Chamber and one hundred and fifty to two hundred dead in the House Chamber. It is absolute chaos, as you can imagine."

"My God, that sounds terrible. The explosions were probably caused by the missiles launched from here. Based on my experience at Boeing, I believe each missile can carry about five hundred pounds of explosive and has a range of about five hundred miles. If I find out more, I'll call you. I'll be returning to Nashville as soon as I can."

"Ian. Please keep me informed. I'll see you soon. Goodbye."

"Goodbye governor." Ian then pressed the OFF button and returned the phone to his jacket pocket.

****

While the Red Moon team members were making their way to their respective homes, the Marines at Camp Lejeune were going crazy trying to figure out what exactly happened.

It was only one hour after the attack on the Capitol that members of the newly created National Police Force and the FBI arrived at the Camp to investigate the situation. They dusted everything for fingerprints and looked for any other clues and details, such as DNA. They discovered the two knapsacks left behind; one of which contained a copy of the Koran and the other one had Arabic plans for the attack. They also made plaster imprints of a set of tire tracks found close the Camp and of the footprints that led to and from the Camp's security fence.

The NPF lead official issued an all points bulletin for the six men. Road blocks were set up on the road to Charlotte. All flights out of Charlotte had been canceled, along with all flights in and out of the United States, for at least the next twenty four hours.

Right after the attack on the Capitol, the president had ordered all flights grounded throughout the United States, until further notice. Bus stations and Amtrak stations on the East Coast were monitored very closely.

Ian didn't inform any of the National Guard commanders, Marines or the FBI of his observations. However, when he returned to Nashville, he relayed his thoughts and opinions of the missile attack to Martha Cartwright, the governor of Tennessee.

38

Aftermath

The Secret Service hustled the president, together with his wife and children, through the security tunnel to safety. They then transported them to a secret location, outside Washington, where they would be safe, until the exact nature of the threat was identified.

In the meantime, the Capitol building and surrounding area was completely cordoned off. Most of the eighteen hundred Capitol police were called in and those officers, who could be contacted, were asked to report to duty immediately. The Washington, D.C. police were also everywhere, checking for evidence and keeping unauthorized people away. Helicopters and ambulances were transporting the dead and wounded to area hospitals, which were soon all overwhelmed with the casualties.

The police were handling the chaos, fairly well. The Dulles International Airport and Reagan Washington National Airport were shut down, to prevent the perpetrators of this heinous deed from flying out of the area. At this point, it was still not clear what caused the explosions at the Capitol. Television networks were receiving phone calls from several eyewitnesses, who said they had seen two planes, both without a cockpit, traveling at a high rate of speed, as they hit the Capitol. None of this was confirmed, as of yet. A report also came in from Camp Lejeune that two missiles had been launched from a facility, close to the U.S. Marine base. On top of that, an airliner had called in to air traffic control that they had almost hit a flying object, near an altitude of twenty thousand feet. The object looked like a plane, but it didn't have a cockpit.

The president quickly called a cabinet meeting for that afternoon, so he could decide on how to handle the crisis. Only two-thirds of the Cabinet was able to attend. At this meeting, it was decided that the president should declare a state of emergency immediately, and issue an order that the Washington airports remain closed, for at least twenty-four hours. In addition, the train station and bus station should be closely monitored for potential suspects, trying to flee the Washington area.

After sifting through the many reports, the FBI determined that the Capitol explosions were probably a result of being hit by missiles launched from a base, near Camp Lejeune. Based on the reports coming from the Camp, it appeared that they were probably fired by Islamist terrorists, who had already fled the area.

As a result of this FBI report, the Secret Service concluded it was probably safe for the president to return to the White House. The roof of the White House would be guarded twenty-four hours a day by agents with Stinger missiles, in case the terrorists did try to attack it.

As soon as the president was back in the White House, he asked Valda Lewis and Andrew Taylor, his chief of staff, to come to the Oval Office. They discussed the events of the day and the cabinet meeting, and then the president asked Andrew to contact the other cabinet members, who could not attend, and apprise them of the decisions. He left the office to make the necessary calls.

After turning off the recorders in the Oval Office and Andrew Taylor had left, the president turned to Valda Lewis and said, "Well, it seems that the false flag operation was a complete success. I must make a speech to the nation tonight and declare that I'm issuing an executive order, creating a state of emergency. Please make the necessary arrangements for it to take place, on all the major networks, this evening at 9:00 pm."

"I'll have the White House communications director contact all television and radio networks and schedule it. Do you already have the speech written?" Valda asked.

"Yes, I do," replied the president.

The nation was in shock, just as it had been on 9/11. Only this seemed a lot worse, because half the nation's leading politicians were either dead or wounded.

"Who would take charge and how could the terrorists be stopped, from more destruction in the U.S.?" Americans wondered.

Most were frightened for the future and for their well being.

39

Fiery Crash

John Norman was the first to leave the safe house. He drove off, in his new white Honda Odyssey van, for his home in Franklin, Tennessee. He was looking forward to seeing his wife and two children again, after the months of separation. He called his wife on an unregistered cell phone, which could be monitored by the NSA. However, they could only determine the location of the phone, not who owned it.

"Hi Honey, I'm on my way home. I should be there in a few hours, if I'm not held up by the traffic."

His wife responded, "I'll be glad when you're home. Did you hear the news?"

"No," John replied. "I haven't been close to a television or radio. What's going on?"

"Two explosions have rocked the U.S. Senate and House of Representatives Chambers. There are scores of dead and wounded in both facilities. Please hurry home."

 "Okay, I'll get there as soon as I can."

As he proceeded down the road, he turned on the radio and heard all the news, about the chaos in Washington, D.C. He wondered what went wrong. *"They were supposed to hit* the Pentagon. *Had the team had been deceived? Did Hisham know what was going on? Were the incorrect coordinates supplied?* There were so many questions and no one to supply the answers.

John went via Greenville NC, Raleigh, Winston-Salem, up Rte I-77 and then Rte I-81 South, to Knoxville, TN. From there he took highway I-40 to Nashville and then I-65 to Franklin. It was approximately six hundred and sixty miles and the drive took him about eleven hours, with a short stop. He stayed clear of Charlotte and kept religiously to the posted speed limits. He saw many State Police cars on the way, but none of them stopped him and there were no road blocks.

He arrived at his home around 9:00 pm and walked in the house. His wife greeted him with a hug and a kiss.

"I've missed you," she said, "and so have the kids." At that point his two kids came running in shouting "Daddy's home" and they gave him a big hug. He thought, *"This is why I was involved in the missile plot. It was for them."*

He took his wife into the bedroom and said, "Honey, I got paid today. Here's two thousand dollars."

He did not mention the other forty-eight thousand.

"In three months, I should have enough money, so we can forget how the military treated me, when I retired. Those politicians in Washington only think about how they can line their own pockets."

"I agree with that," she replied

She took the money without question, relieved that she could pay some bills and buy groceries. She didn't ask what was going to happen in three months. She would concern herself about that when the time came. She lived from day to day, paycheck to paycheck, on his measly U.S. Air Force retirement check and any additional money he brought in from his odd jobs.

"Maybe things would get better soon," she pondered.

****

Meanwhile, Mike Thornburn started on his long journey back to Prescott, Arizona and his girlfriend, if she was still there at his apartment. His quickest route was west on I-95 and I-10. It was basically freeway all the way to Phoenix. He would then swing north, up to Prescott. It was approximately twenty-six hundred miles and would take three to four days, with stops overnight. He could not afford to speed or get sleepy.

Mike left the safe house at 10:15 am in his new red Ford Mustang, with its temporary license plate and tracking beacon. As he headed for Florence and Route I-95, he didn't notice the car following him. It stayed far enough back, so that it wasn't obvious someone was tailing him. He planned to make it as far as Pensacola, Florida, and then stop for the night. Using an unregistered phone, he dialed his apartment to talk to his girl friend, but she didn't answer.

He thought to himself *"Maybe she's left for greener pastures."*

As Mike proceeded down the highway, he turned on the radio and found a news station. This wasn't hard since almost all of the radio stations had transitioned to a news format, and the radio hosts or DJ's were talking about the explosions, at the U.S. Capitol. As soon as Mike heard the news, he realized that he had been misled, about the targets for the missiles. At first, he became depressed, and then angry, at the fact that he had participated in an attack, on the seat of the Federal Government, and not the Pentagon.

He wondered, *"Did Hisham or any of the team know what the real targets were? Whoever was running this mission might have other plans also. Since he knew about the attack and who was involved, was he vulnerable?"*

He thought it was best to mail most of the money and the Swiss bank account information, to himself in Prescott. He stopped in Live Oak, Florida and went to the local post office. It wasn't very difficult to find with its U.S. flag flying at half mast. He entered the post office and asked for a small flat rate box. He took it out to his car and filled the box with the forty-five thousand, in one hundred dollar bills, plus the account number for the Swiss bank. After he wrote his own address on the front of the box, he took it back into the post office and mailed it to Prescott, Arizona.

He then swung back onto I-10 and headed for Tallahassee, about seventy-five miles to the west. As he pulled into Tallahassee, Florida, he decided to get a cup of coffee and a piece of pie. He was getting a little sleepy, but wanted to make Pensacola before stopping for the night. The coffee would help to keep him awake. He pulled into a restaurant, just off the freeway, sat down at the counter and ordered a coffee, together with a piece of cherry pie.

About a minute later, a nicely dressed, middle-aged man came in and sat down by him. They started talking about the day's news. It turned out his name was Joe and he also was travelling toward Pensacola. Mike decided that he had to make room for the coffee, he was about to drink, so he asked Joe, "Would you mind saving my seat? I'll be back in a minute. I need to go to the men's room."

"Sure thing," said Joe.

Mike went to the rest room. While he was in there, Joe reached over and dropped a drug into Mike's steaming cup of coffee, which had just arrived. He quickly stirred the coffee, to make sure the sleeping pill was well mixed in. Joe smiled to himself and thought of the money he would receive, for such a simple job.

Mike returned shortly from the rest room and said to Joe," Thanks for keeping my seat."

"You're welcome. Your coffee and pie arrived, while you were gone," said Joe.

Joe sat there slowly drinking his Coke. Mike quickly ate his pie, and downed it with the drug laced coffee. He thought the coffee had a slightly strange taste, but figured it was just a bad pot of the brew. He had to rush to get to Pensacola, so he could find a motel for the night.

After he finished his snack, he went to pay his bill at the register. As Mike rose from the stool, he said, "It was nice talking to you, Joe. Maybe I'll see you down the road somewhere."

Joe sat there alone, for a short time, finishing his drink. He then quickly got up and went to pay his tab. He walked outside and climbed into his car. As he did, he saw Mike pulling out of the coffee shop parking area. He slowly took off after him, trying not to attract his attention. He followed Mike onto Route I-10, toward the city of Pensacola.

As Mike drove, he thought to himself that the coffee did not do a very good job in keeping him awake. Pretty soon, he felt very drowsy. All the time, Joe was following him in his car, taking care to stay far enough behind. Mike's car started to speed up as he fell asleep. He never woke up. His car hit a bridge abutment and burst into flames, twenty miles short of Pensacola. Joe saw what happened and, judging by the inferno that followed, he knew Mike could not have survived the crash.

Joe thought to himself, "*Well, the boys in Chicago will be happy to hear the news. I just made myself an easy ten grand.*"

He turned around and sped off at the next exit, as an ambulance and police car raced toward the wreck.

****

Gerry Davies left the safe house in his new silver Mustang, a few minutes after Mike did. He was going to his home in Lebanon, Pennsylvania and his long time girlfriend. He had been with her, since he left the marines, after serving time in Iraq. Since he got out of the Corps, he had trouble finding full time employment, but his girl friend was a nurse and made good money. Now, Gerry felt flush with the fifty thousand dollars and would feel even better in December, with the ten million stashed away in a Swiss bank account. He was bitter about the U.S. Government's lack of concern for men who put their lives at risk, for their country and then who came home jobless. He now realized how the Vietnam veterans must have felt, when they returned home.

He drove up route I-95 to Richmond, Virginia and then highway I-64 to Staunton. From there he proceeded on I-81 to Harrisburg Pennsylvania. From there, it was a short drive to his home in Lebanon and his girlfriend Diana. It was around five hundred and fifty miles and he arrived home at 7:30 pm, without any speeding tickets.

Diana was waiting for him. She gave him a long drawn-out kiss and then steered him to the bedroom. Both of them could hardly wait to take their clothes off.

Later, Gerry gave her five thousand dollars and said, "That was the best lay in a long time."

She laughed, took the money and gave him a slap on the behind saying, "You're a naughty boy". He nodded and grabbed a beer. Little did he know, at the time, that he would not have the chance to make love to her many more times.

****

Pasco Martinez and Chris Smith, the other two members of the Red Moon team, left the safe house almost at the same time, in their brand new vehicles. They were headed somewhat in the same direction. Pasco was headed for Miami in his dark blue Odyssey, while Chris was going to Atlanta in his black Explorer.

Pasco's drive home, via I-95, was over eight hundred miles long and so he decided to stop in Jacksonville, on the way. His wife, together with their three children, was waiting for him at their home. On the way, he called them to let them know that he would be there the next day. They hadn't seen him in a few months, but she'd forgive him for the extra one night, when he gave her some of the fifty thousand dollars, to pay their bills, including the house payment.

Chris's drive to Atlanta, where he resided, took him through Florence, Columbia and Augusta; a distance of approximately four hundred and fifteen miles. Since he didn't have to stop overnight, he would be able to make it by 6:00 pm. He had no one waiting for him at his apartment, since his boyfriend left him a few months ago. On the positive side, he could spend all the money himself.

Colonel Alan Burgess, leader of the Red Moon team, was the last one to leave the safe house. He had parked the SUV, the one driven from Illinois and used for the Camp Warrior raid, in the safe house three-car garage. He had the Atlas supplied new dark blue Ford Fusion, waiting for him in the driveway and he would use it to take him back home. After the last team members had driven off, he quickly got into the Ford, started it up and drove off down the road, which led to the freeway. He was glad to be going home to Roanoke, Virginia. He was divorced, and therefore he had no one to call. He and his wife had an amicable divorce five years ago, and their one child had recently graduated from Virginia Tech and had a well paying, engineering job.

Alan headed north from the safe house and then cut over to route I-40. When he reached Winston Salem, he drove north on highway I-74 and then I-77. Where I-77 met I-81, he travelled eastward and drove to Roanoke. It was a total of three hundred and fifty miles, and he made it easily by 5:00 pm.

He parked the Atlas provided vehicle, at a nearby shopping center, disconnected the battery and walked to his home. He would never use that new car again, believing it might be bugged. Alan went into his house, on the outskirts of Roanoke, and immediately took a shower.

He then climbed into bed and drifted off to sleep, dreaming "*I made one hundred grand today and, in two*

213

months, I can go to Switzerland, to collect my twenty five million dollar retirement fund."

The next morning, he called an automobile transportation company and had them pick up the Ford Fushion that he had parked the night before. He met them there and connected the battery, so any transmitter would start sending out a signal again. He paid the company to transport the vehicle, to a wrecking yard in Riverside, California. Atlas would think he was driving to California, by following the transmitted signal. Alan Burgess had taken precautions so that Atlas and the White House had no idea where he actually resided.

40

State of Emergency

Before he went on the air, Valda whispered to the president some news, concerning Al Jazeera.

"Mr. President, for your information, Atlas Communications has put out the phony report, purported to be from Ayman al-Zawahiri, head of Al Qaeda, that they're claiming responsibility for the attack. This report has been fed to all the major news networks, including the Arab Al Jazeera organization. They're all reporting it, as we speak."

Tuckwell responded, "Great, I'll be able to add that information to my speech tonight."

At 9:00 pm eastern time (6:00 pm pacific time) on Friday, the 9th of September, the same day as the attack on the Capitol, President Tuckwell went on all major television networks and spoke to the nation.

Before the president appeared on television in the Oval Office, sitting behind the large oak desk, he was preceded by the playing of the U.S. national anthem. Then, at exactly the prescribed time and on cue from the White House communications director, President Tuckwell appeared and starting speaking:

"My fellow Americans, I am speaking to you at this grave time for our Nation. This morning, it appears that two missiles were launched by Islamic terrorists, from a secret base, near Camp Lejeune in North Carolina, and they subsequently hit the Capitol building. The terrorists managed to infiltrate the base, overpower the guard, alter the programs on the missiles and actually launch them. This attack is far more serious, than any previous terrorist assault, carried out against this country. It was aimed at the symbol of American democracy and has taken the lives of many of our leaders.

In the warhead explosions and the ensuing chaos, scores of U.S. Senators and Congressman have been killed or wounded. Even Vice President James Valpy has been seriously wounded.

We will hunt down these Islamic terrorists and Jihadists, who have carried out this dastardly deed. They will be caught and prosecuted to the fullest extent of the law. None of them will escape, even those that live in foreign countries. As I speak, Al Jazeera, the Arab TV network, is reporting that Al Qaeda, under the leadership of Ayman al-Zawahiri, is claiming responsibility for the strike on the Capitol.

In order to keep our Nation secure during the next few months, I have today declared a state of emergency, which will give more power to this administration, so it is able maintain law and order. I do not take this action lightly, but some freedoms, under the Constitution, may have to be set aside, until the emergency is over. The NPF has been given additional powers, to apprehend any person or organization that is a threat to our national security.

Tonight, I ask you to pray for all those who have lost their lives, the wounded and of course the families who have lost their loved ones. It will take a long time for the healing process, and this administration will provide the resources to help all of those victimized, by this act of aggression.

On this day of infamy, all Americans, from every walk of life, must unite in our resolve for justice and peace. America has faced before, with fortitude, dangerous times and enemies, such as the Battleship Maine, Pearl Harbor and other terrorist attacks. I'm sure that we will do so again, with this Islamic missile strike on the Capitol.

Just as we have never forgotten previous disasters, none of us living   today or future generations will ever forget this day. We must go on with our lives and defend freedom, whenever we can. This great country is the land of hope, for all freedom loving people and will remain so.

As new details come to this administration's attention, I'll speak to you again, so that you are kept well informed.

Thank you and good night. May God Bless America."

After he was off the air,   "God Bless America", sung by Kate Smith, was played. The president thought this was a great "touch", to end the speech with.

Valda Lewis walked over to the president and congratulated him, on his well delivered speech. "Mr. President" she said, "that was excellent. The right tone and sincere enough to make any American agree with you. Adding that piece about Al Jazeera and Al Qaeda was a great touch, and it should convince the average American that it was a terrorist incursion."

All of the Red Moon Team, along with millions of Americans, had turned on their televisions on Saturday at 6:00 pm to hear the president's speech. Actually all except one, named Mike Thornburn. His charred remains were in a Pensacola morgue, as the coroner tried to identify who he was. His driver's license and the temporary vehicle license on the rear window of the car were unreadable. They'd been completely destroyed. It might take weeks before they identified the remains and notified his living relatives.

Three days later, Mike Thornburn's girlfriend, living at his apartment in Prescott, opened up the United States Postal Service flat rate box addressed to Mike Thornburn, which he

217

had mailed to himself from Florida. In it, she found an envelope containing the forty-five thousand dollars and the note from the Swiss bank UBS. It listed the account number and the date the funds would be available. She hid it in a safe place and waited two weeks for Mike to reappear. Finally, she went to the police and they started a search for him. The authorities managed to put two and two together and figured out, using DNA, that Mike had died in the Florida crash. When she found out Mike was deceased, she decided to move out of his apartment, taking with her the money and the UBS account note.

The remaining four members of the team were overwrought with shame. They believed that they had launched the missiles against the Pentagon, and instead they had actually destroyed much of the Capitol. They had a dispute with the Pentagon in the way they were treated, after fighting in the Middle East, but did not have any problem with the U.S. Federal Government, in general.

What had gone wrong? Had they been deceived? The coordinates for the attack had been supplied by Hisham. Did he know the truth or was he also deceived?

All these questions went through the minds of the team members individually, as they watched the broadcast.

41

Conference Call

Governor Cartwright of Tennessee watched the speech in amazement and reflected on the words, uttered by the president. She wondered how he could have the audacity to try and take dictatorial powers, by claiming a state of emergency.

She placed a telephone call to the personal number for Chuck Prince, the governor of Texas, a Republican and a good friend. He immediately picked up the phone.

"Hello."

"Hi Chuck. This is Martha calling from Nashville. Don't forget there may be others monitoring this call. You can't be too careful these days."

"You're right governor, I agree," Prince said.

Governor Cartwright continued, "Listen. I'm very concerned about Tuckwell's declaration of a state of emergency and where it might lead. This will give him almost unlimited power and, if we're not careful, it could tear the Union apart."

"I concur, Martha. This guy is really starting to scare me. I think he's power hungry. When he created that National Police Force, back in March, with an executive order on a Friday night, I thought it was an ominous sign. Why does he need a NPF, when the states have their own State police forces? I'm concerned that he's going to use it, to intimidate his political opponents."

"You're right. If he makes many more moves like this, we may be forced to do something about it. With a lot of the senators and congressmen dead, it'll be nigh impossible to impeach him, even if we had the evidence. I heard a rumor the other day that he intends to try and stay in office, even after the end of his term. This would be in direct violation of the constitution. I have no proof of this, but that was the unsubstantiated report I received from my people in Washington, D.C."

"Let's keep in touch, Martha. Yes, we may have to do something. If we can't impeach him, we may have to move our National Guard troops to Washington and remove him from office, in order to save the Union. That would be ironic. In 1861, the North saved the Union. This year, the South may have to save the Union. Goodbye for now. Thanks for calling, and yes, I'll certainly stay in touch."

"Goodbye Chuck, talk to you soon." With that she hung up the phone. She turned to her trusted advisor and said, "What do you think, Ian?"

Ian replied "I think you're both right. You're going to have to monitor this situation very closely and not let it get out of hand. Let me know if I can be of any help. In the meantime, I'll contact some of the people I know in Washington, to see if I can get any additional information."

42

Boat Vanishes

Pasco arrived home late Saturday afternoon, on the 10th of September from Wilmington, after stopping in Jacksonville, Florida for the night. He didn't notice that he was being followed all the way to his house, by a man in a dark, older Ford. His wife and three children were happy he was home, since they hadn't seen him for a few months. His wife was extremely elated, when he gave her ten thousand dollars, with which to pay some bills. She didn't ask him any questions, as to where the money came from, since she had learned, over the years, never to ask too many questions.

The next day, Pasco sat down with his wife, to discuss a boat he wanted to purchase. He had always wanted a boat to go fishing in, and now he had some money.

Pasco asked Maria, "Honey, would it be okay with you if I bought a fishing boat?

"Of course," she replied.

She felt that he deserved it, since he must have put in long hours, for these past few months, to earn the money he had given her. He had always been diligent in providing for her and their kids. She loved him for that.

221

"How much are we talking about?" she asked.

Pasco replied, "It'll not cost more than ten thousand, and I'll be able to depositing thirty-five thousand dollars in the bank tomorrow. In addition, I have a promissory note for a considerable amount of money, payable in December. I'll take out a safety deposit box at the bank and place this note in it, for safe keeping."

Maria replied, "I won't ask you what you did to get this money. However, whatever you do, please consider the ramifications of your actions on the kids and me."

"Of course, I always do," he said, giving her a hug. He had been depressed, since the launch of the missiles, with its resulting casualties and chaos in Washington. He believed that the team had been misled, because they all thought the plan was to attack the Pentagon; not the symbol of the United States Government.

On Monday, he went to the local bank, deposited the money and took out a safety deposit box, so he could keep the dated promissory note, with the USB account number, safe. In addition, he included a personal note to his wife, which read:

My Dear Maria,

If anything should happen to me and I am no longer around, I want you to know that you can obtain ten million dollars, from the USB Swiss Bank in Zurich, Switzerland. This money will be available any time after the 9th of December and will be yours to keep. You will need to take the card with the USB account number with you, when you go to the bank. For the safety of you and the children, do not share this information with anyone; not even your parents.

All My Love,

Pasco

After that, he went to look at a boat that he had seen in the Sunday paper classified section. The used boat was exactly what he wanted, and it seemed to be in reasonable condition. The owner wanted ninety-five hundred dollars, but Pasco offered eighty-five hundred cash, right then and there. The owner took the cash eagerly and Pasco hauled his boat away, taking it to a small inexpensive marina. Here, he had rented a slip and moored it, ready for use.

While all this was going on, he was followed by the man in the dark, older Ford. Pasco was so enamored with his boat that he didn't notice the car following him, wherever he went.

Three nights later, the man in the vehicle drove to a parking lot close to the marina and walked to Pasco's boat, carrying a small black bag. He climbed on it and went down into the small cabin. He took a package out of his bag, turned on a switch, and placed it close to the gas tank, behind a compartment door. The operation only took a few minutes, and he left just as quickly as he came. He hoped no one noticed him, since it was fairly late in the evening. This man was very experienced in handling these kinds of matters. If anyone did see him, however, they would probably think it was the owner. This boat was new at the marina, and no other owners had met Pasco yet.

Two days later on Saturday, the 17th of September, Pasco got up early, after deciding the night before, to take his boat out for the first time and go fishing the next day. His wife declined to go, since she would have to get a baby sitter, for their young children. Pasco drove his new van down to the dock, where he had moored his boat a few days before.

The man in the dark Ford followed him, as he had done before, checking the display now and again that picked up the transmitter, installed in the Odyssey. Pasco stopped on the way to get a quick breakfast, consisting of a sausage, egg biscuit at the local McDonalds. When he arrived at the marina, he carried his fishing gear down to the dock and boarded his boat. He performed a quick check out; everything looked ship shape. However, he noticed it could do with some fuel. He wasn't sure how far out he would be going. Luckily, Pasco had planned for his fishing trip, by filling up the spare gas can the night before. He went back to his van, took the full can of gas out of the rear and carried it down to the dock. He poured the fuel into the tank, using the gas port installed on the boat's deck.

He started up the motor, which purred like a new engine. Everything seemed okay for his trip. He untied the boat and went very slowly through the channel, by the marina. The speed limit was five miles per hour. As soon as he cleared the channel markers, he increased his speed, as he wanted to get out into the ocean and start fishing, as soon as possible.

The man on shore had a small transmitter in his hand. He turned the battery-powered device on. Pasco steered the boat out into the ocean and went about two miles. He dropped a sea anchor and started to fish. The man on shore, using his left hand to hold and focus a pair of binoculars, watched Pasco as he started to fish. He held the small transmitter in his right hand and, with his middle finger, pushed the red button. The package, he had concealed on the boat two nights before exploded, setting the gas tank and the craft on fire. The entire boat lifted up about twenty feet above the water, and then what was left of it, settled down onto the ocean and sank beneath the waves.

The assassin on the shore smiled to himself and walked back to his car. He placed a quick call to a Chicago number and then drove off.

He thought to himself, *"Boy. That was easy money. I wonder what the poor guy had done to deserve it."*

He was a hit man and didn't delve into the why. He'd learned that asking too many questions was dangerous.

The police were notified about the explosion, by another fishing boat. The homicide police investigated the accident as best they could, since the boat was at the bottom and there was not much they could do. The police attributed the accident to a leak in the boat's fuel system. They never found Pasco's mangled body, but they did retrieve a piece of wood, with the boat license number on it, and traced it back to the owner, Pasco Martinez.

When he did not return from his fishing trip, the new widow called the police. They put two and two together and, after talking to the marina owner, determined the victim in the accident was in fact Pasco Martinez, a former U.S. Navy communications expert.

The police decided that no further investigation was required and the case was closed.

The new widow went through Pasco's personal effects, a few days later, and found the remainder of the fifty thousand dollars. She wondered where he got it, but decided it was best not to ask questions, even of the police. The money would remain her secret, since it would come in handy to help feed their three hungry children.

Later, she remembered the safety deposit box at the bank. She went there and found the USB bank account number and the promissory note, dated the 9th of December. She also found the personal note Pasco had written to her.

She wondered, *"Where did all this money come from and what did Pasco do to earn it? I hope no one comes to claim it and take it away."*

43

NPF Enlarged

Valda Lewis and President Tuckwell decided that he should make another speech to the nation, announcing the expansion of the NPF. He had Andrew Taylor, his Chief of Staff, set it up with the major networks for 9:00 pm eastern time, on the 23rd of September. At the signal from the communications director, he started speaking.

"Good evening, Americans. I come before you to discuss a change to the NPF that I have decided is necessary. As I stated in my talk to you two weeks ago, I said that the chaos which the terrorists brought about on the 9th of September, would live with us for some time. In order to combat the lawlessness being created by some segments of our society, I am today expanding the National Police Force. If you remember, we created this organization back in March of this year and placed it under the direction of the attorney general. We're finding that we need more officers to facilitate the arrest of people breaking federal laws. The NPF should not be confused with the FBI that is basically chartered to investigate crimes. They will actively seek out lawbreakers, arrest them and keep them incarcerated, until they can go before a judge and jury.

We don't take this action lightly, but it's necessary in light of the chaos, caused by the attack on the Capitol. This terrorist action has caused problems throughout the country, to a far greater extent, than this administration had imagined.

In addition, we have decided that for a limited time, the NPF may have to arrest and detain some factions of the press, radio and television stations, which spew out false information. These lies create an unsettled populace and riots in the streets. They cannot and will not be tolerated. This broadcasting of false information has been going on far too long and it must be stopped. We will maintain peace and tranquility, even if it means that some freedoms and liberties, we have had in the past, will be curtailed. We still respect the first amendment to the Constitution, but we cannot allow certain organizations to continue to encourage people to break the laws, by inciting them with falsehoods. I am sure that you will understand the need for these measures, when you reflect on the terrible acts perpetrated two weeks ago.

I am distressed to inform you that Vice President Valpy is still in a coma in the hospital, and the prognosis is not good. We must all pray that he recovers and that his family members can withstand the enormous pressure on them. Other members of the House and the Senate are still in the hospital, in various stages of medical needs. We must pray for all of them and hope they recover quickly. We need them to return to their positions, as we need their experience in political matters and governing our country.

God bless you all and God bless America."

44

Robbery and Death

On the first day of October, Chris Smith decided to take a drive in his new vehicle into downtown Atlanta, to visit The Underground. It was a popular shopping center and eating area in Atlanta. It had been a couple of years, since he was last there. It was a great place to visit and spend an afternoon. What he didn't notice was that, all his movements, in the new Explorer, were being monitored by a tracking system, and two men in an older Chevy sedan.

He arrived in downtown Atlanta around three o'clock in the afternoon. He parked the vehicle and walked to the underground "city". It was just as he remembered it. He entered most of the stores, but didn't see anything in particular he wanted to purchase. By 5:30 pm he was ready for dinner and decided to go to the Café Agora, in Buckhead, which served Greek and Mediterranean cuisine. He ordered the Agora mixed grill that consisted of chicken and lamb, with Turkish sauces; it was delicious.

Chris then decided that he would stop at a few bars on the way back to his home, located in the northern part of Atlanta. Perhaps, he could find an attractive young man, with whom he could spend the night. Chris drove from the Cafe Agora to the Southern Peach Tavern, which he knew very well. The old Chevy followed, but went unnoticed.

Dusk had already settled and the Atlanta lights were twinkling, when Chris made his first stop at the Southern Peach Tavern and drank a couple of beers. The place was crowded and he danced with a couple of men, but neither of them was attractive to him. In fact, he thought he might have to just cross this bar off his list. Just a few old bearded men, who must have been fifty or older, were there.

He then drove to Earthquake Ethel's, a new trendy bar a few blocks from downtown. Parking his Explorer in the rear parking lot, he entered the bar. It was fairly dark inside, with all kinds of colored lights. This was a popular place for men of Chris's age. Once an hour, the whole building shook, as if in an earthquake. Whoever designed it did a fantastic, realistic job. He had a couple of beers at the bar and talked with a few friendly males. However, none of them caught his fancy.

"Maybe I'm becoming too particular" Chris thought.

He then decided he would make one last stop, on the way home, at the Soho Club in northeast Atlanta. The old Chevy, that contained the two men, was still following him. Chris parked and went inside. It was swinging, with plenty of music and dancing. One of the men got out of the Chevy and also went into the bar. He appeared to be in his twenties and was good looking.

He went over to Chris's table and introduced himself.

"Hi, my name is Peter. Do you mind if I join you?"

"Not at all, have a seat. I'm Chris."

He was drawn to the young man almost immediately.

"Thanks. How about a beer? I'm buying."

The waiter came over and they both ordered a beer. Peter told the waiter to put it on his tab.

Chris asked him, "Do you like to dance? This is good music they're playing."

Peter responded, "Sure thing, I love to dance," Peter answered flirtatiously. They danced for a while and then drank some more.

Chris bought the next two rounds.

Three beers later, they were both feeling pretty good and Chris thought he might have found a partner for the night.

"Hey Peter, how would you like a nightcap at my place? It's only a few blocks from here."

"Sounds good to me", he replied.

They both paid their tabs and left the Soho Club. Chris was feeling great because of the beer and the fact that he felt he had a partner for the night. What he didn't know was that Peter had slipped a date drug into his last drink and that was why he felt so good.

Peter asked Chris, "Can we go in your car? My old Chevy is running kind of rough. You can bring me back here later."

"Sure, my car is just over there," he said, pointing to his new Ford Explorer.

They both walked over to the vehicle. Chris unlocked the doors and went around to the driver's side. Peter went to the passenger door and climbed in.

Chris placed the key in the ignition switch of the SUV and was just about to start it, when Peter said "Give me all your money." He looked over and saw that he was holding a revolver. He could not believe it and stared at Peter in disbelief.

"Such a nice young man robbing him," he thought.

Chris took out his billfold, pulled out the bills and handed all of them to Peter. It amounted to about two hundred dollars.

The young man smiled and said, "Thank you. I'm sorry about this, but I have my orders."

With that, Peter aimed the gun, with a silencer attached to the barrel, at Chris's temple and pulled the trigger. One bullet entered Chris's brain. As he faded into oblivion, he thought about his parents and what would happen to them. The young man, who was twenty and a native Atlanta boy, quickly got out of the SUV and jumped into the old Chevy sedan.

"That was an easy few bucks," he said to the other man behind the wheel. "Let's go before the police arrive."

Another patron came out of the bar into the parking lot, just in time to see the old Chevy speed off and go down the road. When he went to get into his car, which was parked next to the Ford Explorer, he noticed blood on the SUV window and, at the same time, Chris's limp body. He ran back into the bar and told the manager what he had seen. The manager immediately called the police, who were used to trouble at this bar. They arrived in less than ten minutes and set about to determine what had happened. They decided, after quickly looking in the SUV, to call the homicide squad.

The homicide police came out about thirty minutes later and started to do their investigation. It didn't take them long to identify the victim. What they didn't find out was that he was involved in the missile attack on the Capitol. The officers questioned the bar manager and, after receiving very little information from him, turned their attention to the patron who was parked next to the Explorer.

"Did you hear the shot or see anything unusual?" the officer asked him

"No. I didn't hear anything, but I did see a dark, old Chevy leaving the parking area, at a high rate of speed."

"What color was the car?"

"The parking lot is not well lit and I could not determine the color of the sedan, other than it was dark, probably black or dark blue."

"Did you get a good look at the license plate?" another officer asked.

"No sir. I did see the plate, but could not read any of the letters or numbers, since it was covered with mud."

The officers took the patron's name, address and phone number, just in case they needed to talk with him some more.

Twenty-four hours later, a Michigan State police car stopped in front of Chris's parents' home in Holland, Michigan and gave them the bad news. It had taken authorities just a few hours to trace Chris's hometown. A few days later, his personal effects arrived and hidden, in a set of cowboy boots, was forty-six thousand dollars, along with a piece of paper listing a USB account number and a promissory note, with a date of the 9th of December. They needed the money badly, so they never mentioned it to anyone. They mourned their only son and gave him a quiet memorial service in Holland, Michigan.

45

Cancellation

On the 10th of October, President Tuckwell decided it was time he should speak to the nation again and inform the people that, due to the state of emergency, he had no choice, but to cancel the presidential election. He asked all the major networks, to provide the necessary time to televise his speech at 9:00 pm eastern time (6:00 pm pacific time). As in previous speeches, precisely on time, President Tuckwell sat down in the Oval Office, with the U.S. flag behind him, and spoke to the American people.

"Good evening, my fellow Americans. I am pleased to announce that we've put a stop to multiple disturbances, throughout the nation. Riots have been quelled and perpetrators have been arrested. We have clamped down on any organized opposition, which posed a threat to our Nation. I regret having to take such action, but it was necessary. In addition, we have already arrested certain members of the press that have been broadcasting falsehoods, for the purpose of inciting disturbances. These broadcasts were intolerable and had to be stopped.

Therefore, I ordered the National Police Force to totally shut down Fox News, last week, because they had refused to stop broadcasting falsehoods and lies. The management of Fox News and many of its reporters were arrested and detained. Also, some anti-American newspapers have also been shut down and their reporters have been arrested for the same reason.

Maintaining order and tranquility, for all of the nation's citizens, is of prime importance. We must have continuity of government so that we can maintain this peace.

I have therefore issued today an executive order that states the presidential election, scheduled for the 8th of November, is cancelled. The current administration will continue in office, until the nation's calm is assured. I don't take this action lightly, as it is in direct contradiction to the Constitution. However, this document was written almost two hundred and fifty years ago, and it needs to be updated and modernized, to reflect the issues of the day.

I have assembled a group of lawyers and outstanding American leaders, to review the Constitution and recommend changes, where appropriate. I have asked them to submit their recommendations by the 1st of January, next year. These will then be submitted to Congress and the fifty states for ratification.

I have to report to you that Vice President Valpy is still in a coma, resulting from the dastardly attack of the 9th of September. In addition, there are still some senators, congressmen and aides trying to regain their health. Let us keep them all in our prayers.

I trust you understand the reasons for the extraordinary measures taken today and that you will continue to support our efforts to maintain peace and security.

God bless America.

Goodnight to you all."

Then the U.S. national anthem was played. Valda Lewis walked over to the president and said, "Sir. That was excellent. It set the right tone for the future."

"Yes. I thought it was pretty good myself, if I may say so," said the president. "You know Valda I think we must crack down on Twitter and Facebook. These could be used to organize resistance against our plans. We must either restrict their use or totally shut them down. Look into that for me and let me know the feasibility."

"Yes sir. I'll do that immediately," Valda responded.

46

Fails to Stop

Gerry Davies watched the presidential speech, on the 10th of October, with his girlfriend Diana, and was dumbfounded. How could the president of the United States cancel an election just like that? Didn't the Constitution prevent this kind of action? It was totally undemocratic, only dictators cancelled elections.

He tried calling Pasco Martinez, in Miami and finally got hold of his wife. She told him the bad news, about how Pasco's boat blew up, from a fuel leak.

"Poor bastard," Gerry thought. *"At least he went quickly."*

Two days later, while Diana was at work, as a nurse in the nearby hospital, Gerry decided to drive to Marstown, Pennsylvania, just a few miles away from Lebanon. He had a buddy there, from the old days, and he had not seen him for awhile. He phoned him to make sure he would be in, and to tell him that he would be there around ten o'clock. Then he called Diana at work and left a message, stating that he was going to Marstown and would be back later.

UNBRIDLED POWER

He climbed into his new silver Ford Mustang and started down the road. He didn't notice the dark sedan trailing him from afar. In the car was a man talking on a cell phone, as he monitored the display that showed the location of the silver Mustang. At the other end of the phone, there was a rough looking guy, driving a large, fully loaded gravel truck.

As Gerry drove down the road, he daydreamed about how rich he would be, in less than three months time. He was so deep in thought, that he didn't notice the black car, which was still following him. On the way to his friend's house, he had to stop at a four-way stop sign, located at a crossroad.

He reached his friends house and found a note on the front door. It read *"Sorry, I had to go to my kid's school. Let's make it another time."* Gerry was a little peeved, because his friend could have at least called his cell phone and let him know of the issue, concerning his child.

Gerry decided there was no point in waiting for his friend. He turned his car around and started back home. He took the same route back that he had come on. As he came over the crest of the hill and down toward the four-way stop sign, he didn't notice the gravel truck speeding up behind him. In fact, it was traveling at close to sixty miles per hour. When Gerry stopped at the four-way stop, he looked in his rear view mirror, and saw the large gravel truck, coming down the road at the high rate of speed

"Cripes," he thought. *"If I don't move quickly, it's going to wipe me out."*

He floored his car and, at the same time, did a quick left turn. The gravel truck sped through the four-way stop sign, without even slowing down at all. Gerry escaped unhurt, but he was a little shaken up. He realized it had been a very close call. The rest of the way home, he drove with a sharp eye, on his rear view mirror.

The man in the Ford got on the phone, to the driver of the gravel truck, and told him they would have to try again later.

Gerry made it home safely and had a cold beer, to calm his nerves. When Diana came home, he told her all about the near miss.

The next day, Gerry decided to go into Harrisburg to do some shopping. Diana didn't want to go, as she was tired and wanted to rest. After breakfast, Gerry climbed into his Mustang and started out toward Harrisburg. As previously, he didn't notice the car behind him, which kept quite a distance away, so as not to attract his attention. The driver of the trailing vehicle was in touch, by cell phone, with a man in a large oil tanker.

As Gerry came to a stop sign, he looked in his rear view mirror and didn't see any vehicle coming up behind him. As he took his foot off the brake and proceeded through the intersection, the oil tanker came from the left and hit him on the driver's side. The impact was such that he didn't have a chance. He was thrown out of the car, since he did not have his seat belt on. His head hit the concrete road and he was killed instantly. At least he didn't suffer.

The oil truck sped off down the road and parked over the next crest, in a wooded area. The driver jumped out and climbed into the waiting car. The two men took off and didn't wait for the police to arrive. The driver called Chicago and told the person at the other end, "This is Antonio, in Pennsylvania. The problem has been taken care of."

There was one witness to the crash, but she was not of much use to the police. The witness stated she thought it was an oil tanker and told them in which direction it went. Later, the police found the vehicle, hidden in the woods, about two miles away. However, there were no clues to identify the driver; no DNA or fingerprints. The truck had been stolen a few days before in Harrisburg, and the company that owned it had not even filed a theft report yet.

His death was listed as a hit and run, by person or persons unknown.

From Gerry's driver license, they obtained his address, and an officer went to his house. They rang the bell and Diana came to the door. The police explained what had happened and expressed their condolences. Somehow, Diana was not totally surprised, after his near miss the previous day. She wondered why anyone would want to kill him and speculated that maybe it had something to do with the money he brought home, back in September.

Later, as she was packing and cleaning up the apartment, to move out to a smaller place, she found the forty-five thousand dollars, remaining from the fifty thousand Gerry had earned, and placed it in her suitcase. With the money was a piece of paper, with a USB account number, and a promissory note dated for the 9th of December. She wasn't sure what it all meant, but she took it anyway. Perhaps a lawyer friend of hers could determine what the USB account was all about.

47

Confession

On Thursday, the 13th of October, Alan Burgess called the Tennessee Governor's office on his secure cell phone, stated that he was a retired Air Force colonel and requested to speak with the governor. He explained to the governor's assistant that the matter, he wished to discuss with her, was of the utmost importance and concerned the Nation's security. After a couple of minutes, Martha Cartwright came on the line.

"Normally, I don't take calls from citizens directly, but since you stated that you were a military officer and it was in the Nation's interest, I've made an exception. What can I do for you?"

"My name is Alan Burgess and I'm a retired Colonel of the United States Air Force. I am calling you to request a meeting with you, tomorrow, concerning an issue that is critical to the survival of the Nation."

"Colonel Burgess, as I am sure you understand, I have a very busy schedule. Please call back in thirty minutes on the number you just called in on, and my assistant will inform you, if there is any time that I am free. Good day."

Alan called back in thirty minutes and talked to the Governor's administrative assistant. She said that the Governor could see him the next day, for fifteen minutes at 2:00 pm. She was sorry, but the rest of the day's calendar was filled in. Alan told her that he would be there at the governor's office, at 2:00 pm sharp.

After ending her conversation with Alan Burgess, Governor Cartwright called Ian Black, her principal advisor.

"Ian, do you know a retired Air Force colonel, named Alan Burgess?"

"His name sounds familiar and I believe I've met him, but I can't recall when or where. I came across many officers during my twenty years in the Air Force and many years at the aerospace company," replied Ian.

"Could you please check the colonel out and give me a report first thing tomorrow morning?"

"Sure thing, governor." replied Ian. "I'll check his background and write up a short biography."

In response, the governor said, "Thanks, I will appreciate that. Can you also be here in my office, at the 2:00 pm meeting tomorrow that I have with this Alan Burgess? I'll need you there just in case he brings up some important information, and it's always useful to have another set of ears, at a meeting like this."

Colonel Black checked out the background of Alan Burgess:

> Born: 1954
> University: Notre Dame 1974-1979
> USAF: 1979 -2004
> NSC: Assistant to the National Security Advisor
> Rank: Colonel. Passed over for general due to some remarks he made about Joint Chiefs.
> Assignments: Last One: set up eight missile sites for the Bomarc C
> Divorced: Affair with unnamed woman, wife wanted divorce; one son who attended Virginia Tech.

After Ian saw on Burgess's bio that he worked on the Bomarc C program, it dawned on him he was the Air Force colonel who had visited him at Boeing, a few weeks after the terrorist attack on America. Subsequent to that visit and the finalization of the missile manufacturing contract terms, Ian had only occasional contact with him. He had assigned a program manager to interface with the White House and Colonel Burgess on the "Red Moon" project.

Upon receiving confirmation that he would be able to meet with the governor the next day, Alan Burgess decided that he had better leave immediately for Nashville, since it was more than a six hour drive on I-81 and I-40. As a precaution, he thought it would be best if he went in a rental car. So, he called Alamo and arranged for them to meet him at 10:00 am, in the rear parking area of his favorite restaurant. He then got into his car and drove to the Hales Coffee Shop, ten minutes from his house. There he had an early lunch, paid his bill and talked to the manager, whom he knew very well, about leaving his car overnight, in the rear lot. Burgess walked to the men's restroom, carrying a small overnight bag, and looked out the window. After he ascertained that there were two Alamo cars with drivers in the parking lot, he climbed out of the window and walked over to the cars. He signed the rental car papers that were handed to him by the Alamo representative, climbed into the black coupe and took off for the Tennessee state capital. The other car returned to the Alamo office in Roanoke, with the two men. All the way to Nashville, Burgess kept an eye on his rear view mirror to insure he was not being followed. He planned to stay at the Sheraton in downtown Nashville, near the State Capitol building, so that he would be rested, when he went to see Governor Cartwright at 2:00 pm the following day.

Burgess arrived in Nashville around 5:00 pm, as the sun was just starting to set. The clocks would not be moved back to standard time for about two more weeks. Driving from Roanoke to Nashville gained him one hour, since a few miles, west of Knoxville, he left the Eastern Time Zone and entered the Central Time Zone. He found the Sheraton, which was a block away from the State Capitol Building, registered under an assumed name and went to his room. He tried to get some rest, but found it hard to go to sleep, since his mind was thinking about the past two months and what he was going to tell Governor Cartwright. He made sure the room door was well bolted, just in case someone did follow him.

The next day, Alan had a leisurely late breakfast and bypassed lunch. He was too nervous to eat any more. At 1:30 pm he left the hotel, walked to the Capitol and entered the lobby. The time was ten minutes to two. He went up to the security desk, showed his Uniformed Services ID card and said he was there to see the governor. The guard looked up his name on the daily visitor list, passed him through the security screen and directed him to the elevators.

"Go to the eleventh floor for the governor's office", said the guard.

At the appointed time of 2:00 pm exactly, the governor's secretary knocked on the governor's office door and announced that Colonel Alan Burgess had arrived.

"Please show him in," Governor Cartwright said.

Alan Burgess walked in and put his hand out, to shake the governor's hand. "I'm pleased to meet you'" he said.

The governor then turned to a gentlemen seated back in the corner of the office and said, "Colonel Burgess, I'd like you to meet Colonel Ian Black."

It was then that Ian Black was positive this man was the same Colonel Burgess who visited him at Boeing, several years ago. If Burgess recognized Ian, he didn't let on.

"How may I help you Colonel Burgess?" said Governor Cartwright.

"I appreciate this opportunity to talk with you and I will come straight to the point," said Colonel Burgess. "I was the leader of a group called the Red Moon team. It consisted of six men, including myself, and our objective was to break into a base called Camp Warrior, near Camp Lejeune, in North Carolina. Once inside the camp, we overpowered the guard, reprogrammed two of the Bomarc missiles, with coordinates for the U.S. Senate and House Chambers of the Capitol, located in Washington, D.C. We launched the missiles manually from the blockhouse, and they hit the Capitol building about ten minutes later. A key part of the plan was that the Red Moon team would act and speak as though we were Arabs. In other words, it was designed as a false flag operation, in order to fool investigators.

My contact in the White House was Valda Lewis, so I have to assume the plan was approved at highest levels of the government.

I now regret that I was involved in this operation. I was bitter about being passed over for general and was offered a lot of money. I would have had a comfortable retirement with the money."

During the brief few moments he made this shocking statement to the governor, he nervously shifted from one foot to the other, and at times looked down at the floor.

Ian Black then realized his BFO, back at Camp Warrior was correct. This whole operation was run by Americans, not Islamic terrorists. He had been right all along, but did not have enough collaborative proof, until now.

The governor asked Alan Burgess, "Do you have anything in writing from Valda Lewis, about this operation?"

"No, all instructions were verbal. However, I made two secret audio recordings, in order to protect myself, if need be. Here are two copies for you, to use as you see fit. In addition, there must a written order somewhere, for the transfer of the test missiles and equipment, which were shipped from the Kansas storage base to Chanute AFB.

My understanding was that this attack on the Capitol was to be used as an excuse to declare a state of emergency and to cancel the presidential election."

Governor Cartwright looked at Alan Burgess with a thoughtful look and said, "Thank you Colonel Burgess for coming in and informing us of this situation. We appreciate the details that you have given us on the missile attack and for giving us the two recordings. We will of course have to verify the facts. Do you have a phone number you could share with us, in case we want to contact you for more information? Colonel Black here will see you out and you can give him your contact information. I can assure you it will be kept confidential. Again, thank you for coming in."

With that she shook hands with Alan Burgess and said goodbye.

Ian Black said, "Follow me colonel, I'll show you the way out."

As they walked out of the office toward the elevator, Burgess gave him a card with a phone number written on it.

As he entered the elevator, Colonel Black said, "Thank you for bringing this situation to the governor's attention. We'll be in touch. If you push the "starred" button, the elevator will take you to the main entrance floor. I hope you have a safe drive home."

"Good day, Colonel Black," replied Burgess.

With that he pushed the "starred" button, the elevator doors slowly closed and it descended, taking Colonel Burgess down from the eleventh floor to the main floor.

Ian Black then went back into the governor's office, to discuss the information Alan Burgess had just given them.

"Governor, Alan Burgess has just confirmed what we have suspected all along, since the missile attack. It looks like the president is making a grab for power, with the declaration of a state of emergency and the cancellation of the election. In addition, we have the NPF running wild, arresting people. This looks like the start of a dictatorship, to me."

The governor replied, "I believe you're correct. However, it would be great if we could get confirmation of who was involved in the missile attack, from another source. The two recordings will be useful, if we can confirm whose voice is on them.

"I believe that I'll cancel my other meetings, so we can listen to these tapes immediately. Do you have time right now?" she asked Ian.

"Yes," Ian replied. "Just give me a minute to call my office."

A few minutes later, Governor Cartwright and Ian listened to the two tapes left with them, by the colonel.

"Those tapes leave no doubt about the nature of the missile attack. I have heard Valda Lewis talk before and it certainly sounds like her voice." Martha said. "It would be nice to obtain something in writing about the attack. I think I'll call to my friend, Governor Prince, to determine his thoughts on the Washington situation. I'll immediately have a voice expert examine the tapes and compare them against Valda Lewis's voice."

48

Incriminating Letter

Alan Burgess telephoned John Norman on Sunday, the 16th of October, to see how he was doing. Alan knew John from before, when they were both in the Air Force and he thought highly of him.

"Hello. This is John. Who's calling?"

"This is Alan Burgess. How are you? I'm glad I reached you"

"Hello, colonel. I'm doing fairly well, thanks. What can I do for you?"

Burgess responded. "I was just calling to make sure you're okay. I've been trying to call everyone on the team to check and see how they're doing. I called Gerry Davies the other day and received no response. The line seemed to be out of service. I then called Pasco Martinez's number in Florida and his wife Maria answered. She was very distraught and told me that Pasco had died, when his new boat blew up, a little over a month ago.

After calling around about Gerry Davies, I managed to get hold of someone in the local police department, who told me he had been killed in a vehicle accident. I also haven't been able to connect with Chris Smith in Atlanta or Mike Thornburn in Prescott. John, you know these deaths and the missing team members sound a little suspicious to me. You'd better be careful, just in case."

"Thanks for the warning, colonel. I'll try to telephone some of them myself. I appreciate your call." With that, they both hung up.

Two days later, John Norman called Pasco's widow Maria in Miami, to find out exactly what happened to Pasco.

"Mrs. Martinez. This is John Norman, a friend of Pasco's, calling from Tennessee. I'm sorry to hear the news of his accident, please accept my sympathies."

Maria responded, "Thank you for calling John. It's been a very trying time for me and the children. What can I do for you?"

John replied, "I worked with Pasco for the past few months on a special project and I would like to know what exactly happened. I'm a little concerned for my own safety."

"Well John, he bought a new boat and had it checked out, at the marina service department. He then took it out into the Atlantic to go fishing. From a witness some distance away, the boat just blew up and sank beneath the waves. Other than some debris, there were not many clues left, for the police to analyze. They closed the case and called it an accidental death. They figured there must have been a fuel leak and the fumes ignited. That's about all I can tell you."

John responded, "Thank you for the information. Again, please accept my condolences. If I can be of any help, please don't hesitate to call. I really liked working with Pasco and would do anything to help him and his family."

"Thank you, John. Goodbye." With that she hung up the phone.

Next, John called Gerry Davies's number. He was surprised that someone answered, because he assumed from Alan Burgess's call the line was disconnected.

"This is Diana. How may I help you?"

"This is John Norman, Diana. I'm a friend of Gerry Davies. May I speak to him?"

"John, I'm sorry to tell you that Gerry was killed in a vehicle accident nine days ago. I was just about to close the front door, since I am moving out to my own place. I've already had the phone service here cancelled, but the phone company hasn't turned it off yet. There really isn't much to tell you about the accident. It was caused by an oil tanker, but the police never caught the driver. It was written down as a hit and run."

"Thanks for the information. Please accept my condolences," John said. He hung up and started to sweat, thinking about the two deaths.

John tried to reach the other two men on the Red Moon team, but he couldn't reach either of them, just as Alan Burgess hadn't been able to. Both phones were no longer in service and that seemed a little odd. He called for operator assistant, and they said that they had no new telephone numbers for them.

After hearing both of these reports, John became very suspicious and decided to write a letter to the Governor of Tennessee, to be mailed in case something happened to him.

Although he had not written a letter to a Governor before, he wanted to make sure she received the truth. John Norman's letter to the Tennessee Governor, Martha Cartwright, whom he had a lot of admiration for, was as follows:

****

RICHARD AND BARBARA OSBORN

1801 Cambridge Road
Franklin
TN 37064
October 21

Governor Martha Cartwright
State Capitol Building
Nashville
TN 37243-0001

Dear Governor Cartwright,

If you receive this letter, it means I have been killed to silence what I know. I have therefore written this letter and given it to a friend to mail, in case of my demise.

I was involved in the September 9 attack, on Washington, D.C. We were misled as to the true target. We were informed that the target was to be the Pentagon, and we only found out after the attack that the actual target was the Capitol. There was a team of six men that took over Camp Warrior, in North Carolina, and launched the two Bomarc missiles toward Washington. We pretended to be Muslim extremists, but we were in reality all Americans, who were bitter in one way or another with the Pentagon. We felt the military let us down, after putting our life on the line.

Besides me, the team members were:

Alan Burgess, USAF Colonel Retired – Leader
Mike Thornburn, USA Iraq Veteran
Gerry Davies, USMC Iraq Veteran
Pasco Martinez, USN retired
Chris Smith, USAF Staff Sergeant retired

It is my understanding that this false flag operation was directed by the White House, so as to have an excuse to declare a state of emergency. After reflection, I am not proud of what I have done. Please forgive me.

God Bless America.

Sincerely

John Norman
USAF Sergeant Retired

****

John called Bill, a good friend of his, who lived just down the road. They had grown up as school mates and had gone through all the way, from Elementary to High School together.

"Bill. This is John. I need a favor of you. May I come over to your home and tell you what it is?"

"Sure, good buddy. Come on over."

"I'll be there in about ten minutes."

John drove over to Bill's home and entered after knocking.

"Bill. This is very important. I've written this letter and I'd like you to mail it, if anything happens to me."

With that, he handed Bill the letter.

"Why do you want me to do this? Are you in some kind of trouble or something?" asked Bill.

John replied, "Please don't ask me any questions. Can I depend on you to do this favor for me? It's very important."

"Of course, you can. When have I ever let you down?"

John replied, "Please keep this as a secret between the two of us. For your own good, don't tell anyone I gave you this letter."

"Okay. You can count on me."

They shook hands and agreed to meet in a few days, to play golf at the local country club.

On Saturday, the 22nd of October, John decided to go fishing at a lake in the area, close to his home. He liked fishing, because it was a quiet sport where he could think. He arose at 7:30 am and had a leisurely breakfast with his wife. Their two children were still asleep and would have breakfast later. It was a great morning to go fishing. The sun was shining and the temperature was around fifty-five degrees. It wasn't supposed to rain for the next four days.

RICHARD AND BARBARA OSBORN

At 9:00 am, he loaded his own car, rather than the Odyssey van provided by Atlas Transportation, with fishing equipment and a portable chair. He kissed his wife goodbye and said "I'll be back by noon and then all four of us will go to Burger King for lunch. I'll call you on my cell, when I leave the lake to come home."

He drove off toward his favorite fishing area, Percy Priest Lake, where the fish were generally always biting. It took him about thirty minutes to get there, at the posted speed limit. He parked the car and walked through the oak trees, carrying his equipment toward the lake. It was deserted, so he was able to pick any fishing location he wanted. He guessed everyone was sleeping in that day or getting ready to watch college football. The Tennessee Volunteers were doing fairly well this year, for a change.

He set up his chair in his favorite spot and cast out his fishing rod. As he sat on the bank watching his float bob up and down, he thought about his life, his beautiful wife and children. He knew that he had been lucky most of his life.

Then, he thought about the missile attack and the ten million dollars sitting in a Swiss bank account, which would be his in less than two months. The money would solve all his family's financial problems. He did feel a few pangs of regret about the deaths in Washington, but believed most of those politicians deserved it. They had cut his military pension and did not seem to care about the veterans medical or psychological problems.

At 11:30 am, he decided that he should head home to take the family to lunch. He had not caught any fish, but he enjoyed the peace and quiet. He packed up his equipment and walked back to the car. He was surprised to find the car was unlocked. He was sure he had locked it, as he always did, when leaving it in a parking lot. He assumed he just forgotten to lock it this time. It bothered him a little and put it off to old age. He looked in the car to make sure nothing was missing. Everything looked okay. He loaded the fishing equipment in the car, climbed in and started the engine. He placed the car in "drive" and proceeded down the gravel path, toward the main road.

As he reached the main road, he turned left and drove back toward town and his home. He went about one half mile down the road when a man, following behind him in a blue van, pushed a red button on a transmitter, he held in his hand. The car driven by John exploded into flames and jumped about twenty feet into the air, before settling back down onto the road. John Norman never knew what happened. His life ended in an instant.

The van following quickly turned around and sped off. A police car came along in a few minutes, after receiving a call from a motorist, who came across the wreck. They identified the car license plate and determined who owned it. They drove to his house and told his wife that she was now a widow. She broke down in hysterics and called her sister, who lived nearby.

John's boyhood friend, to whom he had given the letter addressed to Governor Cartwright, saw the police cars outside the house. He went over and talked to the police. They told him that John had been killed in a car explosion and the case was under investigation.

He decided to take the letter to the post office first thing, as he had promised John. He was sorry for his friend's death and wondered what John had gotten himself into. He thought, *"Well, I hope he didn't suffer."*

Tennessee Governor Cartwright's office received John Norman's letter on Tuesday morning, the 25th of October. The governor's secretary opened up the letter and read it. She thought that the governor should see it right away and took it immediately into her office.

The governor read the letter and then called Ian Black, to inform him of its contents. After she had discussed Norman's letter with Ian, she placed it in a file, labeled Edward Tuckwell.

49

Tennessee and Texas

After listening to President Tuckwell's 10th of October speech, hearing Alan Burgess's information, listening to the audio recordings and reading John Norman's letter, Tennessee Governor Cartwright decided that it was time she had a meeting with Governor Prince. She picked up the phone and called the Texas Governor's private number.

"This is Governor Prince. Who's calling?"

"Hello Chuck, This is Martha Cartwright. How are you?"

"I'm fine. It's a pleasure to talk with you again, but I suspect this call is more than just pleasantries, correct?"

"Yes, you're right. This is a business call. I've some important information I'd like to discuss with you, but I can't do it over the phone. If you're free tomorrow, I'd like to fly to Austin to meet with you in person."

"Let me check my schedule with the secretary. Please hold on."

"Sure."

In about a minute, the Texas Governor came back on the phone.

"Martha. I had some minor meetings scheduled for tomorrow that I can move to another day. What time do you think you'll be here?"

"Thanks, Chuck. I'll leave Nashville at around 8:00 am and should be at your office by about 11.00 am. I plan to return home around 3.00 pm. I assume we're free to talk in your office, with no chance of the NSA or others listening in. There's one other point. I'll be bringing my advisor, Colonel Ian Black, with me. Is it acceptable to you that he attend our meeting?"

"Yes. We're free to talk here. I have this office checked for bugs frequently. On the other point, I've complete confidence in Colonel Black. So yes, it'll be fine for him to attend. I look forward to seeing both of you here tomorrow at eleven o'clock."

"I look forward to meeting with you also. See you tomorrow."

With that they both hung up.

After Governor Cartwright hung up the phone, she then dialed Ian Black's number.

"Ian, this is Martha. Are you available to fly with me to Austin tomorrow, to meet with Governor Prince? We need to discuss the missile attack and the current state of affairs, affecting the Nation."

Ian replied, "Yes, Governor. My schedule is totally open tomorrow, so there'll be no conflict. What time will we be leaving?"

"We should be at the airport no later than 8:00 am. I'll meet you there at eight or before. We'll be flying in the State's plane."

On Wednesday, the 26th of October, Governor Cartwright, together with Ian Black, flew to Austin Texas, on the State of Tennessee's government jet. They cleared the runway at 8:10 am and arrived at Austin airport at 10:35 am. On the way, Governor Cartwright gave Ian a short briefing on what was to be discussed there.

When they arrived, they found that Governor Prince had arranged ground transportation for them, and they were driven straight to his office. By 11:00 am, they were being ushered into the Texas governor's office in the State Capitol and served with a cup of coffee.

Approximately thirty seconds later, Governor Prince walked in and offered his apologies for not being there to greet them.

"Martha. It's good to see you again. I hope you don't mind first names behind closed doors." With that, he shook her hand. He then turned to Colonel Black and said, "Glad you could join us. May I call you Ian?"

"Sure. Nice to meet you again, Governor Prince." He said with a smile, as they shook hands."

"Okay, let's get down to business. I assume neither of you came here just for a cup of our great Texas coffee. Let's sit down at this conference table."

Governor Prince led them both over to a large oak table and they all sat down at one end.

"Martha. Since you called this meeting, why don't you lead off?"

"Okay. Ian, as I go through this, you may interrupt me at any time. Let's look at the facts concerning the state of the Nation.

First, the Capitol was hit by two Bomarc missiles from a Camp Warrior near Camp Lejeune, North Carolina. There was a team of six men in black, with ski masks, who broke into the camp and fired the missiles. They knew enough technically to program the missiles and to bypass the cable to NORAD and SOCC.

Second, they spoke with an accent and were, or pretended to be, of Arabic descent. They all used Arabic names.

Third, they left behind an operating manual for some of the Bomarc components, in Arabic, and also a copy of the Koran.

Fourth, none of them spoke Arabic while they were there. The guard who was tied up said they all spoke English, with a foreign accent.

Fifth, an Alan Burgess, who's a former colonel in the United States Air Force, came to my office on the 14th of this month and told me that he was the leader of this group, named the Red Moon team. He also led me to believe that the plan came out of the White House, but he offered no written proof. However, he did give me two audio recordings that he'd secretly made of meetings between Valda Lewis and himself, on the 10th and 14th of March.   We had a voice expert examine the tapes, and he confirmed one of the voices on the tapes is Valda Lewis. The White House wanted a good reason to be able to declare a state of emergency. They felt that blowing up the Capitol would do it. Thus, they created a false flag operation, so the missile attack could be blamed on Muslim extremists. We had him checked out and we've no reason to believe he fabricated this story. Alan Burgess hadn't broken any Tennessee law, so we had no authority to detain him, at that time. We've tried to contact him later, to no avail."

I also received a letter a few days ago, from one of the team members. The letter was to be mailed in case something happened to him. His name was John Norman and he died tragically in a car that blew up, killing him instantly. The police forensic team discovered traces of an explosive, in the remains of the vehicle. They've listed it as a homicide, by person or persons unknown."

"Now, let me play the two recordings for you."

Governor Cartwright inserted the first tape into the recorder she brought with her and then subsequently played the second one.

Governor Prince listened to the recordings and, when they were finished, remarked, "That was indeed Valda Lewis. I'd recognize her voice anywhere. Those tapes indicate that the White House was involved in the missile attacks and will provide the evidence in any investigation or trial.

"Yes, I thought the recordings would be useful, if we need any firm evidence. How am I doing so far, Ian?" continued Governor Cartwright.

Ian responded "Governor, I couldn't have given the details any better myself. The only point I'd like to add is that I visited Camp Warrior, a few minutes after the firing of the missiles. I was attending a meeting at the U.S. Marines' Camp Lejeune on terrorism, when we heard the first missile exhaust noise. We all rushed outside and happened to see the second missile ascending into the sky.

We followed a group of Marines who went to investigate the incident. We drove for about fifteen minutes behind the Marines and then came across this Camp Warrior. I'd never heard of it before. We entered the Camp and found the guard tied up. After he was released, he told the Duty Officer what had occurred.

I thought at the time that the entry into the camp and the missile firing was too neat and tidy. The guard had no warning that they were in the Camp, which meant the group must have had information about the Camp security system. In addition, the guard said that the terrorists only spoke English, while they were there, no Arabic. I've had extensive work experience in intelligence and to me it looked like a false flag operation. It seemed like they were trying to hide their identities and nationalities."

Chuck responded "That sounds very interesting Ian. Martha do you have any other thoughts or information?"

Martha continued, "Yes. As we all know, President Tuckwell has declared a state of emergency and cancelled the election scheduled for the 8th of November. He has also expanded the National Police Force, arrested members of the press and shut down Fox News. It appears to me we're heading toward a dictatorship. We've heard rumors coming out of Washington that he doesn't intend to give up the office and plans to stay in the White House indefinitely. There's no firm documentation on this; just rumors, but all the events, as of late, point to that."

"Do we have anything in writing at all about the missile firings?" Governor Prince asked.

Ian replied, "Nothing concrete, except what's on the tapes. According to Alan Burgess, the Red Moon team leader, all instructions were verbal; nothing in writing. His contact, throughout the entire, mission was Valda Lewis, the president's chief advisor. However, for the training at Chanute AFB, two Bomarc C's missiles, together with test equipment and spare guidance modules, were delivered to the base by an Air Force officer and crew. They were signed for by a member of the Atlas Movie Company that we believe is a front for the mob. These missiles were delivered to the old Chanute AFB and later returned to a storage base, near Wichita. There should be a record somewhere in the Air Force, for these movements and who authorized them. It'll probably take a while to track them down, if they haven't already been destroyed."

"The main issue to me is that I feel the Nation is being threatened by a potential dictator," said Chuck. "Whether or not he caused the missiles to be fired, is up to a court of law to decide. Obviously it could be a case of mass murder. However, his declaration of a state of emergency and then cancelling the presidential election is contrary to the Constitution. I believe we should hold a news conference in the near future, with other governors and demand that President Tuckwell resign the office. If he doesn't, then we should use our National Guards to oust and arrest him. We need to do this, before he gathers too much power and uses the NPF, as an "SS" unit."

"I agree with your suggestion. If you concur, tomorrow the 12th of October, I'll set up a conference call for 2:00PM CST between you, I and other concerned governors. Specifically, I propose that we discuss the issues, with the governors of North Carolina, Wisconsin, South Carolina, Pennsylvania, Virginia, Alabama, Kentucky, Michigan, Oklahoma, Ohio and Alaska, in order to develop a consensus, on what we should do.

"I think that's a great idea, Martha," Chuck said. "How would you like some lunch, while we continue to discuss this problem? I can have my assistant place an order with a nearby deli and get sandwiches delivered, if that's okay."

"Great idea," Martha said. "Make mine ham and Swiss on rye, warm please."

"Make that two of them", said Ian.

Chuck left the room for a moment, to talk with his assistant, and then came back in saying, "Everything's ordered."

They continued discussing the situation in Washington and President Tuckwell. In a few minutes, lunch was delivered from the nearby deli.

Over the lunch, they discussed the events of the past eight months that started with the executive order forming the NPF.

While they were talking, Governor Prince had his assistant call the offices of the other governors to set up the conference call at 2:00 pm the next day. Governor Cartwright would initiate the calls using scramblers. One never knew who would be listening nowadays.

"Before you have to leave," Governor Prince said, "let me review what I believe I've heard, about all the major points in this matter.

One: On the 9th of September, two missiles were fired at the Capitol, on orders from the White House. There's evidence to this fact from an audio recording and the testimony of two participants that this was a false flag operation, carried out in order to blame Islamic terrorists.

Two: On the same day, the president created a state of emergency to get special powers.

Three: The president ordered the creation of the National Police Force on the 25th of March and then expanded it on the 23rd of September.

Four: On the 10th of October, Tuckwell shut down a news organization and also had newspaper correspondents, who were critical of his presidency, arrested.

Five: On the 24th of October, the president cancelled the election, scheduled for the 8th of November.

I believe this is enough to impeach any president, but there're not enough Senators for a quorum."

"That's our understanding too, Chuck. It appears the states must do something to stop this madness in Washington. I believe it's imperative that we take action quickly, while we, and the other governors, are still somewhat in control of our states."

At 2:30 pm, Governor Cartwright and Ian Black rose to leave for the airport.

Chuck came over to them and shook their hands. "Thanks for coming. It's a dire situation our Nation is in. I'll get prepared for tomorrow's conference call."

Governor Cartwright and Ian Black went back to the airport in the vehicle, provided by Governor Prince. They took off at just past 3:00 pm and landed in Nashville around 5:30 pm.

The pilot taxied to the airport reception area where the Tennessee State jets normally were parked, and then the governor and Ian disembarked.

As they walked to their respective cars from the airport reception area, Governor Cartwright said "Thank you, Ian, for your support and advice. You're an invaluable asset to me. Can we meet tomorrow at my office around 1:30 pm? I'd like to talk with you before the scheduled conference call."

"Sure" Ian replied.   "I'll see you then.   Sleep well Martha."

With that, they went their separate ways to their homes.

50

Governors Meet

Precisely at 2:00 pm on Thursday, the 27th of October, Governor Cartwright's assistant set up the conference call to the eleven State governors, plus of course Texas, as agreed upon in yesterday's meeting with Governor Prince. In a few minutes, everyone was on the conference call line.

Martha Cartwright started the discussion. "This is Governor Martha Cartwright. I hope all of us are talking on scramblers, to prevent unauthorized people from listening in."

All of the governors replied to the affirmative.

"Good," said Governor Cartwright. "We can't be too careful these days. Yesterday, I had a meeting with Governor Prince, and we decided that our two States could no longer ignore the events, going on in Washington. It's been brought to our attention, by two participants, that the missile attack on the 9th of September was a false flag operation, to create an atmosphere where the general population would accept a state of emergency declaration. Although, we don't have definite written proof, it appears it was directed by someone in the White House. Valda Lewis, the president's senior advisor, was directly involved in providing leadership for the operation. We've two voice recordings, and she has been identified by a voice expert, as one of the voices. Given all the measures President Tuckwell has put into place, in violation to the principles set down in the Constitution, we've decided that we must resist his grab for dictatorial powers. The last straw was the cancellation of the 8th of November federal election for president and other offices. I therefore suggest a fivefold approach to the issue.

First, make preparations to take our National Guard units to Washington, including planning the operation. This should be done in a way, so as not to draw too much attention, at this time.

Second, on the 12th of November, I will speak to the nation about the issues, concerning this administration.

Third, a group of us will hold a news conference, on the 1st of December, to call for the president's resignation.

Fourth, if he doesn't resign, then we will proceed to march on Washington, with our National Guard troops, to force him from office. This timetable will allow the participating states to make plans and coordinate them for the advance on Washington, with minimal bloodshed and casualties.

Finally, we're instructing our state attorney general to sue the federal government in court, over its constitutional right to declare a state of emergency and cancel the presidential election.

I also suggest that Ian Black, my senior advisor, who has extensive experience in intelligence and organizational planning, with the British Army and the United States Air Force, be the coordinator between the various states National Guards. Are there any comments or changes any of you would like to make to this overall plan?"

One by one each governor on the conference call agreed with the overall plan Governor Cartwright had laid out and asked her to keep them informed, as the situation warranted. They all said that they would have their National Guard commanders draw up contingency plans, for the march on Washington, starting the 3rd of December. In addition, they said that they would keep her and Ian informed of their progress and any issues.

"Thank you all for participating in this call and for your overall approval of the plan of action. I really regret having to do this, but I see no alternative, in order to save our Nation.

Again, thank you for approving the plan. This is a grave situation we find ourselves in, and this kind of decision does not come easily. Any plan of action, we do make, is serious and not to be taken lightly. I'll keep in touch with all of you, on a regular basis. Goodbye for now."

The governors said goodbye in turn, and then everyone disconnected their phones.

51

Governor Cartwright Speaks

Martha Cartwright delivered her address to the country on the night of the 12th of November, at 9:00 pm EST (6:00 pm PST). This prime time slot, on a Saturday night, gave her the largest national audience possible.

"Good evening, my fellow Americans and patriots. For those of you who do not know me, my name is Martha Cartwright and I am the lawfully elected governor of Tennessee. I want to discuss with you the events that have taken place in this great republic, during the past few weeks. Our Nation is a country of laws. Without them, we have no freedom and no liberty. Over the past two centuries, our ancestors fought, and some died, to protect our liberties.

We now are in a situation where we have a president who does not believe in the Constitution, even though he swore to uphold it. He only obeys laws, or parts of them, that meet his goals. History is full of dictators and uncivilized people, who wanted to enslave others, so that they can have absolute control.

We cannot tolerate this seizing of power by Edward Tuckwell. His cancellation of the presidential election was the last straw. Edward Tuckwell should be impeached, for not protecting the constitution, and thrown out of office. Since many of the senators and congressman have been killed or wounded, it is impossible to get a quorum, to even start impeachment proceedings.

Therefore, Tennessee, together with Texas, Kentucky, Alabama, Oklahoma, Michigan, Louisiana, North Carolina, Wisconsin, Pennsylvania, Ohio, New Jersey, Virginia, Alaska and several other freedom loving states, have started assembling and combining their National Guard forces, police and state trooper units, along with ordinary citizens. This is being accomplished under Title 32 of the United States Code that allows governors to declare a state of emergency and call up their National Guards and militias.

Under this law, which was enacted on the 10th of August, 1956, the governors of their respective states can act as commanders-in-chief. If we have to, we will march on Washington, to free this nation from Edward Tuckwell and his cronies, with all their corruption and tyranny.

We are calling for the support of all Americans. No matter whether you are Afro Americans, European Americans, Asian Americans, Hispanics, Catholics, Protestants, Buddhists, etc., you are all Americans. We ask you to support our National Guard members and their families, and, if you are able, join us in this drive on Washington, in order to get our freedoms back. We will root out all this corruption and return the Nation to its rightful owners – you the people.

Let us march together, for freedom and liberty

God bless America.

Thank you and goodnight.

I'll see you all in Washington."

The phones in the Tennessee Capitol building and Governor Cartwright's office began ringing immediately, after her broadcast ended. The calls were from governors of other states pledging their support for the takeover of

Washington. All in all, forty-two states joined the effort to take back control of the government and American freedoms.

52

White House Reaction

Valda Lewis watched the broadcast by Governor Cartwright and thought *"This means trouble and it could become dangerous, if it's not firmly responded to."*

She called Andrew Taylor, the president's chief of staff.

"Andrew. Did you watch the broadcast by the Tennessee governor, which was on television a few minutes ago? This whole situation could get out of hand, if we don't do something quickly."

He responded, "I watched most of it. I think we should call the president and schedule an immediate meeting."

"I concur. Please contact the president and determine if we can have a meeting with him, within the hour."

"Okay. I'll call him right away and get back to you in a few minutes."

As soon as Andrew ended talking with Valda Lewis, he called Karen, the president's secretary, who was working late.

"Karen. This is Andrew Taylor. I would like to schedule an immediate meeting with the president about an important matter. Is he available?"

"Sir, he's upstairs in his living quarters talking to his wife. Is it important enough to interrupt him?"

"Yes, it is. Valda Lewis and I want to meet with him right away, concerning the Tennessee governor's speech that took place, just fifteen minutes ago."

"I'll call him right away, sir."

A few minutes later, Karen called Andrew Taylor back, and said, "Sir, he'll be able to meet with you, in the Oval Office, in thirty minutes."

"Thank you Karen. Would you please call Ms. Lewis and tell her also?"

"Yes sir. I'll call her immediately."

Karen called Valda Lewis's number.

"Yes?" she answered.

The president's secretary replied, "Ms. Lewis. There'll be a meeting with the president in the Oval Office, thirty minutes from now.

As scheduled, right on time, Andrew and Valda knocked on the Oval Office door.

"Come in," the president said.

They both entered and found the president seated at his desk.

"Okay, so what's so urgent?" he asked, a little irritated to be interrupted so late.

Valda replied, "Mr. President. About an hour ago, Governor Cartwright of Tennessee went on television, in a nationwide broadcast, and stated that several states are going to mass their troops, march on Washington and remove you from office."

"Who the hell does she think she is? I am the president and she's just a governor. We'll see who's in charge of this country. Valda, I want you to get hold of the Chairman of the Joint Chiefs, Admiral Trice, and have him prepare the federal troops, for possible deployment around Washington. In addition, inform the NPF to bring as many of their men as possible, to Washington, and create a wall of steel around the White House.   In order that my family is not held hostage, I'm going to send them on a trip to visit Prince Hassain, my old university friend.   We'll meet again tomorrow at 1:00 pm to discuss this matter further. Again, I won't let this woman, from a minor state in the South, try and run me out of office. I am the president of the United States. Do either of you two have any other suggestions?"

"No sir" replied Andrew Taylor "but we'll come up with some additional ideas by tomorrow's meeting."

As they both left the Oval Office, Valda said to Andrew, "I'm not sure, but I think the stress is getting to him. He's becoming unstable. I'll see you tomorrow, before we meet with him"

Valda then turned and walked back to her office. As she walked down the hallway, President Tuckwell came out of the Oval Office and asked her to return, for a private conversation.

The president and Valda went back into the Oval Office, and he closed the door.

"Is there anything the Committee can do to get us out of this predicament? They've supported me for nine years, and I would think that they would want to protect their investment."

"Edward, they've put their trust in me and my contact in Chicago. They're looking to us to come up with a way, to resolve your problems that are self inflicted."

"Valda, you and your Chicago friend persuaded me to run for president, and both of you are therefore just as responsible, as I am."

"Mr. President. I don't see it resolves anything to point fingers. Let's have a good night's rest, and we can talk about possible action at the 1:00 pm meeting tomorrow."

"Okay, but you better not let me down!" he replied angrily.

With that he stormed out of the Oval Office, leaving Valda standing there aghast.

She walked down the hallway and went into her office, closing the door behind her.   She picked up the phone and dialed Leo DiMaggio in Chicago.   He answered the phone, after two rings, and from the caller ID knew it was Valda.

"Valda, what's going on in Washington?   I watched that broadcast by Governor Cartwright."

"President Tuckwell wants to circle Washington with federal troops and reinforce the White House, with more NPF forces.   I'm afraid he's becoming paranoid and unstable. Most of the armed forces are still overseas, fighting in the Middle East.   I'm not sure how many troops Admiral Trice can base around Washington, to prevent the states from seizing the capital.   It all depends on how many states join the march on Washington, which Governor Cartwright has called for.   What do you want me to do?"

Leo responded, "I want you to control Edward Tuckwell and the situation.   The Committee will not look kindly on us if we fail, after all the money and effort put into this program."

"I'll do the best I can, Leo"

"You'd better succeed in squashing this rebellion.   Give me a call every day and brief me on the situation."

"I'll do that," she replied apprehensively.

With that, they both hung up.

"God," Valda thought. *"What a mess!"*

****

The next day, at one o'clock sharp, Valda Lewis and Andrew Taylor went to the Oval Office.   They both had some ideas for what actions should be taken.   The president walked in, a couple of minutes late.

"Well," he said tersely.   "What bright ideas have you come up with?"

Andrew spoke first.

"Mr. President, I've developed six ideas, four of which I recommend be enacted immediately, and the other two kept for future action, since there're problems associated with them.

First, we should immediately instruct the U.S. attorney general to file suit in Federal Court to stop the states from using the National Guards. Under Title 10 of the United States Code enacted in 1956, as Commander-in-Chief, of all forces, you've the right to federalize the state National Guards, in cases of emergencies. This right includes national disasters, rebellions and enforcement of federal laws.

Second, in line with the first suggestion, we should issue an order federalizing all fifty states National Guards, claiming there's a rebellion under way.

Third, we should instruct the Chairman of the Joint Chiefs, Admiral Trice, to prepare plans for roadblocks around Washington, D.C., in case the states' armed forces get this far.

Fourth, increase the presence of Federal marshals, DHS personnel and NPF officers in the rebellious states. The purpose would be to intimidate the states governments and make them believe they could be arrested under the Federal Government's state of emergency.

The other two ideas, which should be kept in reserve, are bring the troops stationed abroad home, to bolster the federal troops in the country. Additionally, we could attempt to use the non-participating states in the rebellion, to put pressure on the states that are involved.

Mr. President, I suggest you issue orders right away to accomplish my first four ideas."

"Thanks, Andrew. I will let you know my decision shortly. Valda, what ideas have you come up with?"

"Well, I've come up with five feasible ideas, which would help control the problems, if enacted with Andrew's ideas.

First, I'd cut off all Federal funds to the rebellious states. This includes road funds, Medicaid funds, disaster funds and the like. This would place pressure on the states' finances, so that they'd think twice about marching on Washington.

Second, I'd authorize flights by the Air Force to buzz, at low altitude, over all state capitols. This would remind them of the Federal Government's power and that you are the Commander-in-Chief.

Third, put out advertisements on television, pointing out to all citizens that any inconveniences they might come across are the fault of their respective state governments, and not the Federal Government. This would place pressure on the governors, by their citizens.

Fourth, I would use drones to spot any movement by the National Guards, so you can use available Federal troops to maximum advantage.

Fifth, I'd prepare and threaten the use of the Navy, to blockade rebellious states' ports, if they do not comply with your order to stand down and end their rebellion.

I would suggest that my five ideas be put in effect immediately, sir."

President Tuckwell thought for a moment and then said, "Andrew start preparations to put in effect your first four ideas, and Valda you prepare plans to put into action your first three ideas.

Tomorrow, I'll give you both my final decision, as to whether to proceed with these actions.

Thank you both for coming."

With that, Valda and Andrew left the Oval Office, looking at each other with a quizzical glance.

As they walked away, Valda said to Andrew, "Well, I guess we have to wait until tomorrow."

With that, she walked back to her office to call Leo and report to him about the meeting.

****

The next morning, the 14th of November, President Tuckwell picked up the phone in the Oval Office and buzzed his secretary.

"Karen, call Valda and Andrew and tell them to be here at 1:00 pm this afternoon, to continue our discussion of yesterday."

"Yes, Mr. President, right away."

Immediately, she contacted Ms. Lewis and Mr. Taylor and told them the president wanted them in his office, at one o'clock.

Exactly on time, both of them arrived outside the Oval Office and knocked on the door.

"Come in," the president said.

They both entered the office, and on a hand gesture from Tuckwell, sat down in the chairs facing his desk. The president looked sternly at them, like a school master does to errant children.

"I have studied the situation this Nation is in and the many ideas, you both presented to me yesterday. I believe that the governor of Tennessee is bluffing and would not dare challenge the authority of the Federal Government. Therefore, we do not need to make any rash moves until our position, vis-à-vis the states, becomes clearer. I do propose that we take three actions immediately, just in case the rebellious states do try something foolish.

First, we will instruct the attorney general to file suit in Federal Court, obtain a temporary injunction and a clarification on the rights of states to use their National Guards, under Title 10 of the United States Code. Second, as Commander-in-Chief of the Armed Forces, I will authorize the Air Force to fly, at a low altitude, over some of the mutinous states, as a show of strength. Finally, we will develop and televise commercials, which support our position and demonize the opposition.

I should point out, Andrew, that your suggestion, about bringing home some of our troops stationed around the world, is not feasible. Our total army today only numbers four hundred and fifty thousand and it is already stretched thin.

Do either of you have anything to add to this analysis and the recommended actions?"

"Mr. President, I believe you are taking this threat, by the states, far too lightly. Once they put in motion their plans to send their National Guards to Washington, it may be too late for us to do anything about it."

"Valda, I think you're blowing everything out of proportion. The Federal Government, with all its resources, is an entity not to be trifled with."

"Mr. President, with all due respect, I fear that the states may move faster than we can react. Shouldn't we take more action now?" asked Andrew.

"Have you ever known the states to act in unison over any issue? They always advance very slowly and generally only a few get together, to act as one."

The president continued, "I've made my recommendations, and I want you both to ensure they are carried out immediately. We'll meet back here in two weeks, to determine if we need to take any additional action; if the situation changes, we will meet at the earliest possible opportunity.

I now have to attend another meeting, concerning the Federal Trade Commission. Thank you for coming."

Then, President Tuckwell abruptly left the Oval Office, leaving Valda and Andrew sitting there, looking at each other in disbelief.

Shaking her head, Valda thought to herself, *I think he's lost it. I need to call Leo, he's not going to believe this."*

53

Northern Cyprus

The alarm clock woke Alan Burgess up at 5:00 am on Wednesday, the 23rd of November. He quickly got out of bed and turned the coffee pot on. While the coffee was brewing, he shaved and then took a shower. This was a big day for him. After he was dressed, he took two suitcases out of the closet and set them on the bed. He then packed them with his clothes, shoes and toilet articles.

He went into the kitchen, poured a cup of coffee, sat down at the kitchen table and looked around the room for the last time. He quickly drank the rest of the coffee, turned off the pot and returned to the bedroom. He closed both suitcases, locked them and carried them to the front door. He made sure he had his two passports, a U.S. one and a Swiss one, credit cards and the maximum allowable ten thousand dollars, in his briefcase. His case also contained a sheet of paper, with the name of the Swiss bank and the account number, provided by Atlas. The rest of the cash, ninety thousand dollars, he had deposited in ten U.S banks, with overseas branches; each deposit being no more than nine thousand dollars. This way the banks would not have to report them to the IRS; the minimum amount for banks to report was ten thousand.

He loaded up his own car, started the engine and drove to Roanoke Regional Airport. As usual, he was very careful and kept an eye on the rear view mirror, to make sure he was not being followed. He parked in the short term parking lot and looked for a cart. Luckily he found one and loaded it, with his luggage and briefcase. He locked the car up for the last time and pushed the cart into the terminal, all the time looking over his shoulder.

He went up to the US Airways counter and purchased a ticket, in the name of Hans Brunner, from Roanoke to Zurich, Switzerland, via Philadelphia. To reduce any tracking of his movements, he used cash to pay for it, rather than his American Express card, and showed the airline customer service agent his Swiss passport. She looked at it and said, "Are you checking both bags through to Zurich, Mr. Brunner?"

"Yes", he replied. With that she gave him the ticket, bag check stubs and his passport. He was home clear!

He looked around and there was no one watching him; neither a suspicious person, nor a Federal Government agent, as far as he could tell. He went through the security gate and walked to the departure area. His flight was soon called and he boarded with the other passengers. The trip to Philadelphia was uneventful, and they landed about eighty minutes later.

Alan then checked the flight board and found out his flight to Zurich was on time. He stopped at a book store, on the way to the waiting area, and bought two books. At the Zurich departure gate, he had to show his boarding pass and passport; there were no problems at all.

In about an hour, they called his flight for Zurich, boarded the plane, with the other business class passengers, and settled into his seat. He knew that he'd soon be out of the control of the United States. The plane took off and he watched the progress of the flight on the seat monitor. Once they reached cruising altitude, of thirty-nine thousand feet, he knew he could finally relax.

During his flight to Switzerland, Alan started to read one of the books and, after a while, put it aside. He started to think about what he had just left behind. *"I'll probably never see America or my son again. I hope he has a successful life as an engineer, gets married and has children. My ex-wife will probably be involved with him and his family. She will be good for them and will be a great grandmother. I wonder what went wrong, as we were so in love when we first met. Did we both change or was it my military career? I guess it doesn't make any difference, one way or the other, now."*

After a little over eight hours later, they landed in Zurich and he passed though immigration, with no problem. He collected his bags at the carousel and walked through the green "Nothing to Declare" door. No one challenged him, and he was in Switzerland. He then found some lockers, where he could store his luggage. He placed his two suit cases in separate lockers, locked them and walked off.

He found the taxi rank outside the terminal and asked the driver to take him to the HSBC office at Paradeplatz 5. The driver nodded his head and drove off. Alan turned around and looked through the back window, to see if anyone appeared to be following. He saw nothing that looked like a tail. The taxi dropped him off at the address, he had given the driver. He paid the thirty Swiss Franc fare with forty Swiss Francs and told the cabbie to keep the change. He entered the HSBC bank and walked to the "Open Account" desk.

"I would like to open a checking account and deposit one thousand dollars to start," Alan said, hoping there would be no problem.

The clerk asked him for his address, and he gave her the address of his friends in Northern Cyprus, where he planned to go. He opened his briefcase and gave her the cash. She gave him an account number and said he could access the account at any HSBC branch. He told her he would be transferring a large sum from UBS shortly. "Would that be okay?" he asked.

"Yes," she replied. "No problem." She also mentioned that they had offices in Northern Cyprus and specifically Girne. This would be the closest branch to his friends' bed and breakfast establishment, up in the mountains, above the town. He thanked her and walked out of the bank.

After leaving the HSBC, he hailed a taxi and asked the driver to take him to UBS at Bahnhofstrasse 45. When they arrived at the address, the cabbie looked at the meter and told him how much the fare amounted to. Alan paid it, with a good tip included, got out of the taxi and entered the bank, carrying his briefcase.

Alan had made arrangements with Valda Lewis that the twenty-five million dollars, promised to him for directing the Red Moon operation, would be available to him on the 9th of November. Now was the moment of truth. He opened up his briefcase and took out the bank account number. He walked up to a bank window and told the cashier he wanted to transfer two million dollars, from his account, to a HSBC account and also withdraw one million dollars in cash. He gave the cashier his account number and she entered it into the computer.

"Yes. We can do that," she said. "However, you'll have to see one of our managers. I don't have the authority to provide such a large amount in cash." She directed Alan to a group of offices, along the far wall.

Alan walked over and told the receptionist what he wanted. She directed him to an office. He entered the office of Werner Scharbart and introduced himself. "Mr. Scharbart, my name is Alan Burgess, as he produced his U.S. passport, and I wish to withdraw one million dollars cash, from my account."

279

"No problem," he said. "Please complete this withdrawal form and we'll get it for you."

Alan completed the form including the account number, and signed it. He handed it to Mr. Scharbart who then departed the office. In a few minutes he came back with a box and asked Alan if he wanted to count it.

Alan thumbed briefly through the one hundred dollar bills and did a mental count. "It looks about right," he said, as he transferred it to his briefcase.

Continuing, he said, "Now I would like to transfer two million dollars from the same account to my account at HSBC."

"No problem," said Mr. Scharbart. "Just fill out this transfer order with your HSBC and UBS account numbers. Endorse it with your signature and we'll take care of it for you. The funds should be at HSBC in about twenty-four hours.

"Thank you very much for your assistance," replied Alan. "It's been a pleasure doing business with you."

With that, he walked out of the UBS bank and took a taxi back to Zurich airport.

At the airport, Alan went to the Turkish Airlines counter and bought a ticket to Ercan International Airport, near Lefkoşa, in the Turkish part of Cyprus, via Istanbul. All airlines have to touch down in Turkey, before going on to Cyprus. This is because Northern Cyprus is not recognized by any country, except Turkey. This makes Northern Cyprus a great haven, for those who want to hide out. There are no extradition treaties with countries such as the United States, United Kingdom, France, Germany, and other major Western nations.

After he had his ticket, he retrieved his two bags from the lockers and checked them in for the flight to Ercan. The plane was scheduled to take off in two hours, so Alan had time to get something to eat in the airport. The flight to Cyprus would take about six hours, with the stopover in

Istanbul. Alan called his friends, who ran the B&B overlooking Girne and informed them, as to when he was scheduled to arrive. They said they'd be able to pick him up.

The plane took off on time and, approximately six hours later, landed at Ercan International Airport, a few minutes late. Since he carried a US passport, he didn't need a visa for a stay of up to ninety days. If he wanted to stay longer, he would figure that issue out later. He still had to go through immigration and customs at Ercan, but they gave him no problem. He showed his US passport and was waved through. The customs guys did not search his bags and he was in Northern Cyprus, with his one million dollars.

His friends, John and Hazel, were at the airport waiting. They helped him with his luggage and then drove him to their mountain bed and breakfast, about thirty miles away. Their inn was extremely profitable, since it was close to Girne and the United Nations personnel would come up there, for some rest and recreation.

Alan Burgess could now really finally relax for the first time in months, since Northern Cyprus was reasonably safe from the IRS, G-men of the USA, and hopefully from the Chicago men.

He stayed at his friends B&B for a few days, while he went shopping for a car and a house, overlooking the ocean. He had always wanted one and now he had the money to get it. He went by taxi to the nearest HSBC bank, opened up an account and had them transfer funds, from his account in Zurich. He then went shopping for a car, so he could get around and ended up purchasing a three-year-old, Ford. He didn't want to draw attention to himself, by driving around in a brand new luxury vehicle, like a BMW or Mercedes.

A few days later, he found a large house on the west side of Girne, which was previously owned by an industrial magnate, who had returned to the United Kingdom, to face his accusers for embezzlement. He made the necessary down payment and took out a loan for the rest. Again, he didn't want to pay cash, since it might draw too much attention from curious Northern Cyprus Turkish authorities.

He moved into the house in December, about two weeks before Christmas, after thanking John and Hazel for putting him up. Two days before Christmas, he met a beautiful, dark-haired girl, named Dilara, who was half Turkish and half Lebanese. She worked at the HSBC bank, where he had his money. He was immediately taken by her, and she was taken by his bank account, of which she had detailed information.

After a few dates, he asked her to move in, and she accepted the offer. He gave her one hundred thousand dollars to keep and wrote her in his will, in case something happened to him. She would never get the bulk of his estate, since it would go to his son. However, she would receive enough money, plus the house, so that she would never have to be concerned about money problems.

54

Call to Resign

On Thursday, the 1ˢᵗ of December at 8:00 pm CST, the governors of Texas, Tennessee, Michigan, North Carolina, Oklahoma, Wisconsin, Virginia and Ohio held a joint news conference in Nashville, Tennessee. It was broadcast throughout the Nation, by all the major networks. Martha Cartwright spoke initially for all the governors and then opened it to questions.

"Good evening. First, I would like to start this press conference, with a short statement, that has been written and approved by all the governors, present here today. I've also checked with thirty-four other governors, who are not able to be here today, and they have all approved, what I'm about to say.

President Tuckwell swore, almost eight years ago and again four years ago, to uphold the constitution. He has failed to do this. We have good intelligence that the attack on the Capitol, almost three months ago, was a false flag operation. It was made to look like the attack was carried out by Islamist terrorists. This was not true. The attack was conducted by a group of Americans, who launched two Bomarc missiles from a base called Camp Warrior, near Camp Lejeune, in North Carolina. From all the information we have, the attack was planned and approved by the Oval Office. The evidence, we have, implicates the president, and he cannot hide behind the phrase: plausible deniability.

This situation is akin to what happened in Germany, in 1933, when Adolf Hitler and the Nazis wanted to have absolute power. They devised a plan, whereby a man would set fire to the Reichstag and then claim he was a Communist. They found a willing participant, in the name of Marius van der Lubbe, who was later hung for the crime. This fire gave Hitler the opportunity to reduce civil liberties and imprison many of his opponents, including Communists. We believe this was President Tuckwell's intention, with the attack on the Capitol.

Therefore, we call on President Tuckwell to resign immediately and face whatever prosecution, our laws allow. If he doesn't do so, we will "march" on Washington, with the National Guard units of all states involved, and remove him from office. We do not take this step lightly. We realize there could be some violence in doing so. However, the freedom of our citizens is paramount, and this evil man must be driven from office. Thank you for your forbearance. I will now open it up to questions, from the press."

"Albert Jones, Associated Press: Governor Cartwright. What evidence do you have that this was a false flag operation, conducted by Americans?"

"We can't give out all the evidence we have, since the situation is still fluid. However, I'll let my advisor Ian Black answer that question, and give you as much information, as he is permitted."

Speaking with a slight British accent, Ian Black responded to the AP question. "We conducted an interview with the team leader, who gave us some tape recordings. We also received a letter from a team member that has confirmed the team leader's account, of the missile attack. In addition, with the help of the North Carolina governor, we located a safe house used by the team, on the outskirts of Wilmington, North Carolina, which contained incriminating evidence. That's all I can say at this time."

"Dennis Brown, NBC News: Where's the team leader now? What's his name? What do you know about him?"

Ian Black answered, "The team leader used to be a colonel in the Air Force and we believe that he has since fled the country. We're still trying to locate his whereabouts. I can't give out his name, at this time."

"We've only time for one more question," Governor Cartwright announced.

"Charles Tolputt, CNN: What has happened to the other members of the team?"

Martha Cartwright replied, "We're not exactly sure, but we think that some of them may have been assassinated, in order to prevent them from talking. We'll give out more information as it becomes available. Thank you all for coming. God bless America."

55

Vice President Dies

In the Bomarc missile attack on the Senate wing of the Capitol, at 9:30 am, on that fateful Friday, Vice President James Valpy had been seriously wounded. He was at the Capitol that day, because there was going to be a critical vote on the immigration bill, and his deciding vote might have been needed, to break a tie.

Actually, the Senate never got to the point where the voting started, before the missile hit. Valpy was rushed to the local Washington hospital, with other wounded senators. The doctors did the best they could for him, but he was unconscious with a major head injury.

He lay in a coma for almost three months, and his doctors tried everything, to bring him out of it. They'd brought in neurologists, to see if they could help. His wife was consulted during the entire hospitalization.

Finally, on the 26th of November, Dr. Wilkerson, the attending physician, approached Mrs. Valpy. "Helen, we've tried everything that we can think of and we get no response from James. We believe that he may be brain dead," said

Dr. Wilkerson, a family friend. "At some time, we may have to accept the worst."

Helen replied, "I understand you've done your best and that the situation is grave. Please give it one more week and then, if there is no improvement, I will give my permission to take away the life support systems, and let God decide."

On Friday, the 2nd of December, Vice President Valpy gasped his last breath and died in the arms of his loving wife. His two adult children were in the hospital room, gathered around his bed. Helen was prepared for the worst, as doctors had told her some weeks before that the prognosis was not very good.

What irony. The president, along with Valda Lewis, had killed his own vice president.

After consulting with Valpy's wife, the president set the funeral, at Arlington, for the following Tuesday, the 6th of December. The president did not attend the funeral, due to a supposed, previous engagement, or maybe his conscience bothered him.

Helen didn't mind, since she had never cared for President Tuckwell anyway. She thought he was an opportunist. The entire cabinet was at the funeral, and it went off without a hitch. The honor guard fired a volley of shots and the bugler blew the Taps. The flag taken from the coffin was folded and given to the grieving widow. It was all very ceremonial and poignant.

Vice President Valpy was laid to rest in the Arlington National Cemetery across the Potomac, from Washington, DC.

President Tuckwell could not submit a nomination for a new vice president to the Senate until the senators, who had been killed in the September attack, were replaced, which suited him just fine.

287

56

National Guards Advance

On the 2nd of December, the White House press secretary announced, at the daily briefing, that President Tuckwell had no intention of resigning. After hearing this, Martha Cartwright, and the other concerned governors, decided that they didn't have any choice, but to amass their Army and Air National Guard units. The mission was given the codename of *Operation American Freedom*. In order to call up the National Guards, all governors, first had to declare a state of emergency and then call their individual states' forces up.

As required by U.S. Code Title 32, Martha Cartwright declared a state of emergency. She then called General Bree, authorizing him to assemble the Army National Guard troops and associated equipment, in preparation for the drive on Washington. At the same time, she called the Air National Guard commander and informed him, as to what was going on. The governor requested that he provide air cover, wherever possible, for the Army National Guard.

Chuck Prince, the governor of Texas, followed Cartwright's lead and declared a state of emergency. He then authorized General Pawsey, who was head of the Texas ARNG, to assemble troops and equipment, for the march on Washington. In addition, Governor Prince called the Texas ANG commander and asked him to provide air support, as appropriate, for the Texas armed forces.

The governors of Tennessee and Texas placed a conference call to Steve Bingham, the governor of Virginia.

"Governor Bingham. This is Governor Cartwright and Governor Prince on this three way conference call, and we'd like to talk to you about the actions, we've taken today."

"Governors, it's great to hear from you. How may I help you?"

"Since the president has refused to resign, we see we now have only one choice to save the Nation, and that is to force him from office. Accordingly, Tennessee and Texas have declared a state of emergency and we've called up our National Guard troops and airmen. Are you in agreement with our course of action? If so, do you plan to declare a state of emergency and call up your National Guard?"

"Yes, I concur with what you have done," replied the Virginia Governor. "I also plan to declare a state of emergency and call up both the Virginia ARNG and ANG, within the hour."

"Governor Bingham. Do we have your approval to move our troops through your state and, more importantly, are you willing to allow our troops to camp on your state property? In addition, we will need to land our planes at Langley AFB and park in your ANG area. Will that be acceptable to you?"

"Yes, of course. You may move your troops through our state to the Washington, D.C. area. Please keep me informed, as you progress with *Operation American Freedom*. Virginia wants to be involved with the saving of our Nation."

"Thank you, Governor Bingham. Yes, we'll certainly keep you informed, as we proceed. There's one other subject I'd like to bring up. In our discussions with the other governors, they've agreed with my appointment of Colonel Ian Black, as my personnel representative and coordinator of the plan of attack. He's well qualified, respected and has my total confidence. He has served in the British Army and the United States Air Force. He'll coordinate the plan of action, with the generals in command of the Army and Air National Guard units."

Governor Bingham replied, as all the other governors had. "If you have complete confidence in this man, then I do too. You have my approval. Good bye Governor Cartwright, let's keep in touch."

With that, the conference call ended and they all hung up their phones.

Tennessee, Texas, Kentucky, Louisiana and other states agreed that Tuckwell had to be ousted from office, and they assembled their National Guard. Tanks were loaded onto transporters, planes were made ready and troops loaded onto trucks. The march on Washington was about to begin. It would take about three to four days to gather the necessary troops in Washington.

One paramount question was what would the regular army troops do, when faced by the states' forces? The answer would come, when they approached Washington, D.C.

As the Texas National Guard soldiers assembled, they started moving up Rte. I-40, to the East. As they did, they picked up reinforcements from neighboring states, along the way. When they reached Nashville, the Tennessee troops joined the convoy. Ian Black, the Tennessee Governor's advisor flew in a Tennessee ANG plane ahead of the convoys, to scout out any opposition. The F-15E was flown by an experienced pilot, with the codename Buck. Later, this plane landed at Langley AFB, with the other ANG planes.

From just east of Knoxville, they proceeded up interstate I-81 into Virginia. Troops from Kentucky and South Carolina joined the convoy as it neared their states. At Staunton, Virginia, half of the soldiers went on Rte. I-64 to the Richmond area and then up Rte. I-95 to Fredericksburg. The rest of the National Guardsmen continued up Rte. I-81, to the junction with interstate I-66. There, they headed down Rte. I-66 just a few miles, to the Front Royal area and halted, within seventy-six miles of Washington.

Several states fighter aircraft landed at Langley AFB, part of the Joint Base Langley-Eustis, and taxied to the Virginia ANG site. So far, there was no resistance from the regular army or air force groups.

While all these forces were advancing on Washington, President Tuckwell was trying to persuade the Joint Chiefs, to mount a resistance campaign and put the National Guard troops to flight. One of the problems faced by the Joint Chiefs was that many of their regulars were still in the Middle East fighting wars, which had been going on for some time.

Finally, they gathered some Marines from North Carolina and regular combat soldiers from Pennsylvania and Massachusetts. They approached the National Guardsmen at their camps in Virginia, in order to force them to surrender. However, just as in 1917 during WWI, when Russian soldiers, who were sent to stop deserters from going home, instead joined up with them and revolted against the Czar. Likewise, some of the Federal troops and Marines, who had enough of the politics in the capital, joined the National Guardsmen, for their march on Washington.

On the evening of the fifth, the tanks were unloaded from their transporters and prepared for the next day's advance on Washington. Ian Black and the National Guard commanders got together to discuss the plan for the next day. It was agreed that all television stations and major radio stations must be taken over and controlled. The two airports, train stations and bus stations should be closed for twenty-four hours and the major road arteries would be controlled by roadblocks. After an agreement was reached as to which units would perform the tasks, the commanders left to give instructions and get a little sleep. One order, which was issued to all the troops, was that no one was to fire, unless fired upon. This was critical, because the fewer the casualties, the less resistance there would be from the local population. Also, the crisis would be over sooner, if no blood was shed.

57

The Battle

At 3:00 am, on the 6th of December, the ARNG tank crews started up the engines of their Abrams tanks and made sure that the United States flag was flying in a prominent position, with their appropriate state flag underneath. At 3:30 am, Group A started up Rte. I-66 from Front Royal and Group B started up Rte. I-95 from Fredericksburg. Both Groups were racing toward Washington, at speeds up to forty miles per hour on the open highways. By 5:30 am, they were approaching Washington and, by 6:00 am, they were at the planned points outside the four television stations, and ten radio stations. They also blocked access to the two major airports, train stations and bus stations. Other troops were setting up road blocks on the major arterial roads in and around Washington. In addition, troops and tanks were on Pennsylvania Avenue and were surrounding the White House, plus what was left of the Capitol.

In the meantime, Ian Black had taken off from Langley AFB in the F-15E again, flown by Buck. The purpose was to scout out for opposing forces which might be starting to assemble. Dawn was just breaking and in the dim light, they could see a few columns of troops starting to proceed toward Washington. However, there didn't seem to be any coordinated advance, between the units. Ian's F-15E was followed by a flight of six F-15's from the ANG forces at Langley and they buzzed the Washington, D.C. area, to show the White House and federal forces that the states' National Guard troops were serious, about surrounding the city.

As the general population, of Washington and surrounding area, was waking up that crisp December morning, they were astonished to hear a message on their popular television or radio station, every fifteen minutes. It was Ian Black, the Tennessee Governor's representative, reading a recorded statement, in his British/American accent.

"Good morning. My name is Colonel Ian Black, United States Air Force and I am the personal representative of the Tennessee Governor, Martha Cartwright. Due to the corruption of this administration and its blatant disregard for the Constitution, a majority of the states have found it necessary to take action, to force President Tuckwell from office. He was asked to resign a few days ago and refused to do so. Tennessee, Texas, Virginia, Ohio, Michigan, Wisconsin, Oklahoma and thirty-five other states have found it necessary to take military action to save the United States and return the government to the people. We recommend that all DC citizens stay home today, in order not to become a casualty or a hostage. All Washington television stations have been taken over, along with radio stations, airports, bus stations and rail stations. We hope this action will only inconvenience you, for a short time. We will keep you informed, as actions warrant it.

We also appeal to the regular United States Army, Marine, Navy and Air Force units, to join us in this effort. We have no quarrel with you and we'll welcome you with open arms. This also includes members of the NPF, FBI and other law enforcement agencies.

God bless America. May we be one united people again?"

With that the stations played the National anthem and other patriotic music.

By 7:00 am, some regular army and marine units were advancing on Washington, to square off against the states National Guard units. As the regular Federal troops entered Washington, there was some shooting between them and the National Guardsmen. At 9:00 am, Ian Black finally managed to connect with Admiral Anthony Trice, the Chairman of the Joint Chiefs, on the telephone.

"Admiral Trice, this is Ian Black, the personal representative of Tennessee Governor Martha Cartwright. Thank you for taking my call, sir. I'm here with Generals Bree and Pawsey and the other commanders of their respective states' National Guards. We have no quarrel with you or your troops. We're here to protect the United States and its people, from this corrupt and power hungry administration. Please ask your troops to withdraw or join us in this quest for freedom. We don't wish to fight your soldiers. Our men and women have been instructed not to fire, unless fired upon. However, we don't plan to withdraw and, as we talk, more National Guardsmen are on their way to join us."

Admiral Trice replied, "Colonel Black, I also have no personal quarrel with you, but I take my orders from the legal commander-in- chief, the president of the United States. I'll tell my men to stand down and not advance any further, until 12:00 pm. In the meantime, I will consult with my staff and the administration, and then call you back at that time."

"Admiral Trice. That's agreeable with us. I'll await your phone call at noon. Good bye, sir." With that they both hung up.

At 11:30 am, the FBI director, Albert Laine, issued a bulletin that was a preliminary report, on the explosions at the Capitol, on the 9th of September. It was read over most of the television and radio stations, around the country. The short report read as follows:

The FBI, after a thorough investigation that is still ongoing, has determined that the explosions at the Capitol, on the 9th of September, were caused by two Bomarc missiles fired from a Camp Warrior, near Camp Lejeune, North Carolina. The launching of the missiles was accomplished by a group of six men, dressed in dark clothes and ski masks. They tried to convince the marine guard that they were Arab terrorists, by speaking in a foreign accent and calling each other in Arabic names. The FBI has determined that these were actually not Arab terrorists, but Americans acting as Arabs. In some circles this is called a *False Flag* operation. We have a few names of the Americans, called the Red Moon team, and we are trying to ascertain the identity of the others. We believe some of the team members are already dead, but the ring leader fled the United States, some time ago. We are trying to locate his whereabouts and bring him back, to face the full extent of the law.

The funding and planning for this operation appears to have come from within the White House. A further investigation on this link is ongoing. However, this administration has much to answer for in this matter, and we'll get to the bottom of it.

Signed: Albert Laine, FBI Director

Within thirty minutes of the issuance of this bulletin, the Federal Army and Marine forces started to move away from Washington.

Admiral Trice called Colonel Black at 12:30 pm. "Colonel Black, we've heard the bulletin issued by the FBI and my staff has recommended that our troops return to their bases. However, our forces have been ordered not to support or oppose your National Guard units. I hope you understand our position."

Colonel Black responded "Thank you for calling, Admiral Trice. I totally understand your difficult position under the Constitution. I'm glad there will very little bloodshed over this. We're still having a few problems with the NPF, but we hope to have them resolved very soon. Please contact me again, if your situation changes. Thanks again for your call. Good day, sir."

Colonel Black was still concerned about the few diehard snipers of the NPF. Hopefully, they could be neutralized soon. He then called the commanders of the National Guard units and informed them of his conversation with Admiral Trice.

He then called Governor Cartwright to apprise her of the situation. "Governor Cartwright, everything is pretty well under control here. The Federal troops have backed off and returned to their bases. I've been in touch with Admiral Trice, and he's assured me his troops will give us no more resistance. We're still getting some sniper fire from the NPF, but we're slowly eliminating the threat. I'll call you again in a couple of hours; around 3:00 pm, if that's okay with you. I'm meeting with General Bree and General Pawsey and other commanders shortly, to discuss the next course of action."

Governor Cartwright responded, "Colonel, you're doing a great job there. Keep up the good work. I'll wait for your next update." With that she disconnected and Ian Black went back to planning the next moves.

What would happen tomorrow, the 7th of December and the day of infamy, was anyone's guess?

Later, in the afternoon on the sixth, Ian Black consulted with the generals and his boss Governor Cartwright again. It was decided that Ian Black would go to the White House that evening to request a meeting with the president and/or his chief advisor Valda Lewis. If that didn't work and the president refused to surrender, it was agreed that they would give President Tuckwell an ultimatum the next day, at 9:00 am.

Surrender or we will come in by force and arrest you.

At 6:00 pm, Ian Black and General Bree were driven by a guardsman, in a Tennessee National Guard Humvee, to the Southwest appointment gate, of the White House. They were followed by another Humvee, filled with six, heavily armed guardsmen. The grounds of the White House were swarming, with Secret Service and NPF officers.

A uniformed guard came to the driver's window and asked, "What do you want? This is a secure area. Do you have an appointment; if so, with whom? Otherwise you must leave this area immediately."

Ian Black got out of the passenger seat and walked around to the security guard, slapping his swagger stick against his thigh. He was dressed in his USAF colonel's uniform, which was legal under the USAF rules for retired officers. He looked at the guards name tag. It read Sgt. Coles.

Colonel Black spoke slowly, with an authoritative voice, "Sgt. Coles. We wish to see the president, and we represent the states that are here to take this country back."

After looking at Colonel Black's name tag and staring at the swagger stick he held in his hand, the officer responded, "Sorry sir. You're not on the list of officials authorized access to the White House. I can't give you permission to enter."

Ian looked at him directly in the eyes and slapped the Colt Model 1911 45-calber semi-automatic pistol, hanging on his right side. "This is my appointment card and you had better call the White House right now and get us access," he replied.

Sgt. Coles glanced at the weapon Colonel Black had at his side and said, "Please wait a minute, while I place a phone call." He went to the gate house and called the White

House. In a minute he came back and said, "The president is indisposed at the moment. However, Valda Lewis and the president's Chief of Staff Andrew Taylor will meet with you; just you Colonel Black, without your sidearm."

Colonel Black looked at him sternly and, pointing his swagger stick at the officer, said "Sgt. Coles. First, I haven't been without this sidearm since 1964, and I'm not about to give it up now. In addition, General Bree and I come as a pair. I represent all of the state governors and General Bree represents all the National Guard units. We also need the driver to take us to the front portico of the White House. So I would suggest that you get back on that phone and talk to whoever you talked to before."

Sgt. Coles gave Colonel Back an ugly stare and walked back to the guardhouse. In a minute he came back, looking like someone who just lost a battle. "You may go in. Drive up to the front portico, and someone will be waiting for you." With that Sgt. Coles signaled to another guard, to open the gate.

Colonel Black climbed back into the Humvee and told the guardsman to drive on. They drove up to the front portico, and there waiting for them was the Chief of Staff, Andrew Taylor, and a Secret Service agent. The other Humvee loaded with armed guardsmen stayed outside the White House Southwest Gate.

Colonel Black and General Bree climbed out of the Humvee and went to meet Andrew Taylor. They shook hands and Taylor led them through the White House front door, to a first floor conference room. The Secret Service agent followed them into the room and stood in a corner.

In a minute, Valda Lewis walked in and shook hands with Colonel Black and General Bree.

"Colonel Black, I assume?" Valda said in a cold, but wavering voice. Please sit down." They all sat down around the long oval oak table, facing each other.

Valda continued, "I understand that you, Colonel Black, are the spokesman for the rebellious state governors."

"Ms. Lewis", Ian replied rather sternly, "This is not a campaign moment. Trying to demonize the governors, will not be helpful in a meeting, where a serious discussion is needed. We're here to negotiate the surrender of President Tuckwell, to the governors' troops. Are you and Mr. Taylor willing to discuss this matter?"

Valda looked at Andrew Taylor for a moment and then said, "I believe you're wasting your time here, Colonel Black. President Tuckwell has no intention of resigning or surrendering, now or in the future. He is the lawful president of the United States."

Colonel Black responded, "He may be the president at the moment, but he has broken the laws of the United States and has not upheld the Constitution. In addition, he has been an accessory to the murder of senators and congressmen. We have talked with the leader of the group called the Red Moon team and received a letter from another member. We also have the names of the other four conspirators. It appears most of them have been murdered, to keep them from talking. The leader of the team has already left the country, but we will track him down and bring him back for trial. So you see Ms. Lewis, we know more than you think. Your plan, to cancel the election scheduled for last month, and for Edward Tuckwell to remain in office, will not work. By the way, I also know that there is a secret international Committee that is ultimately responsible for this calamity. I've actually been following rumors of such groups for years. Have you ever heard of such cliques?"

Valda replied angrily, "Of course not. I have never heard of any groups, cabals or cliques, plotting to manipulate a country's government or markets."

Colonel Black then asked, "Well, do you think that the president has any knowledge of such a group? He has a vast organization for gathering information."

Valda responded, "How would I know what he has heard of or what information he has received? I'm not privy to all government secrets. He has never mentioned anything about such groups to me."

Colonel Black replied, "Well, years ago, back in 1962, when I was an officer with the British Intelligence Corps, I overheard a conversation in a West Berlin café. Two men were talking about manipulating the Italian Government and financial markets. One of the men was a German named Lutz Schiller."

With that Valda Lewis gave a slight gasp. She recognized the name Schiller and assumed that Karl Schiller on the Committee might be a relative; a son or nephew.

All this time, Andrew Taylor, Tuckwell's Chief of Staff remained silent. Colonel Black felt a little sorry for him, as he looked shocked about the revelations.

Valda finally spoke again after regaining her composure. "Gentlemen, I can assure you that President Tuckwell has no intention of resigning. I believe you're wasting your time here. You have no firm proof, to support your allegations. I suggest you leave immediately."

At that, Colonel Black rose and said, "I see General Bree and I are, in fact, wasting our time and yours. You leave us no alternative. Good evening, Ms. Lewis and Mr. Taylor."

With that Colonel Black and General Bree walked out of the conference room, followed by the Secret Service agent and went to the front door of the White House. They climbed into the Humvee and had the driver proceed back to the White House Southwest Gate. The gate opened as they approached it, and they drove out onto the streets of Washington, followed by the other Humvee loaded with the Guardsmen.

They went back to their camp on the outskirts of Washington and gave a short briefing to the other generals and Governor Cartwright by telephone.

The rest of the evening and night was fairly peaceful. However the commanders warned their troops, to be on the lookout for snipers and looters.

Meanwhile, that evening, back at the White House, Valda called Leo to inform him of the visit by Colonel Black and General Bree.

"Leo. The president was just delivered an ultimatum from a Colonel Black and General Bree. They demanded that Edward Tuckwell resign immediately and leave the White House. They also seem to know about the false flag operation and something about a mysterious group, trying to control Governments. What do you want me to do?"

Leo responded, "I want you to stay at the White House tonight and keep an eye on the president. I understand he can't leave anyway, because the states' troops are watching Andrews AFB and the Marine One helicopter at the Quantico, for any sign of him trying to flee."

Valda said, "Alright, I'll stay here tonight and call you tomorrow as events unfold. By the way, Colonel Black mentioned a group back in the 1960's that had a member called Lutz Schiller. Do you think Karl Schiller could be a relative?"

Leo answered, "I don't know. Next time I see Karl I'll ask him. I have to go now, Valda. Call me tomorrow and let me know what's going on, or sooner, if necessary. Goodnight."

With that they both hung up.

****

At 9:00 am, on the next morning, the 7th of December, a Humvee drove up to the Southwest Gate with Colonel Black, a driver and two armed guardsmen. A Secret Service officer came out of the guardhouse to the vehicle and asked Colonel Black what he wanted.

"I'm Colonel Black representing all the governors of the *Operation American Freedom* coalition and I'm here to present an ultimatum to President Tuckwell." With that, Colonel Black gave the officer an envelope with President Tuckwell's name on it. "Please insure that this envelope is presented to the president immediately. It calls for his unconditional surrender without delay to General Bree, General Pawsey and me. If we don't receive a reply by 11:00 am, we'll start preparations to break down the gates and fences, which surround the White House, with our tanks. Do you understand?"

The officer nodded and went back to the guardhouse. Colonel Black saw him pick up the phone and talk to someone. A couple of minutes later, another Secret Service officer came down to the guardhouse at the gate and carried the envelope back up the driveway to the White House.

As the morning progressed, the Secret Service was also warned not to interfere. Ian Black informed them that they were there to take President Tuckwell into custody and not to harm him. He met with the head of the White House security detail at the Southwest Gate, William Conrad, and explained the situation to him.

Having received no surrender of President Tuckwell at noon, two tanks pushed down part of the fence and main gate. The troops outside were then able to enter the grounds of the White House. A few NPF officers fired on the tanks, to no avail. They then quickly slipped away, so as not to be shot by the tanks' machine guns.

Most of them had served at one time, in one branch or the other of the military, and had no desire to fire on other American servicemen. In addition, most of them had no real loyalty or love for Edward Tuckwell, who seemed to always treat them with distain.

General Bree, General Pawsey, Ian Black and about twenty ARNG troops, with loaded rifles, entered the White House and proceeded toward the Oval Office, while the remainder of the troops stayed outside. After Colonel Black had met with the head of the White House security detail earlier in the morning, the Secret Service officers were instructed to stand down and not interfere, when Colonel Black and the National Guards came to arrest the president.

58

Day of Infamy

When the phone rang, it startled Leo, although he'd been anticipating the call for some time. As he picked up the receiver, he noticed his palms were wet, with sweat.

"How had it failed," he thought. *"When was the turning point in the plan? That egomaniac little bastard had ruined everything. All these years, of waiting and planning, had gone down the proverbial drain. What a prick! They should have chosen better, well too late now. There would be another time, if they acted quickly."*

He didn't bother to say hello, as he knew who it was.

"Leo, my contacts have informed me that the states' National Guards are just outside the White House. This is the time to act," former California Senator Harry Thornton told him.

"I understand completely," Leo responded and hung up the phone.

"Damn it," he thought, *"the Committee had decided and left it up to him, to do the dirty work. Well, what had to be done, had to be done, for the good of all."*

Valda sat silently, in her dim office, behind her ornate desk, her head in her hands. She almost jumped from her chair, when her private cell phone rang. She picked up the phone, with her hand trembling, and said, "Valda here."

Leo told her, "It's time to act. We can't wait any longer." she knew what that meant and replied, "It'll be taken care of immediately." With a sigh, she turned off her phone.

She hated doing it; she had grown fond of "the chosen one", over the years. Even as he grew increasingly vain and over bearing, there was something still charming and likeable about him. The Committee had thought they could control him in the beginning, just like a parent thinks they can control a spoiled child. Which in realty was what he was, brought up in a privileged environment and given the best of everything? But the real gift he had been given was the ability to read others and their weaknesses, to get his way. The answers seem to come so easily on how to get around the rules, with impunity. This had been his best asset growing up and in school. He had used it to fool his parents, his teachers, the American public, the Committee and even her, at first. But after he took possession of the highest office in the United States and she had been assigned as his advisor, she gradually saw through the façade. He was as corrupt as the members of the Committee. Well, she thought she had no other choice, it was him or her. The Committee had decided. It was after all their only alternative, so they could try again with someone else.

Valda stood up slowly and, breathing deeply, retrieved the key which was taped under her desk drawer. She bent down and unlocked the large, bottom drawer of her desk. Inside it was a medium sized case, with a brass handle. She took the case and walked toward her office door. As Valda opened it, she turned and looked back at the impressive office, one last time. She had enjoyed the power that she had wielded here. Now it was time to move on. There would be other assignments, she thought, but she doubted if she would enjoy it as much as she had this one. She quietly closed the door behind her and, with the case in her hand, she walked down the wide, long hallway toward her destiny.

In the Oval Office, the president was pacing the floor. William Conrad, head of the Secret Service Detail, had just called with the news that the rebel forces were just outside the White House Gates. None of his guards were left, even the ones he had personally chosen. He was thankful that his family had left the country some time ago, to visit an old university acquaintance in Saudi Arabia. At least they'd be safe in the land of his "friend", Prince Ahmad Hassain, until he could join them. They would put him on trial he thought, but surely his sentence would be short, the Committee would see to that.

President Tuckwell was feeling very vulnerable that morning. His family had already left, Karen, his secretary, had not turned up for work and he hadn't seen any Secret Service officers.

There was a soft knock at the door and he said, "Who's there?"

"It's Valda."

"Come in," he answered.

She slowly came into the room and closed the door behind her. "What are you still doing here?" he asked.

She had been loyal to him through all of this, and he wondered what would happen to her, after he was gone.

The president walked slowly to behind his desk and then turned to face her. He didn't like the look on her face. She placed a black case, with a brass handle, on his desk in front of him, with the handle facing him. He looked at it with horror, surely they didn't mean for him to do, as they had instructed at the beginning, if something like this happened.

"No, I won't do it" he said, partly to himself and partly to her.

"Sir," she said, "your family."

"My family", he said with some surprise, "they're already with Ahmad."

"Sir, Ahmad is one of them."

He could hardly believe what he was hearing.

He thought, *"How could I have not known? Ahmad was my friend. We've been friends, since our university days. No, this couldn't be true."*

However, he could tell from the look on Valda's face that she was telling the truth.

"How could I have been such a fool? I thought I was using them, when all along they've been using me. I wasn't one of them, I was their tool. Now I'm a liability, even Valda has used me; she was not my loyal advisor and friend, as I had thought, but their informant."

He unclasped the lock on the case in front of him and looked inside, there was a pearl handled revolver, lying in a foam form insert. He looked up at her, when she said, "Sir, I'm sorry, I truly am."

With a faint smile on his lips, he replied, "Not as sorry as I am."

He took the gun out of the case and lifted it to the side of his face. She stood motionless in front of him with her eyes closed, trembling. He slowly turned the gun toward her and fired. Her eyes flew open in disbelieve, as she collapsed to the floor.

He then turned the gun to his own head and, just before he pulled the trigger, he heard loud footsteps in the corridor. Then the President of the United States shot himself.

As Ian Black, General Bree, General Pawsey and the Guardsmen marched briskly down the corridor toward the Oval Office; they heard the first shot ring out and then the second. They immediately broke into a run. As they approached the door and cautiously opened it, they saw a woman's body lying in a pool of blood on the floor, in front of the president's desk. General Bree looked around the Oval Office and then walked behind the president's desk and there on the floor lay the man, they had been coming to arrest. He could hardly believe his eyes. The man that had seemed above it all, in his arrogance and corruption, lay on the floor with a bullet wound in his temple. Blood was dripping down his cheek and ear, to pool on the expensive rug. The general knelt down beside the fallen president and felt his pulse; there was nothing to be done.

General Bree said, "There's no pulse. He's gone."

At the same time, General Pawsey felt the pulse of Valda Lewis.

There was none. He echoed, "She's dead too. No pulse here."

There would be no trial, no impeachment, no public disgrace or humiliation for Edward Tuckwell to face; just a private funeral, with a few personal relatives attending.

"*What a coward*," thought General Bree. But then he wasn't surprised, men like him would only face their wrong doings in the hereafter. In their life on this earth, they felt that they could do no wrong. They felt that everything they did was for the good of the masses, regardless of how many people suffered to achieve that goal or what nations faced ruin. This kind of man had no true loyalties, only to themselves.

With the president's death and that of Valda Lewis, they had lost a very important link to the group that was trying to destroy the United States of America. This international Committee would try again, you could be sure. However, this time the United States would be ready; the Nation would be vigilant and beat them at their own game. Too bad Tuckwell had taken the cowardly way out; they might have offered him a deal, if he had helped them.

Ian walked outside the White House and called Governor Cartwright.

"Governor, it is all over. The president and Valda Lewis are both dead. It appears Tuckwell shot her and then committed suicide, in the Oval Office. We will stay here with the National Guards, for a couple of days, to insure that there is no violence or looting, and then we will return to our appropriate states."

"Ian, you have conducted a commendable job. I, and the Nation, owe you a debt of gratitude. See you soon."

"Bye, governor."

The date was Wednesday, the 7th of December. The same day a memorial service was being held in Pearl Harbor, to commemorate the bravery and sacrifices of U.S. servicemen, in 1941.

59

The Swearing-In

On the next day, the 8th of December, at 10:00 am, the Speaker of the House of Representatives, Clive Knight (R), was sworn in as the president of the United States. The swearing-in ceremony took place in the Oval Office of the White House, with the Supreme Court Chief Justice, Andrew Nash, doing the honors. There were several members of Congress in attendance as witnesses, plus a pool of press reporters. It was a somber day, as no previous sitting president had ever committed suicide, in the Nation's history.

Washington, D.C. was still full of the states' National Guard troops, who were helping to keep the peace, but there were very few disturbances. In general, the capital was peaceful, cold and sunny, as on most mornings in December.

At 9:00 pm eastern time, President Knight went on television, with a nationwide address.

"Fellow citizens of these United States, I can announce tonight that the nightmare of the past few months is finally over. Yesterday around noon, President Edward Tuckwell took his own life, and today I was sworn in as interim president, under the rules of succession, set down in the Presidential Act of 1947. I am calling for a special presidential election to be held on Tuesday, the 3rd of January, in which you, the people, can select a new leader. I must tell you now that I will not be a candidate, for the office of president. If my party remains in the majority, then I will return to my previous position, as Speaker of the House.

I have suggested to both the Democratic and Republican parties that they hold mini conventions, two days from now, in order to select a candidate to run in this election. Only surviving U.S. senators, congressmen and state governors will be attending these conventions, due to the limited time available to organize them.

I have decided that the country will select the next president by majority, popular vote. The Electoral College, which is called for in the 12th amendment to the Constitution, will not be used, as there is not enough time to select electors. I realize that this is outside the Constitution; however, both of the major parties have agreed that this is the best approach, given the circumstances. I have also suggested that the parties should only nominate a candidate for president, and the winner would select the losing candidate, as their vice president. Both parties have agreed to consider this proposal, but many members have reservations, about the idea. I suggested it so that we could have a period of reconciliation, after the election.

I'm also rescinding several of the executive orders, issued by President Tuckwell, in the past few months. The National Police Force will be disbanded, and some of the members will be allowed to return to their previous jobs, within the government. In addition, all those people, arrested under the state of emergency, will be set free immediately. Fox News and any newspapers, which were shut down, will also be able to start operating again.

I plan to lift the state of emergency tomorrow. Let's hope and trust that this nation will return to the civility it has always had, except for the past few years. We must respect the opinions of all people, even though we don't always agree with them.

Fellow Americans, tomorrow will be the start of a new day in the United States. I look forward to seeing all of you participating in the upcoming presidential election. America will need you to go to the polls, on the 3rd of January, and vote for the candidate of your choice, who can lead this nation back to greatness.

Goodnight and God bless you all."

With that, the broadcast ended and America looked forward to the special presidential election, to be held the following month. Surviving senators, congressmen and governors started planning to attend the mini conventions, to be held on the next weekend.

60

Party Conventions

The special conventions were held the weekend of the 10th and 11th of December. The Republicans held their get together in Dallas while the Democrats decided to meet in Chicago. Both were scheduled at cities, close to the center of the country, in order to allow attendees to travel, on fairly short notice. In the end, it was left up to each party to decide who could attend and vote for the presidential candidate, of their choice.

Democrats started flying into the "Windy City" on Friday, the 9th of December, for their mini convention. They allowed all twenty governors, one hundred and forty congressman and twenty-two senators to attend. In addition, they permitted five senators from each state legislature to attend and vote. Altogether, there were approximately four hundred and thirty attendees at the gathering, who were authorized to select a candidate.

There were still a few U.S. senators and congressmen who were not well enough to attend, due to the wounds they received when the missiles hit the Capitol.

The first day of the convention was used to develop the rules for nomination and voting for presidential candidate. The Democrats decided to ignore President Knight's suggestion that they only offer a presidential candidate. After a vote on the issue, the Democrats decided to put presidential and vice presidential candidates on the ballot. Also, included in the first day was the development of a party platform. As usual, the Democrats called for more spending on social programs, more jobs programs and universal health care; one payer system, like the British NHS, that had already been started by Tuckwell. There was no discussion on where the funding, for any of these programs, was going to come from. The party platform was approved by an overwhelming vote, although, there were a few dissenting voices. They were drowned out by the large majority.

On the second day, four names were offered up for nomination, as the Democratic candidate for president. The leading candidate was Hedley Dodd, Governor of Delaware. Two other Governors, Paul Beaumont and Scott Hyde, and one U.S. Senator, Henry Varcoe, were also offered up as candidates. On the first ballot, Dodd received forty-five percent of the votes and the other three candidates split the remaining fifty-five percent amongst themselves. On the second ballot, Paul Beaumont threw his support behind Hedley Dodd. This was enough for Dodd to get fifty-one percent of the votes and enough to carry the day.

As is normal at these conventions, Hedley Dodd was sitting in his hotel suite, watching the voting at the arena, which was broadcast on CBS and CNN. As soon as he saw that he had won his party's nomination, he left his suite and headed for the hall. When he arrived, he was welcomed, with rousing enthusiasm. He went onto the rostrum and told the chairman that he wanted to speak to the delegates.

"My fellow Americans and Democrats," Dodd began. "I stand before you, humbled by the honor you have bestowed on me. I will do my best, in the upcoming short campaign for president. I need, by my side, a man who can help carry us to victory. I therefore ask you to nominate and vote for Paul Beaumont, as our vice presidential candidate."

There was a huge roar and cheering in the hall. The chairman called the meeting to order, and the voting took place. It was unanimous, and Governor Beaumont became the vice presidential candidate.

Then the climax of the convention came, with the ceremonial balloon and confetti drop. Governor Hedley Dodd and Governor Paul Beaumont, with their families beside them, stood together on the dais, waving to the crowd of well wishers.

While the Democrats were nominating their new presidential and vice presidential candidates in Chicago, the Republicans were going about their convention, in basically the same way, approximately nine hundred and fifty miles away, in Dallas. The Republicans followed the advice of President Knight and decided to only vote for a presidential candidate.

This get together was mainly covered by NBC, ABC and Fox News. The coverage was not continuous, just as the coverage of the Democratic Convention was not covered, gavel to gavel.

The Republicans came up with their party platform, which included calls for a smaller Federal Government, an "independent" IRS, without political interference, new operating rules for the NSA, a health plan that called for independent personal responsibility, a real jobs program and a tougher military, to handle all external threats to the nation.

On the first day, the final copy of the party platform was completed and approved by a majority of the delegates. In addition, the rules for the selection of candidates for president were voted on and approved together, with an agreement that no vice presidential candidate would be selected.

Going into the convention, Martha Cartwright, the Iron Lady, or as some called her, Iron Martha, was the overall favorite, with Chuck Prince running a close second. Also, in national polls, Martha Cartwright was considerably ahead, of any Democratic possible candidate.

On the second day, Martha Cartwright was in her hotel suite with Ian Black and her campaign manager, waiting for the nominations and voting for presidential candidate to proceed. In the morning, there were several speeches, by various elected officials of the party. After lunch, at 2:00 pm, the party actually started the process of selecting a candidate for president.

Martha Cartwright's name was place in nomination by the governor of Florida, and there was an outburst of cheering, as it was announced. The only other name placed in nomination was Chuck Prince, the governor of Texas, and a good friend of Martha Cartwright.

As the voting started, it became apparent that Chuck Prince would not get enough votes to win. He left his hotel suite and went to the convention floor. He walked to the Texas delegation position and took the mike.

Governor Prince said, "Mr. Chairman, even though I am the favorite son of Texas, I would like to cast all the votes assigned to our state to our good friend, Martha Cartwright. In addition, I ask all states that have already voted for me, to switch their votes to Cartwright. Thank you, Mr. Chairman."

With that, the convention hall erupted into bedlam. Whistles, horns, cheers, all sounded throughout the hall. After a considerable length of time, the delegates finally quieted down, and then the leader for each state, which had cast its votes for Chuck Prince, went to their respective microphones, to switch their votes to Governor Cartwright. Then, the leader of the Tennessee delegation rose and spoke. "Mr. Chairman, I herewith ask that the nomination of Martha Cartwright be acclaimed unanimously." With that, the hall broke into pandemonium again, and it took about fifteen minutes to quiet down the crowd again.

Finally the Chairman spoke, "I herewith ask all delegates to vote AYE or NAY, on the proposal that the selection of Martha Cartwright, as our presidential candidate, be proclaimed unanimous. All those in favor say AYE." There was a big roar of "AYE" from the crowd of delegates. "All those not in favor say "NAY". There was silence. Not one delegate voted against Martha Cartwright. The Chairman continued, "The AYES have it. Martha Cartwright, the governor of Tennessee is proclaimed the Republican candidate for president." Again there was bedlam, throughout the hall, and calls for Martha Cartwright to appear.

On hearing this, Martha Cartwright left her hotel suite and proceeded to the convention hall, with Ian Black and her campaign manager following behind. After about fifteen minutes, she arrived at the back of the stage, where the chairman was waiting for her. They shook hands, and he escorted the nominee to the rostrum.

Again, there was yelling and cheering that went on for another ten minutes. Finally, Governor Cartwright managed to quiet down the crowd.

"Thank you very much. Thank you, I am deeply aware of the responsibility you have given me, and I humbly accept your nomination, for the presidency of the United States of America.

I will leave this hall, with the goal of unifying this country, after eight years of class warfare. We are faced with severe threats, any of which could ruin this country. We face an economy that is not growing, as it should. We have a weakened defense that emboldens our enemies, and an energy policy that precludes us from cutting our ties, to Middle East oil.

I pledge that I will work tirelessly to fix the problems. I will do this without demonizing the other party, as has previously been done. I do not believe in Lenin's six principles that have been in vogue, for the past eight years.

I ask all of you to work together in a bipartisan way and, if I'm elected, I intend to have a very open administration, working with both sides of the aisle. We have plenty of work to do, so I'll finish up this short speech by saying again, I accept your nomination as our party's candidate for the presidency.

My slogan for the coming campaign will be, to paraphrase a great, conservative Republican:

A Real Choice, not an Echo

God bless you all, God bless America, goodnight."

With that, she waved to the crowd and, amid cheers, left the hall, accompanied by her campaign manager and advisor Ian Black.

****

For the next three weeks, both Cartwright and Dodd crisscrossed the nation, holding campaign rallies and speaking to the press. It was a short campaign, similar to those generally held in Europe. This was probably the way all future presidential campaigns would be run. Both Cartwright and Dodd ran clean campaigns, without either of them disparaging the other. Finally, the campaign ended on the 2nd of January, and the next day voting for president began at 8:00 am.

61

Election

On Tuesday, the 3rd of January, the special presidential election was held across the nation, as called for by the interim President, Clive Knight. The candidates for president were; Martha Cartwright, the governor of Tennessee (R) and Hedley Dodd, the governor of Delaware (D). Both had been selected by their appropriate parties at conventions held on the weekend of the 10th and 11th of December. In addition, the Democrats did not go along with President Knight's suggestion, and they nominated Paul Beaumont, the governor of South Dakota, as their vice presidential candidate.

The people therefore had a unique choice, when they went into the voting booth. If they voted for Martha Cartwright, they would elect her as president. There was no vice president name listed on the Republican side. If they voted for Hedley Dodd, they would get him as president and Paul Beaumont as vice president. This made for an interesting and unique election.

Nationwide, based on local times, all the polling stations were opened at 8:00 am and closed at 7:00 pm. Teams of observers were at every election location to ensure, as much as possible, that there were few irregularities. They would also hopefully deter dead people and non citizens, from voting and depositing a ballot.

Predictions started coming in that there would be a high turnout of voters. According to official statistics, only fifty-five percent of the population had actually voted in presidential elections, during the latter part of the twentieth century. In comparison, the number of people who participated in the 1860 contest, between Lincoln and Douglas, was estimated to be eight-one percent.

The press reported that the lines were long outside the polling stations, during the entire day. It looked like the turnout was going to be heavy in every state, even though the election was for president only. The majority of senators and congressmen, who were killed in the attack on the Capitol, would be replaced, either by appointment or special elections. All were subject to their own state laws. Some of the vacancies had already been filled, since it had been three months since the attack, on the 9th of September.

Martha Cartwright planned a reception, in the Hilton hotel ballroom, in downtown Nashville, whether she won the election or not. She had a suite upstairs, where she watched the returns coming in, with her campaign staff and Ian Black.

Hedley Dodd also had a party planned, in case he won the election, in the Dover Downs Hotel and Casino. He had a group of rooms on the third floor, where he could watch the returns come in, with his wife and grown children.

By the time the polls closed on the East Coast, it was estimated that the turnout was seventy-five percent. Exit polls had the election result at fifty-five percent for Cartwright and forty-five percent for Dodd. These results were not announced on television, so as not to influence the voting on the West Coast or inland.

The voter turnout was heavy across the entire Nation. It appeared the country wanted a change, and the people had finally had enough of all the bickering, between the two major parties.

Finally at 9:00 pm Eastern Standard Time, the major networks started releasing the vote counts, as reported by the various states. It became apparent that Martha Cartwright would win the election, by an overwhelming majority of the votes. All the major networks, by 9:15 pm, had called the election for Cartwright. All that remained was to see how large a vote she obtained, versus her rival Dodd.

By 10:15 pm, Governor Dodd entered the Dover Downs Hotel ballroom, to make a concession speech. The crowd cheered as he entered, and it took a while before they calmed down.

Governor Dodd said, "Thank you, thank you. A few minutes ago I placed a call to Governor Cartwright to congratulate her and supporters on their victory.

America has faced a challenging time, and I gave her my assurance that I would do all I could to support the healing process.

I would like to thank Paul Beaumont for all he has done for our brief campaign, and the support he has given me.

In addition, I would like to express my gratitude to the campaign staff and, in particular, my manager. They all spent many hours a day, doing their best, to help us win this election.

You, the fundraisers, volunteers and supporters, who have been the backbone of this campaign; I can't thank you enough."

With that, Governor Dodd waved to the crowd and left the ballroom.

****

A few minutes later, Governor Cartwright and now the President-elect, prepared to speak to her supporters, in the

Nashville Hilton.   The crowd in the ballroom was getting worked up and wanted Martha Cartwright to come and speak to them. A band was playing patriotic music.

Finally, Martha Cartwright entered the hall, with her campaign manager and Ian Black.   The crowd started to cheer and clap. She walked up to the podium, waving and smiling to her supporters.

After the crowd quieted down, the President-elect then started to speak.

"My fellow Americans tonight is a great day for all of you, whether you are Republicans or Democrats. This great victory will allow us to restore this country, to its former greatness.   No more apology tours.   It will take time, but we're going to make our country economically strong again. The economy comes first, so that every American can have a full time job; not a part time job.

I spoke with Hedley Dodd a few minutes ago and accepted his concession of the election. I thanked him for running a clean campaign, which the country was looking for. I told him it was my opinion that the American people wanted all the interparty bickering to be greatly reduced. I wished him God speed in his continued governorship of the great state of Delaware.

Thank you for all your support in this hard won race. Without you we could not have succeeded.   Bless you and God Bless America."

With that Martha Cartwright left the rostrum and strode into the crowd, shaking hands and thanking as many people as she could.   As she did this, the band started playing the Tennessee Waltz.

****

The final vote count, after all the states' ballots had been counted, was as follows:

RICHARD AND BARBARA OSBORN

Martha Cartwright	70,453,201	55.16%
Hedley Dodd	57,267,109	44.84%
TOTAL	127,720,310	

Total Voter Turnout	75%
Registered Voters	170 million

62

Election Speech

On Tuesday, the 19th of January, at 9:00 pm, President-elect Martha Cartwright gave a speech to the Nation, over television and radio, on all the major networks.

"I speak to you from the governor's house, here in Nashville, Tennessee. The last four months have been a very trying time for this Nation and all Americans. The previous president acted like a dictator and made life in this country intolerable.

I am going to correct his actions and take this country in a totally different direction. Already, the interim President, Clive Knight, has rescinded many of the executive orders, issued by the previous administration. This country has been governed by a president and his advisors, who lived by illusions, over the past eight years. The idea that you can create an economy, with borrowed money, and you can create jobs by government edict, is totally unrealistic and unsustainable. Let me make it perfectly clear, I am deeply concerned about the level of unemployment. This Nation, fifty years ago, was a shining example for the rest of the world. Our most precious asset is our educated and experienced workforce.

The more money the government takes out of the economy, the fewer private jobs are created. Today, government employees are earning more than private workers and yet also have more health and pension benefits. This situation cannot continue, without a collapse of the economy. As Margaret Thatcher, Prime Minister of Great Britain, is purported to have said, "Any housewife can balance a budget," and America can also.

On another subject, if the Federal Government expenditures were the solution, we would have solved our problems years ago. It's not the solution, it's the problem. All the money spent by the government has to come from somewhere. It either comes from taxes or it is borrowed. There is no such thing as a free lunch. Someone has to pay.

To paraphrase another quote by Margaret Thatcher: Our goal is to let all the people feel that they count more and more, in the success of this great Nation of ours.

The class warfare, of the past few years, has to stop, before this Nation is destroyed by recrimination. Charges of racial bias must also be reduced, before it consumes us all. Political correctness doesn't help this country solve its problems. We must face the issues of the day with honesty and real integrity. To this end, a few days ago, I called the Democratic presidential candidate, Hedley Dodd, and asked him, in the spirit of conciliation, to serve as vice president in our administration. I can tell you now that he has graciously accepted my offer, and he will become the vice president on the 20th of January.

Let's all get to work and solve our problems together, so we can all attain a better standard of living and a stronger nation.

As far as our standing in the world, we plan to end this era of appeasement. As the world found out in 1938, appeasement does not offer one peace. It only delays the inevitable conflict with aggressive powers. From now on, we will treat our allies with respect and our potential enemies with wariness.

We must get our economy back on a sound footing, and then we can build the military up, to what is needed to defend this Nation. Our allies must also do the same. They can't expect the United States to be the world peace keeper. Western Europe and Japan must take their place in the world and support the basic principles, including freedom and liberty, of the Western world.

The previous administration was involved with a Committee that was made up of foreigners, from many countries. This was and is an intolerable situation. My administration will try to identify the people involved and, where possible, will have them tried in our courts. The false flag operation, that launched the missiles and caused so much damage at the Capitol, was organized by this Committee and the late president.

I am proposing the creation of a new organization, similar to NATO, but including all the peaceful countries of the world, which have the same basic beliefs, as we do. The United Nations has outlived much of its usefulness and it has become an expensive, debating society, ever since the Suez Canal Crisis and the Hungarian Revolt, in the fall of 1956. Within the first month of my administration, a commission will be formed, consisting of scholars and statesmen, which will be charged to come up with a charter. The treaty will list the rules, regulations and commitments of all countries, invited to join the organization. Terrorist countries and dictatorships need not apply to join, as they will be rejected. Each country invited to join will pledge to uphold the freedom of religion, press and basic civil liberties. Just as in NATO, an attack, on one of the members, will be an attack on all. Again, this will be a worldwide organization, where a country that wishes to join, will have to pledge to meet all requirements and be voted in, by the existing members.

I will be keeping you all informed and up to date, as we proceed down the path of reconciliation in the United States.

Let me close by saying – I pledge to you, as the new president, that I'll work tirelessly for all Americans, no matter if you are rich, poor or middle class.

Thank you, goodnight and God bless."

As soon as she had finished talking, Ian Black walked over to her and congratulated her on an excellent, well delivered speech. He had helped her write some of the speech, but it was the President-elect who had polished, edited and given it the correct emphasis.

63

The New Beginning

Friday, the 20th of January, was a cold blustery day, with a few snow flurries, in Washington, D.C. The temperature hovered around ten degrees Fahrenheit, so everyone was wrapped up warmly in overcoats, hats and scarves. The crowd, which was made up mainly of senators, congressmen, governors and foreign dignitaries, was assembled in front of the Capitol building, for the swearing-in ceremony of President-elect Martha Cartwright and Vice President-elect Hedley Dodd. The main, domed part of the Capitol had not been hit by the missiles, so that the front of the building looked undamaged.

This was to become a historic day, where leaders from two different parties, were to be sworn in, as president and vice president, in a spirit of bipartisanship. The front row had been set aside for the governors of the states, who had been active in the removal of President Tuckwell and his administration.

The Supreme Court Chief Justice Andrew Nash stepped forward to his assigned position on the rostrum. President-elect Martha Cartwright stepped forward and stood facing

Nash. Then Ian Black, her trusted advisor and confidant, stepped forward holding an edition of King James Bible, which had been in Cartwright's family for decades. He stood back a little and was between the Chief Justice and President Cartwright. She placed her hand on the bible and, following the Chief Justice's lead, Martha Cartwright swore to faithfully execute the office of President, to the best of her ability. In addition, she promised to preserve, protect and defend the Constitution of the United States of America.

After the ceremony, President Cartwright was congratulated by the Chief Justice and other dignitaries, close to her. Then Hedley Dodd stepped forward and, with her holding the bible, was sworn in as vice president.

After both of them had been administered with the oath of office, President Cartwright stepped forward to the microphone, to begin her inauguration address.

"Chief Justice Nash, Vice President Dodd, and fellow Americans: I stand before you, with deep humility. You have given me the overall task of turning this nation around. You have placed your trust in me and believe that I will do the right thing for all Americans.

I agreed to have the other party's presidential candidate, Hedley Dodd, as vice president, in order to demonstrate that I'm serious about having both parties working together, to meet the overall goals.

Our Nation is one of laws, and I pledge that I will not sign any law, which does not pass the Constitutional test. In addition, I'll not sign any executive order, without consent of the leaders in Congress. We will eliminate or reduce some agencies, whose tasks can better be carried out, by the individual states.

This administration will not tolerate corruption in Washington. In addition, we will create some checks and balances, to prevent any future repeat of a grab for power, by any politician.

I realize it's very cold out here and I'm keeping this address very brief and to the point. In fact, it's my belief that we should keep all of our speeches short, so we can actually get some business done, for our Nation.

In summation, I take this oath of office extremely seriously and will do my utmost to carry out my duties, within the scope of the Constitution of the United States of America.

Thank you, let us all get to work; I plan to.

God bless America."

With that President Cartwright stepped back from the microphone and shook the vice president's hand.

Then the president and vice president left the reviewing stand and walked down Pennsylvania Avenue, to the cheering of the crowds lining the route. The cold didn't seem to have dampened their spirits, as there seemed to be a general feeling of relief and hope for the future.

After walking for a few minutes down the Avenue, they climbed into the presidential limousine and went to the White House. Once there, President Cartwright held a brief meeting with Vice President Dodd and former President Clive Knight. The purpose of this meeting was to discuss the handover of presidential responsibilities and general administrative tasks, which needed immediate attention. In addition, there was a discussion about having a complete investigation concerning the attack on the Capitol, and they also reviewed the plans for its reconstruction.

64

Cyprus Revisited

After Martha Cartwright and Hedley Dodd were sworn in as president and vice president respectively, President Cartwright delivered a short, but inspiring, speech, to the assembled crowds and the Nation. She vowed to get rid of the corruption in Washington and to set up procedures, with checks and balances, so that the country would never again go through the nightmare, of the past few months. Never again could the United States of America have a leader like Napoleon Bonaparte, Adolf Hitler or Edward Tuckwell.

Then, three days later on Monday, the 23rd of January, she held a meeting at the White House, with leaders from both parties to help develop ways to prevent a repeat of the Edward Tuckwell's grab for power.

Before being sworn in, Martha Cartwright had asked Ian Black, her advisor, if he would be willing to be her secretary of state. He was seventy six years old, but he was still in good health. He agreed to take on the duties as long as he could retire in two years, and obviously assuming the U.S. Senate approved his nomination. President-elect Cartwright agreed to those terms and was glad to have him on board. She knew she could trust him, and it would leave her more time to handle other affairs of state.

On Thursday, the 26th of January, she delivered her first State of the Union speech, to a joint session of Congress. In this speech, she outlined the goals that she and the vice president had in mind, to bring liberty and freedom back to all Americans, regardless of race or religion. This included restricting the power of the Federal Government, including harmful regulations, which interfered with the normal lives of Americans. In addition, she stressed the need to get the Nation's finances under control. This would require sacrifices by everyone but, in the end, every American would be able to prosper and hold their heads high. She ended the address by stressing again that all Americans should be undivided by class, religion or race.

****

A few weeks later, Secretary of State Ian Black went to Antalya, Turkey, to attend a Middle East conference of foreign ministers, hosted by Turkey. The purpose was to try and find ways to bring peace to the area, after decades of fighting. After the conference ended on a Friday at noon, without any major breakthrough, the Turkish Foreign Minister, Hakan Turan, invited Ian Black to go on a weekend trip with him.

"Ian, how would you like to go to my villa, for the weekend, overlooking Girne, in Cyprus?" asked Hakan. They used first names in private, as they had become well acquainted with each other, over the past few weeks.

"That sounds great. I haven't been in Cyprus since the late 1950's. Did you know I was a lieutenant in the British Army Intelligence Corps, during the Enosis crisis?"

Hakan responded, "Yes, I have heard you made quite a name for yourself, fighting the EOKA terrorists."

Ian replied laughing, "I wouldn't say I made much of a reputation for myself. However, I did get a promotion out of it. How will we get to Girne? I went there a few times, during my British Army days, although it was called Kyrenia back then."

"We can fly to Ercan International Airport from here this afternoon and come back Sunday afternoon. Once we get there, we will go by car to Girne, which is only a relatively short distance, as you probably already know. In total, it's about forty-five kilometers from the airport to the town center and another two kilometers to my villa. My home is in a beautiful location, overlooking the ocean and the town. We can fly in my government provided plane. There'll be no problem using it, since we can talk business on the way. It's about one hundred and eighty miles, which will take about thirty minutes by jet."

"That sounds great," Ian said. "I'll have to go back to my hotel and pack a bag, so I can bring a few clothes and personal items with me. Will you be able you pick me up there?"

"Of course, I'll be glad to do that. What hotel are you staying at?"

"I'm at the Marmara Antalya," Ian replied.

"Okay, I'll pick you up there in about an hour, on the way to the airport," Hakan Turan responded.

"Thanks, see you then."

Hakan came by The Marmara Antalya hotel one hour later in a large black Mercedes, which then drove them both to the Antalya airport. The foreign minister had called ahead so that the plane and crew were ready for the flight. They climbed into the Turkish Government owned Cessna Citation, which was standing by, at the Antalya Airport, ready to leave. They took off and headed in a southeasterly direction toward Cyprus. It seemed that they had hardly taken off, when the pilot announced to the passengers to prepare for landing. When they touched down, the pilot taxied to a VIP parking area, where there was a car waiting for them.

Since Ian was with the Turkish Foreign Minister, neither of them had to go through customs or immigration. The officials at Ercan knew Hakan Turan very well. They were waved through, by the airport administrator who had met the plane, and they walked to the waiting Mercedes. The limousine drove toward and through the Kyrenia Mountains and, thirty minutes later, started down toward Girne itself. The view was magnificent, and the town glistened in the bright sunlight, with the blue Mediterranean acting as a back drop. They went through Girne and then turned left to go to Hakan's villa, situated on a cliff overlooking the ocean and the harbor.

They had an enjoyable evening and agreed, over dinner, to go fishing the next day on board Hakan's large boat, moored in Girne harbor. They caught a few fish on the trip, which they brought back to the chef, to cook for Saturday's dinner.

On Sunday, they both got up late and had a leisurely breakfast, after which it was time to head back to Lefkoşa and return to Turkey, on the Hakan's government plane. At around 11:00 am, the chauffeur loaded their bags into the trunk and they drove off down the hill, toward Girne and Ercan International Airport.

The trip took them back through the town center and through some narrow streets. As they proceeded down Sedat Simavi Caddesi, some distance behind a large vehicle, their Mercedes came to a sudden screeching halt. The car in front of them had hit a well dressed gentleman, who had started to cross the road, toward a tall, attractive woman. She had been standing on the opposite curb, waving at the man, and he had stepped into the road, forgetting to look in the correct direction. Since he was an American, he was used to traffic coming from the other way. The large, white,

Lexus SUV hit the American and flung him a few yards, where his head hit the street surface.

Hakan and Ian jumped out of their car and rushed to the man, lying on the street, to see if they could be of any assistance. As they approached the man, who was groaning and only half conscious, Ian thought he recognized him. Finally, it dawned on him that it was Alan Burgess, the retired United States Air Force colonel, who headed up the Red Moon team. Alan Burgess was trying to talk, so Ian bent down to listen, to what he was trying to say.

"I'm sorry about the attack on the Capitol. Perhaps it did some good, since Martha Cartwright is now president," he whispered. He then died, just when the ambulance and police arrived. There was nothing they could do for him.

Dilara, Alan's girlfriend, who was the woman on the pavement, also went over to him, but there was nothing she could do for him either. She was alone again, but considerably richer, than before she met him.

Now that Alan Burgess had been killed in the traffic accident, the entire Red Moon team had been eliminated.

Ian and Hakan climbed back into the limousine, which continued down the main road through the mountains, toward the airport.

Ian turned to Hakan and asked, "Would you mind if we make two quick stops on the way? First, I want to go at a flower shop and then pay my respects at a cemetery, near Ercan."

"No, not at all, just tell the driver where you want to go." Hakan replied.

Soon, Ian saw a flower shop, on the side of the road, and asked the driver to stop. He got out of the car and went inside. He purchased a dozen yellow roses, climbed back into the car and told the driver how to get to the cemetery.

It wasn't long before they arrived at the Greek cemetery that Ian remembered so well. It was now, however, located in the Turkish zone of Cyprus. He got out and walked some distance, over to a plaque in the ground. It read Aphrodite Palas 1938-1958. Ian laid the yellow roses on the grave and said a short prayer. He ended it, by softly saying, "Bye for now, my love. I said that I'd always love you and I'll do so for ever."

Ian glanced over at two adjacent grave sites, where a man was trimming the grass around them. He stood up and read the names on the plaques. They were Aphrodite's father and younger brother. The old man, who appeared to be like in his early eighties, looked up at Ian and said, "Hello, may I help you?"

"Hello" Ian replied in Greek. "Do you know these people?" he asked, pointing at the markers.

"Yes, they're my father, brother and sister," he replied, with tears welling in his eyes.

"You must be Minervo," Ian said.

"Yes, how did you know?"

"My name is Ian Black and I served in the British Army here years ago. I'm sorry for all of this," Ian replied, looking around at the three graves.

The old man got up, shuffled over to Ian and gave him a hug.

"All is forgiven," he said.

"Your sister and I…….," Ian started to say, but Minervo interrupted him. "I know that also; as I said, all is forgiven."

Ian shook his hand and returned to the car. The driver took Ian and Hakan to the airport, and they flew back to Turkey. This was the last time Ian ever visited Cyprus.

EPILOGUE

Approximately one month later, on Saturday, the 22nd of April, Vice President Dodd died of a heart attack, at the age of sixty-two, while presenting a speech at his alma mater. It was very sudden, and he had not complained of any chest pains previously. They rushed him to the hospital, but it was too late. He was given a state funeral at Arlington, with the president and all the cabinet members attending.

A few days later, President Cartwright held a meeting in the Oval Office, with her Secretary of State, Ian Black. He was ushered into the office, by President Cartwright's personal secretary.

"Good morning, Ian," said the president. "Thank you for coming. I know you're busy, taking care of the nation's foreign affairs."

"No problem, Madame President. However, visiting this room brings back the bad memories of four months ago. What can I do for you? I don't think you asked me to come here, to have a chat about old times in Tennessee."

"First of all, Ian, we're too good of friends for you to call me anything but Martha, in private. In addition, you're correct; I asked to see you for a special reason. I've given a lot of thought about whom I should submit to the Senate, for approval as vice president. Since the untimely death of Hedley Dodd, the Speaker of the House of Representatives is the next in line for succession, if something should happen to me. I have decided that I would like you to be my vice president. What do you think about that?"

"Well Martha, I'm greatly honored for the trust you have in me. However, I have three reasons why I wish you would not submit my name.

The first is that I'm a dual citizen. Yes, I am an American by birth, but some people may have a reason to distrust me. By law and under the Constitution, it would be legal for me to be vice president and, if need be, president. However, for you to have a vice president that is half English and half American, it could present some political problems.

The second reason is I believe that I would be too old for the job. Yes, I'm in good health, but I've noticed that I am slowing down.

Finally, I'd prefer to remain as secretary of state for the next two years, or as long as you can put up with me. My skills are a much better match for the secretary of state position, than vice president."

President Cartwright thought for a moment and then said, "Okay, I respect your wishes. I understand your reasons for being reluctant to take on the position. You've done an excellent job as secretary of state, for the past few months, and I do want you to continue. Can you recommend anyone for vice president? Of course, any name or names you mention will remain just between you and me."

Ian responded, "One person I can recommend is Chuck Prince, governor of Texas. He's young, energetic, honest and extremely bright, and I believe that he would make an excellent vice president."

The president replied, "Thank you for your recommendation. I had already been thinking along the same lines."

"Martha, there is an issue I would like to discuss with you, if you have the time, and I also have some information that might be of interest to you."

"Yes, I have some spare time, before my next appointment. What is it you would like to tell me and also discuss with me?" she asked.

"First. I wish to inform you that Alan Burgess was killed in a road accident, in Girne, Cyprus. As he walked across the street, he was hit by a car, in front of the vehicle I was riding in. It appeared that he'd been hiding out in Northern Cyprus, for the past few months. Before he died, he asked to be forgiven, for causing so many deaths in the Capitol attack."

Martha responded, "I'm sorry to hear he met an untimely death. I would have preferred that he had been brought back to the United States and tried in a court of law."

Ian Black continued, "There're two subjects that I'd like to bring up, both of which are connected. The strength of our diplomacy depends on two major factors – the economy and the strength of our Armed Forces. If we're weak in one or the other area, our friends and enemies will not take us seriously. I know you're trying to turn around the economy that has been sadly lacking, for the past eight years. We must do it and then build up our Army, which has also been hollowed out, as of late.

The British deluded themselves, with the help of Prime Minister Neville Chamberlain, into thinking that they did not need a strong army to control Adolf Hitler. They believed diplomacy was the way to control him, as in the 1935 Anglo-German Naval Agreement. History showed their thinking was all wrong, as we well know. We can't let any more terrorist countries or organizations develop nuclear weapons, or else we'll be in 1939 all over again."

The president looked out the window at the bright spring day for awhile, and then said, "I completely understand what you're saying and I'll do my best to achieve the first and prevent the latter. I value your frankness, Ian. This job, as president, is not for the faint hearted or a weak person."

President Cartwright went on to become one of the most respected and successful presidents that ever sat in the Oval Office. Her deceased husband would have been proud of her.

This page intentionally left blank

	Bomarc A	Bomarc B	Bomarc C
Nomenclature	CIM-10A	CIM-10B	CIM-10C
Prime Contractor	Boeing Airplane Co.	Boeing Airplane Co.	Classified
Booster Rocket	Liquid	Solid	Solid
Booster Manufacturer	Aerojet General	Thiokol	Classified
Booster Nomenclature	LR-59-AG-13	XM-51	Classified
Ramjet Manufacturer	Marquadt	Marquadt	Classified
Ramjet Nomenclature	RJ43-MA-3	RJ43-MA-7 RJ43-MA-11	Classified
RamJet Fuel	80 Octane Gasoline	80 Octane Gasoline	80 Octane Gasoline
Range	260 Miles	440 Miles	500+ miles
Speed	Mach 2.8	Mach 3.0+	Mach 4.0+
Fuze	Proximity	Proximity	Contact or Proximity
Atomic Weapon	W40 (10 kiloton)	W40 (10 kiloton)	W80(<150 kiloton)
High-Explosive	1000 lbs	300 lbs	500 lbs
Altitude Limit	65,000 feet	90,000+ feet	100,000+ feet
GPS Guidance	No	No	Yes
Terrain Contour Matching	No	No	Yes
Active Radar	Yes	Yes	Yes
Pulse Doppler Radar Mfr.	Westinghouse AN/DPN-34	Westinghouse AN/DPN-34	Classified
Data Link	Ground	Ground	Satellite
Data Link Manufacturer	RCA	RCA	Classified
Mapping Capability	No	No	Yes
Cruise Missile Capability	No	No	Yes
Length	46′ 10″	45′ 1″	45′ 1″

POSSIBLE BOMARC C INTERCEPT OPTIONS

Nomenclature	Name	Description	Mission	Max. Speed	Range
F-15C	Eagle	Fighter	Intercept	Mach 2.5	1200 miles
F-22	Raptor	Fighter	Intercept	Mach 2.5	470 miles
F-35	Lightning	Fighter	Intercept	Mach 2.0	600 miles
AIM-7/B	Sparrow	Missile	Shoot Down Planes	Mach 2.5	20 miles
AIM-7C/E/F/	Sparrow	Missile	Shoot Down Planes	Mach 4.0	20-30 miles
AIM-9	Sidewinder	Missile	Shoot Down Planes	Mach 2.5	35-110 miles
AIM-120	AMRAAM	Missile	Shoot Down Missiles	Mach 4.0	>20 miles
THAAD	THAAD Missile	Missile	Take out high alt. ballistic missiles	Mach 7.0	<125 miles
MIM-104D/E	Patriot	Missile	Take out high alt. ballistic missiles	Mach 5.0	12-100 miles
CIWS/C-RAM	Phalanx	Radar Controlled Gatling Gun	Shoot Down low altitude missiles	N/A	2.2+ miles
FIM-92	Stinger (Redeye)	Shoulder launched Infrared Seeking	Shoot Down Aircraft/helicopter	Mach 2.2	3.0 miles

343

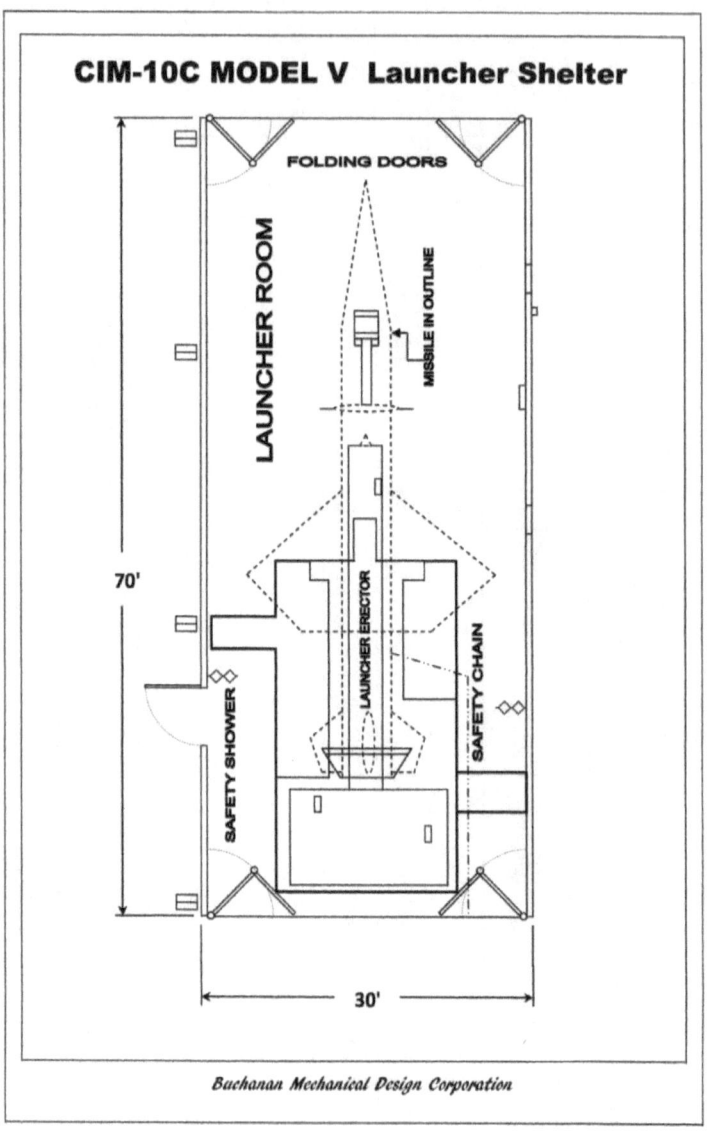

CIM-10C MODEL V Launcher Shelter

Buchanan Mechanical Design Corporation

Bomarc C Missile on Erector in Shelter

Bomarc C Missiles Ready for Launch

GLOSSARY OF ABBREVIATIONS

ADLO	Air Defense Liaison Officer (Rome, NY)
AFB	Air Force Base
ANG	Air National Guard
ARNG	Army National Guard
ATCT	Air Traffic Control Tower
BFO	Blinding Flash of the Obvious
BND	Bundesnachrichtendienst (German Secret Service)
BOFFIN	Chief Engineer (English slang)
DSMAC	Digital Scene Matching Area Correlation
FAA	Federal Aviation Agency
GPS	Global Positioning System
HSBC	Hong Kong & Shanghai Banking Corporation
IEFD	International Economic & Finance Development
INS	Inertial Navigation System
JSS	Joint Surveillance System (USAF & FAA)
NCA	National Crime Agency (Great Britain)
NORAD	North American Aerospace Defense Command
NPF	National Police Force
NSA	National Security Agency
NSC	National Security Council
RPG	Rocket Propelled Grenade
SOCC	Special Operations Control Center (Rome, NY)
TERCON	Terrain Contour Matching
TRACON	Terminal Radar Approach Control
UBS AG	Union Bank of Switzerland & Swiss Bank Corp.

This page intentionally left blank

THE AUTHORS

Richard Osborn

He was born and raised in England, survived the bombing in World War II and attended the King's School in Canterbury. He has served in the British Army – Royal Artillery and the United States Air Force. He is a graduate of California State University at Los Angeles and of the Thunderbird Graduate School of International Management. In civilian life, he worked at General Dynamics, Aeronutronic Ford, Hughes Aircraft and Tektronix. He is a licensed pilot and has conducted numerous seminars for Tektronix Inc. in the Far East and Europe. Now he is writing fiction and non-fiction books in Knoxville, Tennessee.

Barbara Osborn

She was born and raised in Virginia. She attended art classes at the University of Georgia and studied art history at the University of Tennessee. She has travelled extensively in Europe and the Mediterranean. After living in England for awhile, she came back to Knoxville, Tennessee remarried and retired. Currently, she and her husband are co-writing fiction and non-fiction books.

AVAILABLE NOW

The Osborns' novel is about a young British lieutenant, Ian Black, who comes face-to-face with EOKA terrorists. He falls in love with a nurse at the hospital and saves the Cyprus Governor from assassination. Ian survives an attempt on his life but to his horror faces a tragedy. He returns to England after helping to save the Cyprus peace treaty.

On Her Majesty's

CYPRUS MISSION

An **Ian Black** *Novel*

RICHARD *and* **BARBARA OSBORN**

BRITANNIA-AMERICAN PUBLISHING
ISBN-13:978-0692294246

RICHARD AND BARBARA OSBORN

AVAILABLE NOW

Ian Black is transferred to Berlin after graduating from the Advanced Intelligence Corps Academy. He arrives just in time to be involved before and after the construction of the Wall. He befriends an East German politician's mistress and assists a Czechoslovakian ice skater in her defection to the West. Ian follows the Russian troop movements in the East.

On Her Majesty's
BERLIN MISSION

An **Ian Black** *Novel*

ACHTUNG!
Sie verlassen jetzt
WEST-BERLIN

RICHARD *and* BARBARA OSBORN

BRITANNIA-AMERICAN PUBLISHING
ISBN-13:978-0692780855

AVAILABLE NOW

After resigning his commission in the British Army and going to the United States, Ian Black meets with General Carter in Washington. He is offered a commission in the USAF and works in the Air Force ISR Agency as a Captain. Due to his experience in Berlin, he is transferred to the USAFSS Section H during the Vietnam War.

BRITANNIA-AMERICAN PUBLISHING
ISBN-13:978-1981773022

RICHARD AND BARBARA OSBORN

AVAILABLE NOW

This book by Richard Osborn delves into the history of the last one hundred years and examines the major blunders and appeasements that took place during 1914-2014. At the end of each chapter, the author analyzes the blunders and what effect they have had over time. In the last chapter, the top blunders are reviewed and their effect on the West.

TWILIGHT

FOR
THE

WEST?

A CENTURY OF
BLUNDERS AND APPEASEMENTS
BY NAÏVE, NEOPHYTE POLITICIANS
1914-2014

RICHARD OSBORN

United States Air Force Veteran·
British Army – Royal Artillery Veteran

BRITANNIA-AMERICAN PUBLISHING
ISBN-13:978-0692418413